Private detective Terry Luvello has just been handed the biggest case of his career. During confession, a man has twice declared his intent to commit murder. In both cases, the murders later occurred in exactly the way the unknown man had described.

Hoping to keep the church connection out of the newspapers, the parish pastor asks Terry to find the killer and act as his liaison with the Cleveland Police and Detective Hannah Page. While dealing with their own growing attraction, Terry and Hannah race from Cleveland to New Orleans to catch a brilliant and ruthless killer acting on his own twisted compulsion.

Those who know Terry describe him as intelligent, obsessive, and annoying, often all at once. To solve this case, Terry must also put his uniquely wry sense of humor into play, coming to terms with a longstanding grudge against the Catholic Church and his identity as a transgender male.

AND GOD

LAUGHED

TERRY LUVELLO, BOOK ONE

JOE RIELINGER

A NineStar Press Publication

www.ninestarpress.com

And God Laughed

© 2022 Joe Rielinger
Cover Art © 2022 Jaycee DeLorenzo
Edited by Elizabetta McKay

First Edition, August 2022

ISBN: 978-1-64890-527-8

Also available in eBook, ISBN: 978-1-64890-526-1

CONTENT WARNING:
This book contains sexual content, which may only be suitable for mature readers. Recounting of a sexual assault (off page), death by murder, use of guns, transphobic behavior, misgendering of MC.

To my wife Lisa, my daughter Rachel, and my son Andrew. Without your patience and understanding, this book would never have been written. I love you guys!

To Scarlett and Scout. You may be golden retrievers, but you're better people than I will ever be.

PROLOGUE

Dark spirits flourished in ancient folklore—demons whose sole purpose was to bend victims to their will and punish those who failed to comply. This inhuman rogues' gallery included the Dybbuks, who haunted the dreams of early Jews, and the Afreets, who tormented characters in numerous Middle Eastern legends. Other cultures used different names, but these spirits could be found in the mythology of virtually every civilization since the dawn of recorded history.

As a child in Catholic grade school, I had a simpler name for my dark spirits. Ignoring my classmates' more colorful descriptors—I just called them nuns.

Believing I would benefit from a Catholic school education, my parents enrolled me in Saint Jerome's Grade

School in the fall of 1999. Located in a middle-class neigh-
borhood in the city of Cleveland Heights, Saint Jerome's
was a huge concrete and brick monolith that once housed
nearly eight hundred students. The student population was
down to two hundred fifty at the time of my arrival, and
the school shut some classrooms due to lack of use. Those
enrollment declines continued after my graduation, and
the bishop of Cleveland eventually closed Saint Jerome's
and several other Cleveland parishes with the goal of "bet-
ter allocating limited church resources." The fact that these
resources were later distributed to the more affluent sub-
urbs of Greater Cleveland was said by the bishop to be
purely a coincidence.

At the time I attended, Saint Jerome's was also the only
school in the Cleveland Catholic Diocese where nuns were
still a significant percentage of the teaching faculty. In my
pretransition childhood, that should have been an ad-
vantage. Never one to hide their feelings, the nuns openly
favored the girls. Girls generally followed the rules, were
unlikely to mouth off during class, and were far less likely
than boys to cause trouble overall.

To the nuns' dismay, I was an exception to the nice-girl
rule. I preferred playing football with the boys to any of the
more sedate games normally associated with my sex. I also
questioned virtually every point my teachers raised in
class, particularly over matters of religion. My queries re-
flected no interest in Catholic doctrine. It was the nuns' de-
mand for unquestioning acceptance that really pissed me
off.

Adding to my frustration at school was the presence of
my brother, Paul. Known by the faculty as "the good

Luvello," Paul accepted anything the nuns told him with the same loving look displayed by dogs when fed unwanted table scraps after a meal. I wanted more than scraps. I wanted a place at the table.

It was this tendency to rebel, both verbally and physically, that landed me in frequent trouble at Saint Jerome's. My transgressions ranged from openly questioning church doctrine to accidentally, sort of, running down an old nun on the school playground. My friend John still talks about the time our teacher told us Mary spent her entire life as a virgin. To the teacher's chagrin, I asked if that was why Joseph died so long before she did.

The latter incident resulted in my mother's first trip to the school principal's office. When she told my father about her day, Dad almost spit out his coffee from laughing so hard. My mother always blamed him for my irreverent sense of humor.

For all my intentional misdeeds, it was my teacher's reaction to a more honest question that bothered me the most. One of the nuns, Sister Michelle, yelled at our class for not paying attention during morning prayer. In a lecture we heard frequently, Sister told us our behavior was making God cry.

I listened to these daily diatribes with only minimal attention. I knew God couldn't cry as frequently as the nuns claimed. Chronically depressed patients in psychiatric wards don't cry that often.

Whether it was from that thought or just general boredom, I raised my hand after this latest scolding and asked if God could laugh. Without trying to answer my question, Sister Michelle called me up in front of the class and rapped *my hands with a ruler.*

The punishment was minor, far less severe than what I'd received in other instances. What bothered me more was Sister's reaction. My question had clearly appalled her, and I needed to know why.

After class, I gathered my courage and asked Sister Michelle what had been so improper about my query.

Looking surprised, she said, "There are some things you just shouldn't ask."

It wasn't until recently I realized she was right.

CHAPTER ONE

AMOS JOHNSON WAS an enforcer. A triggerman for the Cleveland mob, Amos stood six-foot-four with the physique and ornery nature of a habitual steroid user. His body was his business, and Amos took his business seriously.

Amos also loved tattoos. Known as "Tatts" to his friends, Amos proudly claimed to have visited every tattoo parlor in the city of Cleveland. Fully covered from head to toe, the design on his left forearm was a tribute to his mother.

Amos's other tattoos, not nearly as sentimental, would get him thrown out of any polite gathering in the city. That assumed, of course, someone would be foolhardy enough to try.

Not being part of polite society myself, Amos and his

tattoos didn't bother me at all. We shared the same opinion about the Browns, blues music, and the current state of the movie industry. With the people I met in my business, that was pretty much the best you could hope for. Amos might not have understood me, but he was at least willing to make the effort.

I met Amos almost a year ago during a custody dispute with his ex-wife. His ex, a heroin addict, had run off with Amos's two-year-old daughter, Leann. It wasn't that Amos thought he should take care of his daughter—he knew he wasn't cut out for parenthood any more than his ex-wife. Amos's goal instead was to return Leann to the person who really did have custody, his beloved mother, Amelia. He hired me, a licensed private investigator, to make that reunion happen.

After a lucky break, I was able to return Leann to her grandmother within two days of her abduction. Amos was grateful, but he couldn't pay me much. That was pretty much an occupational hazard, though Amos promised he would be forever in my debt. One year later, that was a marker I needed to call.

My old-school mother would call Amos a thug. I didn't care if Amos was a thug because tonight, he was my thug. Bored and uncomfortable, Amos and I were crouched behind a car on the fifth floor of the main student parking garage at Creesmont College, a small liberal arts school about twenty miles outside of Greater Cleveland.

As colleges go, Creesmont wasn't much. Its history department was rated as one of the top thirty programs for schools of its size, and that was about it for high-level academics at the college. In a move born of desperation,

Creesmont administration decided to take advantage of the school's low academic reputation by investing more in athletics. That bet had paid off, and the school's football team currently ranked in the top five of Division Three schools across the country.

Amos and I were waiting to meet James O'Keefe. Considered a potential low-round pick in the next NFL draft, O'Keefe was the senior quarterback of this year's Creesmont football team. Six-foot-three, movie-star handsome and outwardly friendly, he was every girl's dream date. Unfortunately for those girls, James preferred rape to relationships.

My client, Jenna Adamcheck, was a third-year English major at Creesmont. To earn extra money, Jenna had signed up as a tutor for the Creesmont Athletic Program, and her first client was James O'Keefe.

With a long-term boyfriend at another school, Jenna had little interest in James's early attempts at seduction. Her indifference only piqued James's interest, and Jenna was surprised two weeks into their arrangement when James showed up at her dorm room requesting an unscheduled tutoring session. Jenna reluctantly allowed James into her room, where he then continued his courtship by pushing Jenna onto her bed and ripping off her sweater top.

Jenna was no shrinking violet. Taught by her father to always fight back, she aimed a well-placed knee at James's crotch. The knee connected, and James, now in considerable pain, fought to regain the upper hand.

Jenna, however, was not through. Furious, she grabbed the fork she was using for dinner and aimed it at James's left eye. While she missed, the fork drew blood as it gashed her assailant's left cheek. Unsure how to deal with a woman who hit back, James ran from Jenna's room. Cursing and in pain, he plotted his revenge.

Thinking she had resolved the incident, Jenna didn't report James to Creesmont administration. That was a mistake; although, it did initially appear James had backed off.

Three days later, Jenna found the windshield of her 2018 Kia Forte smashed and a typewritten note placed on the driver's seat. The message read, "Sluts always pay in the end." Alarmed, Jenna reported the incident to campus police along with her suspicions as to the culprit. Without evidence, those suspicions were promptly ignored.

The day of her police report, Jenna saw James watching from a distance as she exited her last class. When James saw her looking back, he smiled his brightest student-athlete smile before making an obscene gesture. Over the next few days, James began following Jenna everywhere she went on campus, always keeping a discreet distance to avoid any verifiable claims of harassment. After three more days, James's stalking took a different turn, and Jenna began finding posters with her picture hanging by the entrance to her dormitory. She showed me the ones she'd torn down, and "slut" was one of the nicer words James used.

Jenna realized the harassment would ultimately lead to another attempted rape, this time potentially including James's friends. Believing the campus police were useless, she decided to enlist outside help. Not having a lot of money, that led her to me.

Amos and I were waiting for James just before midnight on the top level of the campus parking lot adjacent to the Creesmont athletic dormitory. Just as he had the previous three nights, James pulled into the lot at precisely eleven forty-five, fifteen minutes before the football team's curfew.

I had realized two things while watching James both on and off campus: James was a creature of habit, and James was in love. The object of his devotion, his 1965 burgundy Ford Mustang hardtop, would have caught any man's eye. The 1965 was the original Mustang released by Ford. It was truly a sight to behold, and demolishing it would make me resent James all the more.

Every evening James parked his car in the same spot on the top, fifth floor in the student parking garage. There were plenty of spots lower down, but James clearly didn't want to risk another car denting his beloved Mustang.

Amos and I waited for James behind the only other car parked on the fifth level. Neither of us worried about surveillance cameras. Using a pellet gun, Amos had previously taken care of the fifth-floor cameras along with those on several other levels. I knew campus security, usually harried and understaffed, would assume their destruction had been the work of vandals. They would replace the cameras when time and budget allowed.

Its cameras now disabled, the fifth floor was the perfect place for a confrontation. Amos and I would have James all to ourselves, and I intended to have some fun.

James quickly exited his car before turning to take one last look at his Mustang. I stepped out from behind my hiding spot.

"You've been a bad boy, Jim."

He wasn't expecting company, and he didn't know how to react. He tried bluster.

"Who the fuck are you?"

"Never mind that, Jim. Didn't your mom ever tell you

not to pick on girls?"

The idiot thought I was referring to myself. "I don't give autographs to queers."

Still basking in his witty comeback, James finally noticed the tire iron swinging in my right hand. Unfortunately for James, he failed to see the brass knuckles in my left.

At five-foot-seven and a hundred forty pounds, I had a survivor's aversion to fair fighting. James's lack of attention went uncorrected until the knuckles connected with his liver.

Few blows are more excruciating than a punch to the liver. James didn't lose consciousness, though he collapsed in pain on the parking lot floor. It was a sight Jenna Adamcheck would have paid extra to see, but I had much more planned for our evening. I kicked James to get his attention.

"Damn it, Jim, you took that punch like a trooper. I'm glad you didn't pass out. Now you can watch what we do to your car."

I waved my hand, and Amos stepped into view, all six-foot-four, horrifying inches of him. Amos had a tire iron of his own, and he used it to terrifying effect. He started with the Mustang's windshield, moved around to the side windows, and then to the rear. In just sixty seconds, there wasn't a section of glass that hadn't been demolished. Amos then switched his attention to the car's hood and trunk. Five minutes after he started, the Mustang looked like a refugee from a demolition derby.

Watching Amos work on his beloved car, James looked utterly defeated. I bent down to refocus his attention.

"Jim, I need you to listen to me." He heard my voice, but he could only watch his car. Two more quick kicks, and he was again facing me.

"You've been bothering Jenna Adamcheck—that will stop right now. I need you to understand me, Jim. This is strike one. You talk to Jenna, you look at Jenna, you post even one more note about Jenna, and that will be strike two. Strike two means my friend over there will take his tire iron to your knees. How many guys do you think get drafted by the NFL with two broken kneecaps?"

He didn't respond, so I kicked him again, this time in the groin.

"I asked you a question, asshole. You think you'll get drafted with two broken knees?"

James shook his head weakly. I kicked him again for emphasis and pulled out my Glock. James now lay in a fetal position on the concrete floor; it was the perfect time for show-and-tell.

"Now, let's talk about strike three. The game we're playing here, it's three strikes, and you're dead. You might think a queer like me would never shoot you. Who knows, maybe you're right. But I want you to take a good look at my associate."

Amos stepped into James's line of sight. Seeing him, James started to noticeably whimper.

"You're looking at a man who kills people for a living. He wanted to kill you tonight, but I talked him out of it. If anything happens to Jenna, that protection goes away, and you are a dead man. That warning includes your moron football friends as well. If anything happens to Jenna, if she even trips and falls on the sidewalk, I'll assume you are responsible."

Tatts swung his tire iron menacingly. "You should at

least let me break his knees. Enough with the three strikes shit."

I bent down once more, only inches from James's face.

"You see, Jim? You owe me your life, and I haven't even asked you to thank me."

James muttered something unintelligible. It reminded me of one more thing he needed to know.

"I almost forgot something very important, Jim. Thanks for helping me remember."

I turned to Amos. "Show Jim what you have in your hand."

Amos smiled and again began swinging the tire iron. Lying next to his car, James curled himself into a little ball for protection. Before Amos could go full-on crazy, I said, "The other hand, Tatts."

Amos grunted with disappointment, but he held up his other hand. In it was a small object, the miniature camera I'd given him when we met earlier that evening. James looked confused, so I explained.

"Let's talk about the cops. For a guy in your position, they might seem like your salvation. They find us; they arrest us, and your troubles are completely over. Hell, you'd be back to raping women before you know it.

"If I were you, Jim, I'd rethink that little strategy. You see, all the time I was kicking your ass, my associate over there was taking pictures. I'm sure he even got some of you crying like a baby on the parking lot floor.

"Now, getting beaten up by a big guy like my friend, your buddies might understand that. They might even show you some sympathy. Imagine, though, if those pictures get out, and everyone realizes you were messed up by some five-foot-seven transgender guy. Imagine if that transgender guy also said he beat you up because you two were in a relationship, and he found that you were cheating.

"What would your teammates think? What would your family think? Hell, imagine what the NFL would think—you know they investigate everyone they draft. At that point, we might as well take out your knees; you wouldn't need them for football anymore. You could try denying everything, but people would always wonder. No one would ever look at you the same.

"So if someone insists on calling the cops when they see the condition you're in, I would just tell them a couple of guys snuck up from behind and started whaling on you before you could react. They might not believe you, but stick to your story, and they won't have much choice.

"Do we understand each other, Jim? Are you gonna mess with Jenna Adamcheck anymore?"

He shook his head no, but I kicked him anyway. No particular reason; it just felt right.

Amos and I watched James stagger toward the parking lot exit. We then left ourselves, making sure to take the side exit without an attendant.

As we walked toward our respective vehicles, Amos said, "You know, I've seen him play. He's got a pansy arm. No way he makes it to the NFL."

"I've seen him play too. He couldn't even make it in Division One. Fortunately for us, he doesn't know that."

"You shouldn't have let him call you a queer. You're more of a guy than he is."

"Don't worry, Amos. I know exactly what I am."

It was the first real lie I'd told that evening.

CHAPTER TWO

I CALLED JENNA Adamcheck the next morning and let her know that James O'Keefe would no longer be a problem. For her sake and mine, I avoided detailing the previous night's events. After reminding Jenna to call me should anything else go wrong, I hung up and thought further about the lie I'd told Amos. At age twenty-seven, I still didn't fully know who the hell I was.

To be fair, there were some certainties. For my first twenty-two years as the daughter of Clair and Alan Luvello, I'd led a remarkably normal life in a remarkably normal midwestern town.

All that normality ended five years ago. Since then, I've been Terry Luvello, a transgender man working as a licensed private detective. While I hated the word transgender—it

sounded like something from a bad Frankenstein movie—
I'd made my peace with it long ago.

Had the last five years invalidated my first twenty-two?
I never thought they had. Beyond gender, my true identity
was a more complicated question. I'd been a daughter, a son,
a sister, and a brother. I had a best friend who'd stuck with
me through it all.

If pressed for an answer, I'd say I was an investigator. I
loved solving puzzles, and that was true long before I received my detective's license. It was what I liked to do, and
I was good at it. Throughout all the changes in my life, it had
been the one constant.

Not that being transgender didn't affect my daily routine. Every transgender male or female had their personal
list of annoyances. Depending on the individual, their list
might include family rejection, employment discrimination,
stereotypes, and other issues affecting the transgender community.

My own list had only one item. I called it "dealing with
idiots." While admittedly broad, it included an ever-growing
list of subcategories.

That was no insult to my hometown. I've always believed living as a transgender person was easier in a city like
Cleveland. Like most Cleveland residents, I complained
about the city, its sports teams, its wildly variable weather,
and its dysfunctional city government. Like most Clevelanders, I also wouldn't dream of living anywhere else. My downtown studio apartment was in the middle of a high-crime
neighborhood, but I lived in the heart of the city, and my
neighbors left me alone. What more could I have asked?

Life in Cleveland was certainly far less glamorous than

say, Los Angeles or Miami. On the plus side, it was also more real. People here were far too busy working, raising families, and dealing with the day-to-day realities of life to worry about a transgender male living in their midst.

Still, there were idiots. As a licensed private detective, I carried a gun for a living. For the most part, that made the idiots easier to deal with.

A phone call interrupted my moment of self-reflection. Expecting my friend, John, I picked up my cell phone without glancing at the screen. My mistake—the call was from my mother.

I loved my mother dearly, but she typically only called when she wanted to go clothes shopping. From the time I announced I was transgender, my mom took it upon herself to expand my wardrobe of male clothing, particularly in the area of men's suits. While I never found an occasion to wear those suits, that never seemed to bother my mother. Regardless of the unwanted clothing and the logjam in my closet, I appreciated her support nonetheless.

To my surprise, this call was about something different. After inquiring about my health, Mom announced, "Your brother Paul is going to call you this evening. He wants to talk with you."

"Mom, you know what happened the last time Paul and I spoke."

Three years my senior, Paul was what one might charitably call a doctrinaire Catholic. Being anything but charitable, I once referred to him as the world's first male nun. The fact that I said it to his face when he was standing next to his wife Lydia probably didn't help. The conversation occurred when I was twenty-two, and Paul and Lydia had just begun a lecture on the evil of doubting God's plan for my gender. Our relationship degraded from there, and Paul and I have barely spoken in the five years since.

"What could Paul possibly say to me at this point?"

"I don't know. He wouldn't tell me anything. Just give him a chance, please?"

I agreed to hear Paul out. It was close, but I figured five minutes wasted on the phone with my brother beat a couple of hours in a clothing store. I considered just sitting back and waiting for Paul's call but decided to text John and see if he wanted to come over and watch the baseball game.

John Travers became my best friend after we met on the playground at Saint Jerome's Grade School. The playground had separate sections for the boys and girls, established with the typically nunnish idea that the two sexes should never interact. The church parking lot served as the boy's section, while the girls played in a smaller, grassy field closer to the school building.

According to the nuns, this division gave the boys a larger area to play sports like football and baseball. While no one spoke about this openly, the different playing surfaces also served to minimize injuries for the girls and maximize attrition among the boys. For the nuns, that was a win-win.

Having no interest in jumping rope, I gravitated to the boy's section, hoping to play football. John eventually talked the other boys into letting me play, and he and I have been friends ever since.

While I was a social outcast, John had girls flocking around him even in grade school. The other boys also liked John, and he was the center of virtually every social group. When we got to be teenagers, John went on numerous dates with an assortment of girls, but he still spent much of his time hanging out with me.

After college, John parlayed his skills into a career in advertising. It was a field I never much cared for, but he sought my input on every campaign. That continued even after I told him one of his logos—I called it "Fred, the wonder pigeon"—resembled a bird rising from a dog food bowl.

John was also the first person I told about my plan to transition. After hearing me out, he told me I'd always been a better male companion than his more traditional male friends. Later on, I made John stay in the room when I made the same announcement to my mother. Thinking back, that was probably not very fair—I was sure Mom assumed we were announcing our engagement.

Though he called me a wimp, John was also supportive when I changed my mind about the medical procedure that would make my decision permanent. It wasn't that I intended to go back to being female, but hospitals terrified me. My father had died in one, and I could never quite forgive them for that. John was right though. I guess I was a wimp in thinking about it.

Unfortunately, John was unavailable for the game. Adding to my misfortune, Paul called just a moment later.

"Hey, Terry," he said in his fake-jovial tone. "Did Mom tell you I might be calling?"

"Hi, Paul. I thought the church frowned on contacting the Antichrist."

"Can we have a normal conversation? I'm asking for your help. I need you to go to my parish and speak with the pastor there."

I couldn't believe it. Five years with virtually no conversation, and Paul was calling to convert me.

"Are you insane? You know if I walk into a church, it will end badly for them and me."

"This is about a case, not religion. Father Lawrence came to me because I mentioned that my sister, sorry, my brother," he said hurriedly, "was a private detective."

This was suddenly getting interesting. "What does he need me to do?"

"I don't know. Father Lawrence wouldn't tell me. He just asked if I could get you in to meet him at Saint Edmund's as quickly as possible, preferably on Monday morning."

"Tell him I'll be there at nine o'clock."

I hung up before Paul could respond.

CHAPTER THREE

I DROVE TO Saint Edmund's in my ten-year-old, less-than-trusty Honda Civic. Soon after I purchased the car, my mother encouraged me to give my new vehicle a name. After considering a variety of expletives, I eventually settled on Hannibal Lecter since the car has tried to kill me on more than one occasion. While many have a love-hate relationship with their automobile, mine was more hate-hate. If it weren't for my complete and abject poverty, I would have traded it in long ago.

On the way to Saint Edmund's, I experienced the usual Cleveland traffic jam. Long-time Cleveland residents know there are four seasons in every year: almost winter, winter, still winter, and orange barrel season. We were well into June, so the orange construction barrels were out in force.

While annoying, the delay gave me time to review what little I knew about the church and its patron saint.

Saint Edmund's was a Jesuit church in the Cleveland suburb of Westlake. The parish was named after Saint Edmund Campion, known as one of the "Forty Martyrs of England and Wales." The English had considered Catholicism to be a treasonous offense, and Campion had served as a spy for Rome. Not at all forgiving, the English eventually executed Campion for his efforts.

I wouldn't know any of this if I hadn't attended Saint Robert Bellarmine, a large Jesuit high school located close to my Cleveland Heights neighborhood. Saint Bellarmine was famous as the priest who ordered Galileo to quit saying the Earth revolved around the sun. Like Campion, Saint Bellarmine also ran afoul of the British, this time over the Oath of Allegiance required of all English subjects. The Oath placed the English king over the pope in authority, a big problem for the Roman hierarchy.

Thinking about Bellarmine, I wondered how some saints had achieved that designation. Sometimes it seemed like the Oscar lifetime achievement award, a gift for hanging around in the business long enough and not pissing off the wrong people.

That realization aside, I'd enjoyed my four years at Saint Bellarmine's. The Jesuits welcomed my many questions, and they threw their own right back at me. They were blunt and occasionally sarcastic, two traits I've always appreciated.

Paul didn't value the Jesuitical bluntness the same way I did. I still remember him coming home one day as a freshman complaining, "Father Ned told me I smile too much. He

said you couldn't trust anyone who smiled as much as I do."
I couldn't help but laugh. Paul had finally moved to my position on the great Catholic totem pole.

The other unique aspect to the Jesuits was that their
priests, churches, and schools all reported up through their
own provincial structure, separate from the Catholic diocese. That gave the Order a degree of freedom with no interference from the local bishop—convenient for many reasons, particularly if one was trying to keep secrets.

I wore one of my mom-purchased gray suits for this
meeting, its maiden trip outside my closet. While I still preferred jeans, this suit had multiple pockets in both the pants
and suit coat. I often wondered why women wore the clothes
they did. If I'd realized how utilitarian men's clothing was, I
might have started wearing it years before I actually did.

Construction delays aside, Hannibal, my new suit, and
I arrived just five minutes past my nine o'clock appointment. I exited my car and got my first good look at Saint Edmund's and its architecture.

The Cleveland parishes I knew tended to be of two
types. The older ones, such as the one I attended as a youth,
looked as though they'd been designed by an architect in the
middle of a particularly nasty hangover. Churches of this
type tended to be gigantic brick buildings with little style,
identifiable only by a large entrance door and a cross either
in front or on the roof.

The newer suburban parishes were even less recogniza-
ble than the older types. I'd driven past one the previous
week that resembled a fat rocket ship. I wasn't sure what
type of building it was until I noticed the sign out in front.

In contrast, Saint Edmund's appeared almost Eastern

Orthodox in styling with two prominent steeples and an ornate dome in the middle. To ensure no one could misunderstand its purpose, the church had three crosses, one on each steeple and a third, larger cross on the dome itself.

After making sure to leave my gun locked securely in my car, I walked over to a small brick building to the side of Saint Edmund's that appeared to be the parish office. I pressed the buzzer, and a secretary unlocked the door. Unlike the more senior staff employed by many Catholic parishes, my welcomer was a surprisingly cute brunette. Her name tag announced her as Miss Catherine Lambert, and she looked to be in her early thirties. Wanting to make an impression, I tried to sound official.

"My name is Terry Luvello, and I have an appointment with Father Lawrence at nine o'clock."

"You're late," she said in a no-nonsense tone. "Have a seat, and I'll get Father."

My official voice had clearly had no impact. With that, the effect of her appearance wore off quickly.

I'd sworn off sex for some years now, having had only two sexual experiences in my entire life. My first, to both of our embarrassment, was with John. When we were eighteen, John asked me to our senior prom. After dinner and two quick dances, we realized we were both bored out of our skulls and snuck out for a ride.

John brought along a bottle of whiskey he'd stolen from his alcoholic father along with a couple of shot glasses. After parking, we proceeded to drink way too much. The drinking led to a kiss, and the kiss led to the backseat of John's car. The sex that followed was less than fulfilling, and neither of us has ever discussed it much to this day.

My second sexual experience came as a junior in college with a rather masculine girl who lived in my dormitory. If anything, it was even less exciting than my first attempt.

John has tried, on multiple occasions, to fix me up with the more adventurous friends of the girls he was dating. People have said I make a reasonably handsome guy, and my voice was deep enough to sound male. Still, I figured I'd already given it a try with both sexes, and it just wasn't for me. Lately, I've been revisiting that decision more and more often.

Father Lawrence showed up a couple of minutes later, interrupting my sexual reverie. A tall, muscular man in his midfifties, he walked with a rather pronounced limp. Father Lawrence led me a short distance down a narrow hallway to his office, and he motioned me to sit. I figured I should get something out in the open.

"Father, before we get started, did Paul fill you in on my...change?"

"Did he mention you were transgender? Yes, he did. He also said you two had a falling out, and you were, and I quote, 'the most annoying and obsessive person I have ever known.'"

I was impressed. A priest had spoken the word transgender in the same tone of voice one used in saying someone was tall or had brown hair. Given my misgivings about the term, there were days that even gave me pause.

"You're still interested in hiring me?"

"He also mentioned you were the smartest person he knew. I figured smart and obsessive weren't bad qualities for a detective. I'll withhold judgment on the annoying part for now."

To my surprise, I found myself liking this priest. "Fair enough. Paul said you might need my services. Why don't you fill me in?"

Father Lawrence chose his words with extreme care. "This is a delicate matter, and it requires your complete discretion. It involves Father Samuel, a recently ordained priest, who came to Saint Edmund's last December from our New Orleans province. About two weeks ago, Father Samuel came across information that led him to believe"—Father Lawrence hesitated noticeably at this point—"a man intended to commit murder. Specifically, that he intended to slash a woman's throat. Father Samuel notified me immediately. He couldn't identify either the intended victim or the suspected assailant based on what he heard."

He waited for me to digest this information. While doing so, I remembered an item on the local news from the same time period—the Angela Tully slaying. Angela Tully was a Cleveland housewife found murdered in her home. The police had no trouble determining the cause of death; Mrs. Tully was found with multiple stab wounds to her throat. If that wasn't horrifying enough, her children discovered their mother's body shortly after arriving home from school. The timeline for the killing fit with Father Lawrence's story.

"Do you think this might be related to Angela Tully, and can I assume this information was acquired during confession?"

"I wanted to see if you would make the Tully connection. Yes, I do think it's related. The Tully murder happened on a Tuesday, just three days after Father Samuel obtained this information."

I noticed he didn't answer my question concerning confession. Given the rules that I knew to be in place, I didn't expect him to. Father Lawrence was clearly trying to finesse his way around the confessional seal.

"Have you notified the police?" I knew the answer, but I had to ask.

"I haven't contacted the police. After discussing the matter with my superior, Father Thomas, neither of us felt that was possible. You asked about the role of confession in this case, and I suspect you know that is something I cannot discuss. Based on legal statute, the seal of confession protects not only the content of conversations within the sacrament, it goes further in protecting even the existence of those communications. In theory, a priest hearing someone's intent to murder Jane Doe could notify the police that Jane's life was in danger. The priest could not, however, tell the police where they obtained this knowledge or supply any additional information concerning the identity of the person making the threat.

"In this case, that wasn't even an option. As I mentioned, Father Samuel was told nothing indicating the identity of the individual who was threatened, nor did he see the person making the threat or recognize his voice."

"That leads to another question," I said. "With the restrictions inherent in the seal, why am I here?"

"For you to understand your involvement, I need to make you aware of two additional aspects to this case. The first is, regrettably, a political concern expressed by Father Thomas and the bishop here in Cleveland, and yes, he has become involved as well. Both are worried about the perceived connection between this case and the sacrament of confession."

"Okay, you lost me," I said. "I'm not sure I see a political issue here at all."

"If you take this case, you need to start thinking like a Jesuit. You are undoubtedly aware of the broader discussions in this country over issues concerning religious freedom. Those issues include employee insurance coverage for birth control in Catholic-run workplaces, restrictive hiring practices in Catholic educational institutions, as well as the whole discussion of gay marriage. Should the Church's prior knowledge in this case become known, there is a concern it could further weaken popular support for the Church and for religious freedom in general. It could potentially lead to the restriction of a confessional privilege that currently exists in all fifty states."

"With all due respect, Father," I said. "I think you and Father Thomas may be overstating the Church's exposure on this issue. If the threat was truly nonspecific, I am having trouble seeing how anyone could think the Church should have done more."

Father Lawrence suddenly looked exhausted, and I began to see the strain he was under. "That, Mr. Luvello, leads to my second item. Yesterday, there was another threat."

CHAPTER FOUR

WHEN I DROVE to Saint Edmund's, I assumed I was stepping into a routine case, possibly a parishioner with his or her hand in the collection basket. Now, I was in the middle of a murder investigation with virtually no information and a limited ability to ask questions. When I asked Father Lawrence to elaborate on the second threat, he called Father Samuel into his office.

Father Samuel was in his early thirties, older than I would have expected from a recently ordained priest. He was slender in build, with prematurely thinning red hair that provided only patchy coverage to the top of his rather large head.

More interestingly, Father Samuel hardly looked in my direction, offering virtually no acknowledgment I was there.

When he finally did glance my way, the first thing I noticed was his eyes. I'd heard of piercing eyes, but I'd never met anyone whose gaze fit that description. Father Samuel's eyes looked as if they could melt steel. Unlike Father Lawrence, I assumed he felt some distaste for what he viewed as my "sexual deviancy." Either that, or he didn't like my new suit. I would hate to think he glared at everyone that way.

Father Lawrence performed the introductions and asked Father Samuel to describe, as precisely as he could, his conversation the day before.

"I was scheduled," Father Samuel said, "to provide counseling to parishioners after the noon mass yesterday from one to three o'clock." He chose his words as carefully as Father Lawrence, so much so, I expected him to use air quotes.

"Most Sundays," he continued, "parishioners seek counseling the hour right after mass, and yesterday was no exception. Only one parishioner entered my booth after that time, and that was around two-fifteen.

"The other individual, the person you're interested in, came around ten minutes before I was scheduled to leave. From his voice, I would say he was the same individual who made the previous threat. While I can't tell you his exact wording, I can say another murder is quite possible."

I figured I could start asking questions at this point. I was careful with my phrasing.

"Based on your conversation, would you guess the second murder might look like the first—a woman killed by a knife?"

"The threat was to a woman. Unlike our first conversation, the method was unspecified."

My next question was addressed to Father Lawrence. "Father, beyond yourself and Father Samuel, how many priests are there at Saint Edmund's? If it's just the two of you, how often do you both hear confession?"

"We are the only two priests in the parish," Father Lawrence replied. "Regarding our schedule, we normally hear confessions on Tuesdays, Saturdays, and Sundays. Father Samuel bears the brunt of that burden; I cover Tuesdays while he ministers both Saturdays and Sundays. As you can imagine, attendance is far greater on the weekends due to work schedules."

Father Samuel broke in. "To answer what I'm guessing will be your next question, the first threat occurred on a Saturday, and as I mentioned earlier, the second occurred yesterday after mass."

I turned again to Father Samuel, but he continued to keep his gaze focused on Father Lawrence.

"Father, do you see any possibility this individual may be targeting you specifically for these confessions? Has anything like this ever happened previously, either before or after your transfer to Cleveland?"

Father Samuel replied in a clipped tone as if I was accusing him of complicity in the threats. "Trust me, Mr. Luvello, if anything like this had happened previously, I would certainly have told my superiors. Regarding your other question, I see no reason to think this individual may be targeting me."

"While I'm sure you're correct," I replied, "I do need to ask any questions I believe might be pertinent to this case."

Turning my attention back to Father Lawrence, I asked if I could speak to some of the parishioners who attended confession on a regular basis.

"I realize I can't be open regarding my real reason for asking questions. I would suggest we tell these individuals there have been a couple of break-ins at Saint Edmund's over the last few weeks. You could tell them I was hired to investigate."

"That is acceptable," Father Lawrence said reluctantly. "We actually have had a few minor burglaries recently. How do we explain the lack of police involvement?"

That question had occurred to me as well. "Tell them you have a reason to suspect teenagers are the culprits, and you hope to settle the matter privately without getting them in even more trouble."

"All right, let's go with that for now. I believe Father Samuel and I can put our heads together and come up with three to four names. People don't go to confession as regularly as they used to."

Father Samuel asked if he could go back to his room to finish morning prayer. As he was walking to the door, he suddenly stopped and looked directly at me.

"Have you ever been to confession, Mr. Luvello?"

"Not since I was about fifteen, Father. Is that a prerequisite for this case?"

"Not at all. I just wanted to offer my services. Seeking forgiveness for your sins can be cathartic, even for those who don't believe."

"I never said I didn't believe, Father. Maybe I don't think I've committed any sins worth confessing."

Not surprisingly, Father Lawrence picked that point to jump in. "Father Samuel, please leave us. Mr. Luvello, I'd like you to stay awhile longer. We need to talk."

After Father Samuel closed the door, Father Lawrence said, "Mr. Luvello, please don't take offense at this question, but can I ask you when and why you decided you were transgender?"

I usually avoided personal questions, but this one caught me off guard. I started to answer before I could think through my response.

"I don't know, Father. It was about five years ago. I based my decision on where I was at the time and the fact that I've always considered myself a male."

"You looked at the facts, and you made a deduction based on what you knew. Did you ever really trust in your decision?"

"With all due respect, Father, I have no idea where you're coming from. Look at me and look at the clothes I'm wearing. How could you possibly ask if I trusted my decision? Do you think I'm dressed like this because I like men's suits?" My voice had gotten louder than it should, but he was starting to piss me off.

He shook his head and tried again, the lonely Jesuit lecturing the recalcitrant student. "Let me try to put this differently. When you came here, you asked if it bothered me that you were transgender. I told you no, and that was an honest answer. I didn't tell you there were two things that did give me pause. The first was when your brother told me you decided this five years ago and then backed out of the surgery. Second, from what Paul told me and what little I've observed, it sometimes appears you treat your identity as more of an annoyance than something central to what you are. Taken together, those things tell me you may have decided in your head you were transgender, but you didn't trust your own decision."

Spreading his hands in a gesture of conciliation, Lawrence said, "Don't get me wrong, I don't doubt for a second that you are transgender. In the context of this case, however, your skills at deduction are of absolutely no use to me if you don't trust in them yourself. I should also say this relates to you and Father Samuel. I realize he has his issues, and I will speak to him. That being said, I need to know those issues will not get in the way of you solving this case."

I was still angry, but I was also feeling a degree of self-doubt. Introspection has never been my strong suit. Not sure what else to say, I threw his words back at him.

"You may have a point, Father, but now I need you to trust me. While speaking to Father Samuel, an unknown person declared his intent to commit murder. Now, a woman has been killed, quite possibly by the same individual. While I may not like the good Father, I've found that to be true of many clients. That has never kept me from doing my job, and I promise you it won't in this case."

"Fair enough. I will text you the names you asked for, and I'll call each of them ahead of time to tell them you may be visiting. While I can't say how they'll react, I think most of the parishioners here are open-minded. Please solve this thing before anyone else gets killed."

Unfortunately, I failed on Father's last request within a few hours of our meeting.

CHAPTER FIVE

SARAH GRUBER WAS a twenty-six-year-old housewife living in Avon, Ohio, a well-off community populated largely by lawyers and physicians. As they became even more prosperous, many Avon residents ended up moving to more well-to-do Cleveland suburbs like Moreland Hills and Hunting Valley. In essence, Avon was a proving ground. Those truly worthy of one-percent status moved on, while other, younger professionals were always ready to take their place.

In the case of Sarah Gruber, her husband, Ethan, was a legal associate at Traber, Young, and Williams, a prominent Cleveland law firm. As was often true, Mr. Gruber did not come home from work until after 10:00 p.m., the typical weekend and weekday life for any associate in just about any big-city law firm.

In his police interview, Ethan Gruber stated he initially couldn't locate Sarah when he returned home. After a quick search, he eventually found his wife, fully clothed, lying on top of their bed in a pool of blood. Mr. Gruber immediately called 911, and the police medical examiner determined Sarah's death had occurred as the result of a knife wound to her throat.

The ME estimated the attack had taken place between five o'clock and six o'clock that same day. That timeframe ruled out Ethan Gruber as a suspect, as several coworkers confirmed he'd been working until nine-thirty. From the blood trail and other evidence, the medical examiner determined the killer attacked Mrs. Gruber in the second-floor hallway outside the bedroom and dragged her to the bed.

The police thought Mrs. Gruber might have known her assailant since there were no signs of forced entry. Upon questioning from reporters, a police spokesman admitted there were several similarities between the Gruber and Tully murders, but police were unwilling to say the two cases were related.

I first heard of the attack on the evening news, and I immediately called Father Lawrence. Father had watched the same news account and reached the same conclusion—we needed to assume both cases were linked to our confessor. Despite his earlier concerns about issues of church doctrine, we also agreed it was time to alert the police. While doing so, we would take care to stick to the strictures regarding confessional privilege.

I asked Father Lawrence if he wanted me to continue my own investigation. Somewhat to my surprise, he said yes. While he agreed police involvement was necessary, he felt their hurry to solve the case might result in panic or suspicion among his parishioners. In short, he was now asking me to investigate the crimes while also acting as his liaison with the Cleveland PD.

I was skeptical about the new arrangement. For understandable reasons, cops are notoriously suspicious of an outsider's interference in a criminal investigation. That would be true in any case, but doubly so in a high-profile homicide. Father said he would make my role clear to the detective in charge, but I was still dubious.

I drove out to Saint Edmund's the next morning to meet with Father Lawrence and plot strategy. Since the Tully and Gruber murders had taken place in two different cities, our first challenge was deciding where to go with our information. Given the significant difference in size between the Cleveland and Avon police departments, we assumed Cleveland would take the lead in any joint investigation. With that, we decided to call the Cleveland Twelfth District, the precinct with jurisdiction over the Angela Tully homicide.

After finally reaching a human operator, I was connected to Detective Hannah Page, the lead investigator on the Tully murder. I started by explaining who I was and my relationship with Saint Edmund's. I then told Detective Page that Father Lawrence and I might possess information linking the Tully and Gruber murders, information we would be reluctant to discuss over the phone. Father Lawrence had told me he had no desire to meet with a police officer, even a plainclothes detective, on church property. Detective Page agreed to meet with us at the Capstone, a diner located just a few blocks away from the parish.

The Capstone Diner was one of the better-known

establishments in Greater Cleveland, a region with a diner on virtually every major street corner. The Capstone's lofty status was due in part to its unique location next to an old, now unused railroad station.

Their dining area, decorated with old railroad memorabilia, showed Capstone ownership clearly felt that décor was more important than mere embellishments such as food and service. I based my observation on the burned grilled cheese sandwich served more than twenty minutes after my order, along with a dark, bitter drink advertised as coffee.

Detective Page arrived just after our food. She entered the Capstone in a rush, a five-foot-four-inch, brown-haired whirlwind. Quickly scanning the room, she had no trouble picking out Father Lawrence's collar. She proceeded to our table, seemingly without stopping for breath, and sat in the empty chair directly across from me. She was younger than I expected, in her late twenties or early thirties. Interestingly, she wore what appeared to be designer clothing.

"I am assuming," she said, "that you gentlemen are Father Lawrence Donegan and Mr. Terry Luvello. As I'm sure you both guessed, I am Detective Page. Would one of you please tell me why I'm here?"

Luckily Father Lawrence answered because I was distracted by Detective Page herself. Her reddish-brown hair, while short, seemed to go in several different directions at once. On anyone else, I would have described it as disheveled. On her, it seemed to fit, almost as if it was styled to align with her personality. Not beautiful in a conventional sense, she possessed a small, crooked nose that complimented an equally crooked smile. She wasn't just pretty; she was fascinating.

I realized I was staring like an idiot. Luckily for me, Father Lawrence spent ten minutes relaying the essentials of the two threats made to Father Samuel in confession, finishing just in time for the arrival of the detective's order.

In discussing the case, Father Lawrence used the same careful wording from our first conversation at the church. He covered the declarations made to Father Samuel and his obligations under the confessional seal, making sure to emphasize the latter's place in state law.

Detective Page hesitated after he finished. Whether that was from surprise or a vain attempt to digest the Capstone's food, I couldn't be certain. Eventually, she spoke.

"I understand why you're here," she said, pointing to Father Lawrence. "Mr. Luvello, why don't you tell me about your involvement?"

I'd known the question was coming and had prepared an answer. "As I mentioned over the phone, I'm a licensed private investigator. Given the rather sensitive issues in this case, Father Lawrence hired me to explore the possibility our confessor might have some involvement with Saint Edmund's. He thought a private investigator could work more under the radar than someone operating within an official police investigation. It's my job to raise as few alarm bells as possible in the hope that parishioners might then open up more easily. Now that the police are involved, he also asked me to be his liaison with your investigation."

To my surprise, Detective Page had no objections.

"I have a million other leads to run down," she said, "so I can live with your involvement for now. There are, however, two conditions. First, you need to limit your inquiries to the parish itself and the people within the parish. Second, you need to let me know immediately anything you find that might be even remotely relevant to this case."

"I'll be honest with you both," she continued. "Given you have almost no information, even if this is our killer, I'm not sure you're going to be able to find anything of note. I'll pass along what you told me to the Avon police department since they are looking into the Gruber murder. They may wish to contact you as well."

We exchanged cards, and Detective Page left quickly after cautioning me once again about the need to keep her in the loop. I agreed, and Father Lawrence and I watched as she hurried out the door. Once she was out of earshot, Father Lawrence looked at me with a slight smile.

"She's very direct. Not bad-looking either."

I couldn't resist. "Father, remember your vocation!"

"I meant for you, idiot. Your brother said you lived like a monk. Remember what I said about trust? You need to keep an open mind."

There were times I forgot he was a Jesuit. After dropping the discussion of my love life, he handed me a sheet of paper with names and contact information.

"There are four names on this list along with addresses and phone numbers. Father Samuel and I put our heads together, and these were the parishioners we thought would most likely have been present on the days in question. I've spoken to all four individuals, and all are willing to talk with you. As you suggested, I stretched the truth a bit and said your visit involved some break-ins in the church these last few weeks."

He hesitated a bit before continuing. "I also need to give you some background on a few of these individuals. The first name on the list, Joyce Taylor, may be your best bet. She's active, still runs marathons at the age of sixty-two, and strikes me as observant. Miriam Lomax is in her early seventies and not as well connected. Don't get me wrong. Miriam still drives a car, talks politics, and is well-regarded by most other parishioners. She has, however, started talking to God."

"I know I've been away for a while, Father, but talking to God used to be a good thing."

Father Lawrence shook his head. "Maybe it's best you find out what I mean on your own. I've been to her apartment a few times, and sometimes it doesn't even come up."

"What about the other two names?"

"Mrs. DePaulo should present no issues, although she goes to confession less frequently than the other three. According to Father Samuel, she was definitely in church this past week, and he believes she was there the previous time as well.

"That brings us to Mrs. Olivia Moore. You will need to use some caution with that one—not, let me stress, with Mrs. Moore herself. Olivia is a fine woman, in her midforties and widowed for the last four years.

"The issue with Mrs. Moore is her sons, Theodore and Mark. They are in their late teens and live at home with their mother. If I weren't a priest, I would also say they are a fine pair of assholes. I met the sons only once, and it was not pleasant. They are both rather large, and they've spent time in juvenile detention for beating up some of the younger kids in the neighborhood. The only reason I put Olivia on the list is her sons are, from my understanding, rarely home. From what their poor mother tells me, they usually hang out with a gang down by the mall. Still, I would advise you to call before coming over just to be sure they aren't there."

"Don't worry, Father. I've found the right attitude usually gets me through these situations just fine."

CHAPTER SIX

THERE WAS MORE to my comment than bluster. John christened it my "batshit crazy" defense. I discovered it walking home from the bus stop one day after high school.

The route leading from the bus stop to my home went down a long, winding street called Montis Avenue. Montis was once one of the more scenic residential streets in Cleveland Heights, comprised mostly of older yet well-maintained homes.

Never ones to be satisfied with a good thing, city planners decided Montis could be improved. Over the objections of its residents, the city purchased and razed ten houses on each side of the street with the goal of adding an additional exit to the I-90 freeway. The demolition of those homes took place four years before I entered high school.

More than fifteen years later, there was still no sign of the promised exit. Over time, the razed area became an unmaintained dumping ground with tall grass used by teenagers as a hiding place to drink and smoke weed.

I wasn't thinking about any of this when I walked home that day. For reasons long forgotten, I was angry over something that had happened in school, and the fury was still with me as I strode past the vacant Montis dump. Lost in thought, I never noticed as three teenage boys, all older and considerably larger than me, stepped out from behind a tall patch of grass directly into my path.

Not paying attention to your surroundings could be a fatal mistake, but this was a rare instance it might have worked in my favor.

The tallest one, clearly the leader, looked at me and sneered, "Hey, asshole, you got any money?"

Still feeling the effects of my after-school funk, I snarled back in a voice even louder than his, "No, shithead!"

I don't know who was more shocked, him or me. Thinking they must have missed something, the three assholes stepped back from the sidewalk and gave me room to pass. It was then my brain finally caught up with my predicament, and I realized they would catch me quickly if I ran.

With that in mind, I continued walking slowly and deliberately down the remainder of Montis Avenue. When I was a safe distance past the lot, I turned around to see all three of the assholes still watching me. The leader gave me the finger, but he made no move to follow.

Not being a total idiot, I took an alternate route past that section of Montis for the rest of the school year. Later, I also talked my parents into letting me take kickboxing and judo classes at my neighborhood rec center. With practice, I became pretty good at both.

The walk down Montis taught me the key to the batshit-crazy defense—most people are terrified of a lunatic. In the years since, I used the same technique at least four or five times, and it worked on each occasion.

With those early encounters in mind, I decided to make Olivia Moore my first visit. When I called to verify her availability, Mrs. Moore confirmed she'd already spoken with Father Lawrence. Before I asked, she also assured me her children were out, and we could have our conversation in private.

Olivia lived in a small, 1970s-style bungalow a few blocks from Saint Edmund's. When I arrived, she was outside working in her rose garden, roses being one of the few flowers I could recognize. I parked across the street, taking care to ensure my Glock was safely concealed in its holster.

I owned two other guns, but I'd taken to the Glock 19 as my weapon of choice. Wearing men's jeans allowed me to carry the Glock in an inside trouser holster, convenient if you don't want to advertise that you are, indeed, carrying a gun. I wouldn't normally take such precautions when talking to a woman in her midforties, but Father's warning stuck in my head. I didn't want to place all my bets on attitude.

After locking the car, I stepped across the street and introduced myself to Mrs. Moore. She invited me into her home and pointed to a seat on the couch. She then earned a special place in my heart by offering me some of her homemade chocolate chip cookies. My stomach was still rumbling from eating at the Capstone. I needed real food, even if it was only bakery.

Unfortunately, our discussion yielded little in the way of new information. After telling me to call her Olivia, Mrs. Moore verified she'd been to Saint Edmund's for confession on the two days in question. She noticed only one person she didn't recognize—a young woman, possibly pregnant, likely in her early twenties.

After finishing my cookies, I thanked Mrs. Moore and stood up to leave. With an impeccable sense of timing, that was also the moment her sons chose to arrive home.

Theodore and Mark were of a type, both muscular with short blond hair and well over six feet tall. Upon entering, Theodore, the older brother, saw me standing by the couch and sneered, "Mom, why did you let a fag into our house?"

The insult didn't concern me. They were standing between me and the door, however, and I had no wish to become involved in a fight. I considered removing my gun from its holster, but that didn't feel like the low-key course of action Father Lawrence would have advised. It was then that Olivia, my sweet, chocolate chip cookie friend, made any action on my part unnecessary.

In a voice loud enough to be heard in the next county, she said, "You two shitheads get away from the fucking door!"

While she was at least six inches shorter than her sons, they almost knocked one another over in their hurry to comply. I even started to move, and she wasn't yelling at me.

Despite her sons' acquiescence, Mrs. Moore wasn't nearly finished. "Mr. Luvello is a guest in this house. You two apologize to him immediately!"

Both boys quickly, if grudgingly, apologized. After thanking Mrs. Moore for the cookies and her time, I stepped past her now-mute sons and walked to my car—the brave detective saved by a forty-five-year-old mother of two. Sam Spade would have been proud.

I was still considering Sam's reaction when I heard the sound of a loud pop, similar to a firecracker. The noise seemed to pass right next to me at shoulder level. Though not a marksman, I'd visited the range often enough to know a gunshot when I heard one. My first thought was that one of the Moore boys, fresh from being humiliated by his mother, had decided to take it out on me with a weapon.

It was then I saw a movement next to one of the cars parked behind mine. Not wanting to get into a gunfight on a suburban street, I ran the few remaining steps and managed to gain cover with a clumsy dive in front of my car.

Lying there, my gun now out of its holster, I could see little directly in front of me. Glancing toward the Moore household, I noticed Olivia at the screen door, cell phone in hand and no doubt calling the police. She yelled to see if I was okay, and I gave her a thumbs-up. I put away my gun once I heard the sirens, the shooter having presumably run off long ago. Knowing the police would ask, I also pulled the carry permit from my wallet.

When the Westlake police arrived, they asked me some basic questions before speaking to Mrs. Moore and her two sons. Other than the sound of the shot and my embarrassingly awkward dive—the Moore boys were quite descriptive on that one—none of us had much to offer. After the police finished talking with the Moores, they checked our hands for powder residue to ensure none of us had also fired during the exchange.

I wondered how I was going to explain my reason for

being in the Moore home. I had no interest in lying to the police, but I didn't want to relate my true purpose in front of Olivia and her two sons. Fortunately, the cops requested that I come back to the station to answer additional questions. There, I spent the next two hours talking to a Westlake detective about my connection to Saint Edmund's and the potential link between the Tully and Gruber homicides. While he wasn't pleased, he let me go after calling Father Lawrence to verify my story.

My original intent was to visit at least one more individual on Father Lawrence's list, but I decided to rethink. It wasn't the gunshot itself that bothered me. In truth, this was the second time someone had tried to shoot me.

The first had been an intoxicated, overweight husband who noticed me taking pictures of him through the window of his hotel room as he was in flagrante delicto with his mistress. It took three minutes of drunken staggering for him to find his gun, and I shot plenty of additional pictures during his struggle. His soon-to-be ex-wife found one of these shots, a beached-whale-like photo taken after he fell out of bed, to be especially amusing. She eventually had the image pressed into coasters for use by party guests in her now, solely owned home. The gunshot itself did little damage other than to the hotel room window.

Arriving back at my apartment, I called Father Lawrence to tell him I was okay and ask who else might know about the situation at Saint Edmund's. He assured me he'd told no one else except his Jesuit superior and the bishop of Cleveland. I believed him, but that still left a potentially wide group of individuals who were aware of our secret.

I needed to think, and I thought better when I wrote. I

took out my laptop to construct an outline of the case:

<u>Tully/Gruber Murders</u>
1. *June 3rd* – **Saint Edmund Church:** Man confesses to Father Samuel he intends to kill a woman within the next week. Confessor declares he will kill with knife slash to the throat.

2. *June 6th* – **Cleveland:** Angela Tully killed
   a. Throat stabbed
   b. Is this our confessor or a coincidence?
   c. If not a coincidence, why did the killer choose Saint Edmund's? What is the connection?

3. *June 11th* – **Saint Edmund Church:** Man (same voice as in #1 above) confesses to Father Samuel he will murder again. Woman mentioned as victim, method not specified.

4. *June 11th* – **Saint Edmund Church:** Father Lawrence contacts Paul and asks him to set up a meeting with me.

5. *June 12th* – **Saint Edmund Church:** Father Lawrence and I meet
   a. Reasons cited for my involvement vs. police
      i. Broad concern over confessional privilege
      ii. Desire for more low-key investigation
   b. Discussion with Father Samuel

      i. Covers all Saturday/Sunday confessions with Father Lawrence providing coverage on Tuesdays

      ii. States no prior, similar incidents while in Cleveland or at his previous post in New Orleans

      iii. Samuel clearly hostile—reaction to me personally or other reasons?

6. *June 12th* – **Avon:** Sarah Gruber murdered
   a. Throat slashed
   b. Discovered lying in bed by husband, Ethan Gruber
   c. Time of death (5:00–6:00 p.m.) eliminates husband as a suspect
   d. No signs of forced entry
   e. Was there a struggle? Consider asking Detective Page.

7. *June 13th* – **Westlake:** Meet with Father Lawrence, Detective Page at Capstone Diner
   a. Never, ever go there again

8. *June 13th* – **Westlake:** Meet with Olivia Moore
   a. Mrs. Moore attended confession on June 3rd and June 11th
   b. Mrs. Moore noticed nothing unusual on either visit
   c. Confrontation with Moore sons, Mark and Theodore, upon leaving

9. *June 13th* – **Westlake:** Shooting attempt
   a. Incident took place when walking across the street in front of Moore home
   b. Likely shooter location: behind a parked car, 4–5 houses north of Moore home on the opposite side of the street (unconfirmed)
   c. Potential escape route—through the back-yard to the adjoining street
   d. Potential motives
      i. Derail investigation into stabbings/link to Saint Edmund's. Those aware of the investigation:
         • Father Lawrence
         • Father Samuel
         • Saint Edmund's secretary?
         • Detective Page
         • Potentially anyone within Cleveland's bishop and Jesuit Midwest Province offices
      ii. Moore boys' involvement
         • Did Olivia, suspecting their involvement, relay the bogus church break-in story to her sons before my visit?
         • If they were aware of other break-ins, was the shooting arranged to keep me from discovering other incidents involving the boys? The argument against—they were genuinely surprised to see me talking with their mother.

iii. Could the shooting be personal? Prejudice against LGBTQ in the neighborhood? While prejudice exists, highly unlikely

e. Need to call Detective Page and make her aware

My cell phone rang after I closed my laptop. I didn't need to call Detective Page after all. Not surprisingly, she wasn't exactly happy.

"When I said you needed to let me know of anything that might be remotely relevant to this case, didn't you think you getting shot might fit into that category? Why did I only hear about this from the Westlake cops?"

"In fairness, it was a miss. I never actually got shot."

"Keep it up, smart-ass. Do you want to get thrown off this case?"

I apologized. The truth was, I liked Detective Page, and I needed this case. Fortunately for me, she accepted my apology, and we decided to meet for supper and compare notes.

She asked if I liked Mexican, and we chose "Homenaje a Los Gordos," one of the newer eateries in Cleveland's Tremont district. When it first opened, I thought the restaurant's name had flair. That lasted until John, who'd paid more attention in Spanish class than I did, told me it translated to "Tribute to the Fat." You had to admire a place that appreciates its customers.

We planned to eat at seven-thirty. Unsure of what to wear, I donned my best vintage Stevie Rae Vaughn T-shirt, hoping I wouldn't be too underdressed. As it turned out,

Detective Page also dressed in vintage style, wearing jeans and a Star Wars/Luke Skywalker T-shirt that could have time-traveled from the 1970s.

After we were seated, she took a long, disdainful look at my outfit. "Do you have any shirts with guitarists who aren't dead?"

I noticed she had a way of smiling sweetly while sounding utterly sarcastic. "Big talk from a *Star Wars* nerd. You shouldn't make fun of a guy in the Rock and Roll Hall of Fame."

"Don't mock *Star Wars*. Besides, it was you I was making fun of, not the guitarist."

"I would never mock *Star Wars*; I'm just more of a *Star Trek* guy. Captain Kirk got to make out with green alien women. That always had a certain allure."

Our old-movie banter dispensed with, we agreed to call each other by our first names and proceeded to order our meals, a burrito for me and two extra-large tacos for her.

Hannah caught me staring as she wolfed down her dinner. "Don't judge me," she said. "If you'll recall, lunch wasn't exactly five-star. At least this food is edible."

"I am impressed. We should probably ask if they have an eating contest."

She was chewing and couldn't reply, so she compensated by showing me her middle finger.

Actually, the food was good, though the restaurant décor was a little unusual, kind of Southwest glitzy. I told Hannah it looked like Aztec human sacrifice meets Las Vegas. She said she didn't care what they did in their off-hours so long as their food was worth eating.

We moved to discussing the case. After berating me one

more time for not calling after the shooting, Hannah agreed that my incident and our two murders were likely related. I gave her more details regarding my conversation with Mrs. Moore and the shooting, leaving out my embarrassing dive in front of my car. Since I wasn't a direct participant in the police investigation, there were also some questions I hoped she could answer.

"The news report on the Gruber murder mentioned there were no signs of forced entry. What about signs of a struggle?"

"There were some," she admitted. "Mostly overturned furniture. Unfortunately, there were no skin scrapings under her fingernails or anything else linking back to the killer."

"Any sign of sexual assault? The report I heard said she was clothed when her husband found her on the bed."

"She was clothed. No signs of rape."

"I heard even less about the Tully murder. Beyond the stab wound to the throat, were the other circumstances similar?"

"Beyond the neck wounds, they were similar in the sense there were only minimal signs of a struggle and no indications of sexual assault. In the Tully case, the body was found in the first-floor living room."

"One other thing you need to know," she continued. "Your shooting this afternoon resulted in another change. The Cleveland and Avon police departments are now working these cases as a joint investigation with me as the lead investigator. That means the Tully and Gruber cases now both fall under my jurisdiction."

"That works out better for me," I said. "I appreciate not

having multiple go-betweens."

We transitioned to other subjects, and Hannah asked how I became a detective.

"Don't take this the wrong way, but you're different than most detectives I've known."

I knew what she meant, but I could also tell she was genuinely curious. I gave her the CliffNotes version. "In some ways, I fell into the job entirely by accident. I applied to law school after getting my bachelor's. I was admitted, but I decided not to go. I knew law school would typecast me as some sort of crusader for a cause, and that wasn't what I wanted.

"I sat around in my mother's house for a month trying to figure out my next move when her next-door neighbor came over crying so hard I could barely understand her. From what I finally gathered, the neighbor and her husband had divorced the year before, and she and her ex had custody of their daughter on alternating weekends.

"After the daughter's latest visit with her father, the mother went to pick her up and found no one at her husband's apartment. The landlord checked, and the apartment appeared to be empty. The mother called the police, and the cops couldn't find any signs of the father or the baby. After a week without any news, the mother was starting to panic.

"The neighbor mentioned her husband was out of work, so I figured he was staying with a friend or a relative. I asked her about both, and the most likely suspect appeared to be the ex-husband's sister, who lived just over the Pennsylvania border.

"I figured I had nothing to lose. I asked the neighbor to give me a recent picture of her daughter and her ex-husband. I left my mother a note and drove to the sister's address. Though it was out of state, it was only an hour away.

"I won't go into all the details, but I was able to watch the house from a patch of woods overlooking the sister's side of the street. About an hour in, I saw her come home from the store with several bags, one that appeared to contain diapers. That wasn't definitive, but my mom's neighbor had said the sister didn't have any kids of her own.

"It took a homemade smoke bomb, but I was eventually able to trick the father and the sister into coming outside with the baby. I had my Nikon along, so I shot some pictures and contacted the local police. The cops let the sister go, but the father was arrested. My mother's neighbor was able to pick up her daughter the following day."

Hannah was fascinated. "You didn't even know this woman, but you drove all the way to Pennsylvania to help her find her daughter. Mind if I ask why?"

"I was bored sitting around the house, and I hate being bored. After I found the daughter, I realized I liked being a detective and went back to school to get my associate's in criminal justice. After graduation, the school got me hooked up with a PI firm for the rest of the training I needed for my Ohio license. Starting my own business was a tough go at first, but cases eventually started to trickle in. There aren't many private investigators in Cleveland, so I didn't have a lot of competition."

Hannah and I finished our meals, and she appeared uncertain how to proceed. Her next question caught me by surprise.

"You see the couple sitting two tables to our side? Tell

me what you think is going on with them."

I'd already noticed the man and woman she was referring to. They were nondescript in every way, except the man kept taking sips of his water and managed to knock over his glass early on during their meal. The woman looked apprehensive throughout. I thought it might be a breakup, but then I saw the man's other hand, the one not holding his water glass, tapping his pants pocket.

"I'll go out on a limb," I said. "I think he's going to ask her to marry him. The pocket he's tapping is holding the ring."

Thirty seconds after my pronouncement, the man removed a small box from his pocket and handed it to his companion. From her smile, it was easy to see she accepted.

Hannah watched me even more intently. "Okay," she said, "now do me."

I had no experience with women, but I knew this was a minefield. John would call me an idiot, but I decided to be honest. After taking a deep breath, I said, "I think you're an exceptional investigator. You believe that yourself, or at least most of you does. A part of you has doubts."

Hannah's gaze became almost savage in its intensity. I started to apologize, but she waved it away. "You don't even know me. What makes you think I'm a good investigator?"

"Because you noticed the same things about the couple that I did. You didn't ask for my opinion because you wanted to find out about them; you asked because you wanted to know about me and whether I was worth partnering with."

Her smile remained almost predatory. I was wrong—she was enjoying this. "Now," she said, "I get a turn. You think of yourself as a cynic, but you're really a romantic. I saw the way you smiled when that guy proposed. You'd tell me it was because it proved you right, but I think you were hoping for a happy ending. I'll go even further and guess that's the real reason you became a detective. That hope drives you, but you're worried it's also a weakness. You wonder what happens if you run into too many endings you just can't fix."

I couldn't think of anything to say. I wanted her to be wrong. Deep down inside, I even needed her to be wrong. We'd been together for one dinner, and she'd diagnosed a fear I rarely admitted, even to myself. I felt exhilarated and terrified, somehow both at once. After what seemed like forever, I finally found my voice.

"Where do we go from here?"

"If you're willing to follow me, I was hoping we could go back to my place."

CHAPTER SEVEN

I WOULD HAVE followed her anywhere, but two things were working against me. The first was Hannibal, who decided that sixty on the freeway would be his absolute upper limit for the evening. The second was Hannah's own vehicle, a BMW of fairly recent vintage. The car was fast, and Hannah drove it like a fighter pilot on steroids. I could only imagine the number of traffic tickets she'd have received without her detective shield. After numerous dirty looks, Hannah finally slowed down so I could follow at a Hannibal-approved pace.

To my surprise, Hannah lived in a house just a few moments' drive from the street I grew up on in Cleveland Heights. One thing I always liked about my old neighborhood was no two homes looked exactly alike, and the same was true of Hannah's street. Her small, brown colonial had a porch and two large picture windows. She drove into the garage, and I parked behind her in the driveway. She met me as I got out of my car.

"You drive like an old woman."

"I thought women liked guys who went slow. Besides, they say a lot of international sex symbols are driving old, beat-up Civics these days."

She gave me a long, wonderful kiss while we were still standing in her driveway. "Speaking of sex, I hope you're better at that than you are at driving."

I was, I think. Sex with Hannah was a revelation. She had a wonderfully full figure, and she took her time showing me all of it. We turned off all the lights. It wasn't that either one of us was particularly self-conscious; everything just felt more alive that way. It might have been mutual loneliness, the fact we were alike in so many ways, or maybe we were both particularly horny that evening. Whatever the reason, we spent hours experiencing each other in every manner imaginable. I got to know her touch, her taste, and every curve of her body. We spoke little during sex, though she did come up for air at one point to let me know if I wanted to be Captain Kirk, she would be my green alien woman.

Afterward, we turned on the lights and talked. I told Hannah about John and what it was like growing up middle-class in that very neighborhood. She told me more about her parents and growing up rich in Hunting Valley.

"You were right about what you said in the restaurant," she said. "Growing up with hyper-successful parents wasn't always conducive to self-confidence."

"I feel stupid asking this, but who are your parents?"

"My father is Congressman David Page, Democrat, Eleventh District. My mother is Amanda Patterson-Page, assistant district attorney."

I'd only vaguely heard of her father. I was never interested in politics and only read the newspaper for the comics and the sports page. As a detective, however, I was familiar with Hannah's mother. She had a reputation in the law enforcement community as a tough, no-nonsense prosecutor with an interest in running for higher office. If these were her parents, Hannah's political connections ran very deep.

"Most cops in the department," Hannah continued, "assume I was given my gold shield due to family pull. If they knew my parents, they'd know how ridiculous that was. My mom and dad wanted me to become a lawyer. I attended law school for a year before I realized it wasn't for me.

"You wouldn't believe their looks of genteel disapproval when I quit. It was a constant topic of discussion between my parents and their patrician friends. I suppose becoming a cop was a rebellion at first, though eventually, I realized I really liked what I was doing. My parents still disapprove, but I'm good at my job. I deserve to be a detective, and I have no intention of apologizing for that."

"No reason why you should."

"Still, I would be open to working this case together rather than separately. For reasons having nothing to do with tonight, I just think it makes sense."

"So you weren't seduced by my manly charms?"

"No, but I'm open to the prospect."

I caught her looking down at the lower half of my body. "What are you looking for down there?"

"I guess I was wondering what you would look like with

man parts."

"Man parts? What is this, the 1950s?"

"I'll come right out and ask. Did you ever consider a sex-change?"

In a little over twenty-four hours, two people had asked me essentially the same question. One was a priest, and the other was the woman lying next to me in bed. Sometimes my life was like a bad Woody Allen movie.

"If you want to be politically correct, it's called gender reassignment surgery. I signed up to start the process, but I have this overriding fear of hospitals."

"If you change your mind, I wouldn't mind being the first woman to break everything in for you."

"I don't know. There are dozens of women who've already asked. You'd need to get in line."

"Do any of those other women carry a Smith & Wesson?"

With that, we fell asleep. The next morning, Hannah woke me up at seven o'clock with a donut and a glass of milk.

"No bacon and eggs?" I asked.

"I thought about slaughtering the pig out back, but you kept me up too late last night."

I washed up in Hannah's bathroom and brushed my teeth with an extra toothbrush from her medicine cabinet. As she dressed, I snuck into her kitchen and checked out her refrigerator, almost afraid of what I might find. Sure enough, it was filled with juice, a bottle of milk, and a case of Diet Coke. The only actual food items were in the freezer, which was packed with frozen dinners. From what I could see, she favored Mexican and Italian. God help her if the microwave broke down.

The rest of her house was, to use a nice word, disheveled. In truth, it looked like the average trailer park after an F-5 tornado. I poked my head in the laundry room doorway adjacent to the kitchen. After turning on the light, I could barely see the washer and dryer over the large mound of clothes waiting patiently to be laundered. The living room included three bookshelves, but there was clearly a need for more. Beyond the books on the shelves, two large stacks sat on a ledge by one of the front bay windows. At a glance, her taste in reading appeared to be rather eclectic, ranging from mysteries to horror and, somewhat incongruously, English poetry.

Afraid of what I'd find if I kept looking, I went back to the kitchen. Hannah came in a few minutes later, already dressed for work.

I had to ask. "Did you ever consider getting a housekeeper?"

"Why?"

"No reason."

I turned to her at the front door. "Before we go, I need to ask how much of last night was about me and how much was about giving a symbolic middle finger to your mom and dad?"

"I'd be lying if I said I didn't think about their reaction, but I don't have sex just to make a point. We can overthink this and manage to screw up something nice, or we can take it a step at a time and see what happens. I'm in favor of the latter."

"I'm fine with that. I just wanted to know if your father is going to shoot me if we happen to run across each other on the street."

"My father is very pro-gun control. He wouldn't shoot you. He'd hire someone to do it instead."

"Okay then, problem solved."

CHAPTER EIGHT

WE GOT IN our respective cars and drove off, Hannah to the Twelfth District and me to my apartment. Since we were both heading toward downtown, I tried to keep up with Hannah as long as possible. That lasted until we turned onto the freeway, where she left me quickly in her dust.

After a quick stop in my apartment, I figured I would continue meeting with the parishioners on Father Lawrence's list. I managed to get in touch with Miriam Lomax, Father's "not well-connected" suggested source. Miriam agreed to meet with me that morning in her apartment at the Morning Hill Assisted Living Center, an upscale facility located a couple of miles from Saint Edmund's. After Hannibal's gasping, wheezing effort driving me to a night with a pretty detective, I was able to hit over seventy on the freeway to visit Mrs. Lomax. The car did hate me somehow.

Like all assisted living facilities, Morning Hill's buildings and décor sought to convey a bright and cheery impression to both residents and family members. The design ensured the facility's apartments remained fully occupied despite the exorbitant monthly fees charged for the most basic of services. I entered the main office and was greeted by an equally bright and cheery receptionist who likely assumed I was either visiting a loved one or considering moving one there. I wondered if she was paid on commission.

The receptionist continued smiling as she gave me directions to Mrs. Lomax's apartment. It was just past the Stevens Aviary, no doubt filled with bright and cheery birds, on the second floor of the main building. After a ride up the elevator, I knocked on Mrs. Lomax's door and tried to ignore the bird noises that would have driven me crazy if I was ever unlucky enough to live there.

Mrs. Lomax greeted me with a smile. I saw no signs of the instability Father Lawrence had warned about in this slender, well-dressed woman with gray hair. Like many assisted living facilities, Morning Hill allowed its residents to keep small animals. Mrs. Lomax had taken advantage of this nod to companionship and held a brown chihuahua. Once I was inside, she offered me a seat on her couch and a glass of tea. I didn't want to take up too much of her time, so I got right to the point.

"I'm not sure how much Father Lawrence told you about my visit, but I'm here to see if you have any information concerning two break-ins that occurred at Saint Edmund's on June 3rd and June 11th. We believe these break-ins took place during the time Father Samuel was hearing confessions. We wondered if you might have noticed anything or anyone unusual while you were there."

"Do you mean more unusual than Father Samuel? As my late husband used to say, he is one unlikeable SOB. Sometimes I think I hear more from God here in the apartment than I do in church."

I couldn't help but laugh at her mention of Father Samuel. I didn't know if she'd be of any help, but I was enjoying my visit.

"Father Samuel aside, Mrs. Lomax, did you notice anyone unfamiliar at the church on those days? Was anything out of the ordinary?"

"There was one young woman who looked like she might be pregnant. Without a wedding ring, it was easy to guess what she was confessing. Let me see if Betty noticed anything."

Confused, I asked, "Who is Betty, Mrs. Lomax?"

Clearly thinking I was a moron, Mrs. Lomax pointed to her chihuahua. "This is Betty. She comes with me everywhere, including confession. She helps me talk to God."

Without meaning to, I had gone way over into alien territory. I tried to clarify and somehow made things worse. "So, you talk to God through Betty?"

Her look turned to scorn. "Look at her. She's a chihuahua, you idiot, not some sort of cosmic transmitter. I just sometimes hear God speak to me when she's close by. Here, you try."

She gestured for me to come closer to Betty, probably the last place I wanted to be at that moment. I hesitated, but Mrs. Lomax kept motioning. Finally, I moved closer, and the dog started to growl and bare its teeth. If Betty was channeling God, this was definitely the Old Testament version of our Savior. In any case, the last thing I wanted was to get rabies from an animal that looked more like a rat than a dog.

A quick retreat seeming like my best option, I tried backing away from Betty and ended up bumping the coffee table holding my teacup. The cup fell, spilling half a cup of tea onto the white carpeting. Even Inspector Clouseau would have laughed. All I needed was the *Pink Panther* theme song to make my day complete.

I apologized profusely while absorbing withering looks from Mrs. Lomax and Betty, the latter continuing to growl and bare her teeth. I considered offering to clean up the tea, but who knew what additional damage I might cause if I stayed. I thanked Mrs. Lomax for her time and left as quickly as I could. When I walked past the main desk, even the receptionist appeared distinctly less bright and cheery.

I felt foolish and increasingly angry. The anger wasn't aimed at Mrs. Lomax or her God-fearing dog. In evaluating my progress, it seemed like I was checking off boxes on a list pulled from some "Private Investigation for Dummies" handbook. Interviewing people from the church had led me nowhere, and I was wasting time until the next murder.

I needed a new approach. Until I could figure one out, however, I thought I might as well finish talking to Father Lawrence's other two contacts.

So far, my face-to-face interview record hadn't been stellar. My first ended with a gunshot, while my second culminated with an attempted mauling by an overly religious dog. I decided I shouldn't be stubborn. I would conduct my next two interviews by phone.

Joyce Taylor was at home and seemed more than willing to discuss her memories of the days in question. Unfortunately, she had little to add to the previous two accounts, though she did include some choice words concerning Mrs. Lomax's ill-mannered chihuahua.

My last contact, Mrs. DePaulo, didn't answer her phone. I left a message on her answering machine, but I knew this course was a dead end. It was now two o'clock. With nothing left to do, I drove back to my apartment.

Heading home, I again found myself caught in one of Cleveland's frequent road construction delays. To my surprise, however, the holdup proved to be beneficial. Given time to think, I realized what I'd been missing. I called Hannah and left a message. She called me back just after I reached my apartment.

"I was going to call you," Hannah said. "You start, and then I'll tell you what I found."

"I just finished speaking with two other parishioners who remembered absolutely nothing out of the ordinary about the two days in question. With that, did it ever strike you our approach may be too by the book?"

"What do you think we're missing?"

She sounded more than a little annoyed, but I plowed ahead anyway. "Everything we've done up till now—talking to potential witnesses, reviewing the evidence, etc.—it's all been focused on the question of who did this as opposed to why.

"I recognize the "who" answer is ultimately the most important, but if we can figure out why they did it, that might give us our best chance to get there."

"You mean, like, why the confessional?" She sounded a

little more intrigued.

"That's one question, but there are several more. We also don't know why the killer chose Saint Edmund's. The church is in Westlake, but the killings occurred in Cleveland and Avon. What's the killer's connection to the church?

"You could go one step further and ask why he chose Father Samuel. I figured it was because the killer had a work schedule, and Samuel covered the weekend confessions. It didn't hit me until today what a poor assumption that was, given the killings all occurred on weekdays.

"Since I'm on a roll, why did our murderer stab both women in their throats? There must be some significance in that. Also, why take a shot at me? I learned nothing from those women, and I have to believe our killer knew that would be the case. Why would he take that risk?"

"I agree we need a change in direction," Hannah said. "Let me tell you my news, and then we can talk about where we go from here. When you called me earlier, I was with the medical examiner. There's been another murder."

CHAPTER NINE

NANCY LOSANO, SEVENTY years old, lived alone in her Westlake home. Described as a recluse by her neighbors, no one noticed anything unusual at the house until a neighbor across the street reported a "suspicious-looking African-American gentleman" peering through Mrs. Losano's windows. The African-American gentleman turned out to be the neighborhood mailman who wondered why so much mail was accumulating in the victim's mailbox. After questioning the postman, the police broke into Mrs. Losano's home and found her body lying on the living room floor.

Based on the advanced state of decomposition, the medical examiner estimated Mrs. Losano had been dead at least six weeks, easily predating the murders Hannah and I were already investigating. Factors tying this homicide to the later murders included the sex of the victim and the cause of death, a jagged knife wound to the throat. The Westlake location also provided a possible link to Saint Edmund's—the Losano home was just three miles from the church.

Hannah and I agreed to meet at my apartment to plot our strategy moving forward. While waiting for her arrival, I called Father Lawrence. The Losano murder had yet to hit the evening news, and I wanted to find out if the victim was in any way connected to Saint Edmund's.

Father Lawrence was shaken by the news of the latest murder. From the Saint Edmund's parishioner database, it appeared Mrs. Losano belonged to the church and was a regular contributor until five years ago. After that point, Father could find no record of her attendance, though he did note that Saint Edmund's had a "Meals on Wheels" program that served a number of elderly whether or not they were active in the church. He promised to check with the woman who directed the program to see if Mrs. Losano was part of their route.

John was the next person I called. He'd left several messages the previous evening, hoping to come by and play Mortal Kombat.

Video game nights with John typically degenerated into a surreal if not bizarre series of simulated conflicts. After the first hour or so, we invariably ended up ignoring the stated purpose of the game to see how quickly we could kill each other. We both found the experience surprisingly relaxing, though the presence of beer likely hastened that process significantly.

I told John, quite truthfully, that I'd spent most of last

evening discussing my latest case with a detective from the Cleveland Police Department. John didn't push for details, but he asked if he could stop by. As much as I wouldn't have minded the distraction, I told him she and I needed to meet again that night to discuss some new developments.

I knew when I said the word "she" that I'd made a grievous error. John had been trying to find me a girlfriend ever since my transition. When it came to sex, he also had the maturity of a twelve-year-old.

"Whoa, you're actually meeting with a woman? Is she cute? How old is she?"

I had no intention of filling him in on last night's events, at least not until I'd had time to process them myself. "I'll give you the rundown. She's a police detective, and she's cute. She's probably in her late twenties, though I didn't ask for her birth certificate. Personality-wise, think of me in female clothing."

"The personality thing is terrifying. Are you going to sleep with her?"

"I'm hanging up now, John."

"Oh my God, you already have. Are you on a twice a decade schedule? Your mother and I have a bet going. She's going to be thrilled."

Knowing my mom, he might be telling the truth. "If only I had one friend who wasn't an asshole," I said.

"Given that you only have one friend, I guess you're out of luck. I'll leave you to your little rendezvous, but I want the details the next time we talk."

He hung up just as Hannah arrived at my apartment. Before we started discussing the case, she insisted on a tour. Given the size of my living space, our walk-through lasted about thirty seconds.

"You have no pictures hanging," Hannah said. "I figured I would at least see one of your mom."

"I guess I'm not a picture person. Come to think of it, I didn't notice any pictures of your parents at your house."

"That's true, but you like your mom."

We decided to fix supper before we talked about the case. Based on our mutual lack of culinary skills, spaghetti and salad seemed the only acceptable risks. I boiled water for the spaghetti while Hannah mixed together some lettuce, tomato, and cucumber for a salad.

All things considered, the result wasn't too bad. I could never eat much of my own cooking, but Hannah made up for my reticence as she ate her pasta with gusto. We talked in between bites.

"So we have another murder that fits within our narrative," I said. "If you assume they're all connected, you have to wonder why the other two killings were announced during confession while this one wasn't."

"If the Losano murder was his first kill," Hannah replied, "he may have decided later he wanted to make it into a game. Even if that's true, we're still left with your original question—why Saint Edmund's? The church is in Westlake, and the Losano home is only a short distance away. Does the murderer also live in Westlake, and is he connected to the parish?

"The other possibility is the one you mentioned on the phone. The murderer could have a prior connection to Father Samuel, and he's trying to torment Samuel in some way. What did you think when you spoke to him? Is Samuel telling the truth?"

In between bites of spaghetti, I said, "While I don't like him personally, I've no reason to think he wasn't truthful. Father Samuel said he didn't recognize the voice in the confessional. He graduated from the Jesuit seminary in New Orleans, but he said nothing had occurred there that would lead him to believe he was being targeted."

"Does Samuel speak with a Southern or French Quarter accent?"

I realized immediately where she was going, and I could have kicked myself for not thinking of it sooner. "No, he doesn't, and no, I didn't ask if Father Samuel was actually from that area. I can't believe I missed that, but I'll follow up."

"Once you do, call me with the information. I can call the police departments in New Orleans and his home city to see if there were any similar murders when Father Samuel was there."

"I'll ask Father Lawrence about Samuel's hometown. There's also one other detail of note regarding the parish. Mrs. Losano wasn't an active member of Saint Edmund's, but they have a meal program that might have visited her home. Father Lawrence was looking into it, so I'll call and check on both questions."

Father Lawrence picked up on the first ring. After I explained we weren't targeting Father Samuel, he gave me some background information regarding Samuel's hometown. From his records, Samuel was born and raised in Manhattan, Kansas, a small college town home to Kansas State University. Father Samuel wasn't prone to discussing his family background, having fallen out with both parents over his decision to join the priesthood.

Regarding my second question, Father Lawrence couldn't find any record for Nancy Losano in the church's Meals on Wheels client listing. He stressed this wasn't a definitive "no" on that point. The church often received last-minute add-on requests, which weren't entered in program records. Father Lawrence still intended to speak to the woman who ran the program once she returned from vacation.

I filled Hannah in on the details, and she promised to follow up with the police departments in Manhattan and New Orleans. With that, she was still operating under the assumption the killer's connection was to the parish rather than to Father Samuel specifically.

"Now for the other question," she said after we'd finished. "I left a bag of clothes in my car along with a toothbrush. Is there any chance I could stay? I'm hoping you're not the kind of guy who'd make a girl drive home in the middle of the night."

"I don't know. You saw my bed. You'd pretty much have to sleep on top of me."

"I think we can make that work."

We made it work rather well, and I was both happy and exhausted when we finally fell asleep. That feeling lasted until the dream.

I was walking down a long, narrow street shrouded in the kind of fog one finds in werewolf movies set in the English moors. It was night. The street looked nothing like the Montis Avenue of my youth, but I knew it was Montis all the same.

As I continued walking, cracks appeared in the

sidewalk. I started skipping over them like I did when I was a child, the old nursery rhyme seeming like the most critical task in the world right then. Avoiding the cracks was easy at first, but they soon started appearing more and more often. Eventually, I landed on one, and the sidewalk shifted, causing me to fall. Now lying on the ground, I looked up, and the three teenagers I'd encountered in my youth stood right in front of me.

I knew I must say something, but the words wouldn't come. I remembered my gun and reached behind me only to realize I was once again a teenager, wearing nothing but a school uniform and a backpack. Sensing my impotence, the three boys laughed and began kicking me over and over. They say it's impossible to feel pain in a dream, but my body recoiled from every contact. Eventually, the kicking stopped, and the three teenagers stood me up and started ripping at my clothing. Suddenly, I was naked, and the name-calling began. They called me fag, homo, lesbo, and a host of other names I'd heard many times before. I wondered why they hurt so much now.

Eventually, they stopped, and I noticed a tall man moving forward behind the three. The man was huge, so big I couldn't see his face from beneath the fog. The tall man continued forward, and the others handed me to him like an offering.

Now in the man's grip, I was almost unsurprised to feel the knife at my throat. With one quick movement of his hand, my blood began to spurt like a fountain from some demented horror movie. The man laughed, and all of my tormenters turned to walk away. With my throat cut, I was unable to cry out. I watched the group disappear as I died *alone on the sidewalk.*

Before perishing, I felt an emotion I'd never experienced before. For the first time in my life, I felt ashamed.

CHAPTER TEN

I SAT UP quickly in bed and managed to knock Hannah to the floor. Still groggy, she climbed back into bed and asked what the hell I was doing.

"I'm sorry. I had a really horrible dream."

"Just what every girl wants to hear after a night of sex. What was this horrible dream?"

"Ghosts from the past, but do you mind if I ask you a question?"

She didn't say no, so I pulled her close and continued, "Why are you here with me?"

"I thought I was here because you asked me. What the hell are you getting at?"

"You're a smart, sexy woman who could be with virtually anyone. Why are you with me?"

"I figured we'd have this conversation at some point, but I never thought it would be at three-thirty in the morning. I'm going to tell you two things, and then you're going to shut up and let me get some sleep."

She fluffed her pillow and continued. "First of all, for a guy who's pretty self-confident in most aspects of his life, you seem to think you're always wearing a big, scarlet 'T' on your chest. I can't prove this, but I would guess 80 to 90 percent of the people you pass on the street think you are a man no different than any other man. Look at yourself in the mirror sometime. Some transgender men look girlish, but you aren't one of them. You make a pretty sexy guy, particularly with that dark, wavy hair. I'm not saying I wouldn't dump you in a second for George Clooney, but I would at least have to spend a second thinking about it. I wouldn't have realized you were transgender when we first met if I hadn't been checking you out."

"You were checking me out?"

"Don't pretend you weren't doing the same thing. I was just much less obvious. Even the priest noticed you staring."

"I can't deny that, but what's the second thing you were going to tell me?"

Her face grew serious for a moment. "I suggested we go to dinner yesterday because you were cute and seemed intelligent. I asked you to come home with me because of what you told me about your first case and what you said afterward.

"You said you took the neighbor's case due to boredom. While you'd never admit it, I also believe you helped that woman because you cared about her and her child. You drove to another state, for God's sake. Who does something like that?

"What I'm trying to say is you're a smart, sexy, private detective who clearly cares a lot about people. Given that, this shame thing you have going is a little ridiculous, don't you think?"

I couldn't think of anything to say, so I substituted a kiss instead.

"Now if you'll quit trying to knock me off the bed," she said, "I really would like to get some sleep."

I woke up the next morning still feeling somewhat conflicted. Hannah and I had a quick breakfast, and she made me run through every detail of the dream before she left for the station.

After she was gone, I prepared a report on the latest events for Father Lawrence. As I was typing, it occurred to me that at least one part of the dream still bothered me, something with a potential link to this case. It wasn't the dream man and the stabbing—that connection was obvious. What I couldn't wrap my head around was the whole issue of confession.

When I was in grade school, I considered confession my least favorite of the seven sacraments, a ritual whose sole purpose was to embarrass the penitent. The dream managed to bring the feeling back, and I wondered if our killer shared that same perception.

I finished my report and decided to present it to Father Lawrence in person. While I was technically going to give him an update, I thought his perspective on the dream might also be valuable. I'd told Hannah it raised ghosts from the past. I didn't want one of those ghosts—my grade school bias against the Church—to get in the way of how I approached this case.

After begrudgingly allowing me entrance, the Saint Edmund's church secretary greeted me with a glare. Clearly, Miss Lambert had not forgiven my tardy arrival for my first meeting with Father Lawrence. Requesting an unscheduled follow-up was another strike against me. I could only imagine what a third strike might bring, although I was sure the gates of hell would be somewhere in my future.

Father Lawrence was quite happy to meet, though I suspected that had less to do with me than the fact that he'd be missing his monthly finance committee meeting. In any case, he agreed to give me one hour of his time.

We moved to his office, and I summarized where we stood with the case to date. Father Lawrence asked several questions concerning the status of the police investigation and our desire for more information concerning Father Samuel. I still had fifteen minutes of my hour left, so I then moved to the more awkward reason for my visit.

"Father, no matter the killer's motives, the sacrament of confession plays a key role in this case. That's true if he's targeting Father Samuel, the Church in general, or if he wandered into Saint Edmund's entirely by accident.

"I know this sounds ridiculous, but I had a nightmare last night. It ended with me stabbed in the throat, but most of the dream was about shame, my shame, really. The ending was obviously tied to the murders, but the dream also made me think about the connection between shame and confession. Do you agree the connection exists? If it does, do you think it might be related to this case?"

"You may have lapsed," Father Lawrence said, "but you went to Catholic grade school and high school. What did they teach you about confession?"

He had the Jesuitical gift for answering a question with a question.

"I know the basics," I answered. "Confession is one of the seven sacraments, and its key elements include contrition, confession, satisfaction, and absolution. I also know the power to absolve sins was first given to the apostles by Christ."

"You sound like you're reading from a church catechism. Tell me what you think that all means."

"I honestly don't know, Father. That's why I asked you in the first place."

"Then try coming at it from a different angle. The Church teaches we're all made in God's image, correct? If that's true, would God create a sacrament designed to shame the men and women He created to be like himself? Confession is meant to be an uplifting sacrament, not a shaming one. It was designed to take what's good in us and make it even better."

His fingers tapping his desk, Father continued, "My answer to your first question would be no, I don't think there is a link between confession and shame. That doesn't mean, however, there isn't a link between confession and this case. You're far from the only Catholic with a negative perception of the sacrament. Some priests have used confession to shame the penitent. Far worse, some clergy involved in the church sexual abuse scandals used confession to recruit young children. While I believe we've improved significantly in that area, there's no doubt many people still carry a well-deserved grudge against the sacrament and the Church."

It was interesting he mentioned the child abuse angle,

though I couldn't figure out how that would lead someone to commit this particular set of murders. In any case, I'd run over my allotted hour, and Father was due at a meeting regarding a parishioner dispute. I thanked him again for his time.

As I was driving home, I remembered one other aspect of the dream that still bothered me. After the unknown man stabbed me in the throat, I couldn't scream or make a sound. Was that the purpose behind the killer's MO—to keep people from talking? Psychologically, did that also support the whole confession framework I kept trying to construct around this case? I arrived at my apartment more unsure than ever.

As I walked in, I received a call from Hannah. While still waiting for word from Kansas, she'd obtained some interesting information from her counterparts in New Orleans.

"I asked them if they had any unsolved, multiple stabbing cases going back the last couple of years. I told them we were looking for a possible link to a series of murders in Cleveland.

"It turns out they had two sets of cases fitting what I described. The first involved three murders, all prostitutes, killed about eighteen months ago. While unsolved, these cases are likely unrelated to ours. The New Orleans cops believe they stemmed from a territory dispute between two rival gangs. The second set, however, might be worth checking out.

"At first, those cases didn't appear to be related. The victims included a fifty-five-year-old man, a thirty-two-year-old woman, and two college students. The first student was a nineteen-year-old male engineering major at Tulane.

The second was a twenty-six-year-old female nursing student at Louisiana State. All of them were single except for the fifty-five-year-old man. All of the victims lived within a ten-mile radius."

"Other than the fact that they were stabbed," I said. "Why would you think these are connected to our case? Why do the cops even think they're related?"

"I'm coming to the good part. The police didn't see the relationship until they looked further into the victims' backgrounds. It turns out all four were seeing the same psychiatrist, a Dr. Michael Grieve."

"I am assuming the police spoke to Dr. Grieve?"

"It gets better. Dr. Grieve is nowhere to be found. The police obtained a judge's order releasing Grieve's current patient files. Beyond the four murdered patients, two others appear to be missing."

"So, we have a set of murders related to a priest, and they have four related to a therapist. That is something, but New Orleans is a big town. Do we have anything to tie this to Father Samuel?"

"Nothing definitive, but you told me Samuel took his vows in the Jesuit Church of Saint Francis. I looked at a map, and the church is about one mile from the psychiatrist's office. If our killer was Catholic, he could easily have attended Saint Francis. Father Samuel would likely have no idea who or what he was."

"One other question," I said. "Going back to the psychiatrist, how did the police have any idea the victims were all seeing Dr. Grieve? Did a family member volunteer the information?"

"I wondered that too. It turns out the wife of our fifty-five-year-old man mentioned he was seeing a therapist for anxiety and depression. The same thing came up in an interview with the parents of one of the college students. The police checked further, and they found the psychiatrist in both cases was Dr. Grieve. Based on concern for patient safety, a judge then issued a court order allowing the cops to review patient records from the time the murders started. That's how they realized the other two murder victims were also patients of Dr. Grieve and that two more of Grieve's patients were missing."

Hannah paused a brief second before she continued. "There's one other thing I should mention. The first murder, the male college student, occurred one year ago. The last, the fifty-five-year-old man, happened in February. You mentioned Father Samuel came to Saint Edmund's last December. If this is our guy, he killed at least one more person in New Orleans before following Samuel here."

"Is there anything in Dr. Grieve's record indicating he might be the killer? Are the police concentrating on him or a patient?"

"There's nothing unusual in his record, but that doesn't mean he isn't our killer. He is, I'm told, a well-respected physician, forty-two-years-old, who's had his own practice for the last twelve years. His patients speak well of him, and he occasionally taught classes at Tulane.

"The truth is, I don't think the Louisiana cops have any idea who they're looking for. Once they realized the connection between the murders, they devoted significant resources to solving these cases.

"That's as good a lead as any to my last point. When I told them about the cases up here, they asked if I'd be willing to come down to New Orleans to help with the investigation. I ran it past my captain, and he said yes. When I mentioned to New Orleans I was working with a private investigator hired by the church, they said they'd be happy if you came along, assuming you—and I quote—'promise to get your ass out of the way whenever we tell you to.' I'm leaving the day after tomorrow. You'll have to decide pretty quickly if you want to come."

"I'd love to come, but I'm going to have to speak with Father Lawrence. I'm not sure the church can afford to cover the cost of a plane ticket and a hotel room."

"If you're willing, it could just be the cost of the plane ticket. The department is covering my ticket and the hotel room. If you're game, I know a way we could save some money."

"I feel like a kept man. How old are you anyway?"

"I'm twenty-eight, about to turn twenty-nine. Why the hell would you ask me that?"

"I don't turn twenty-eight until August. That makes you a cougar. I always wanted to date a cougar."

"Remember, cougars have claws."

After Hannah hung up, I called Saint Edmund's and managed to get in touch with Father Lawrence. I filled him in on the information from New Orleans and asked him to hold off on telling Father Samuel. I also told him about the invitation Detective Page had received from the New Orleans PD and their willingness to have me tag along. When I asked if the church would reimburse the cost of a plane ticket, I didn't get the reaction I expected.

"You know," he said, "the church isn't paying your bill."

Sensing the reason for my pause, Father added, "Relax,

we don't stiff people. Saint Edmund's isn't paying your bill; the funding is coming from the Midwest Jesuit Province. My superior is as anxious to get this solved as anyone. You can go to New Orleans, but keep me informed. If there's even a hint that Father Samuel interacted with this person, I want to know right away."

I called Hannah and had her text me the flight information. Fortunately, her flight was direct, and there were still some seats available. I then called my mom to let her know I'd be going to New Orleans for an indeterminate length of time. She made me promise to send her pictures via Snapchat. My mother, the smartphone queen.

"Mom, since when are you on Snapchat? You can't even open your e-mail half the time."

"A lot of my friends are on it. You were busy, so I called John yesterday, and he talked me through using the app. By the way, he also said you're dating a police detective. How come I heard that from him and not you?"

Like most mothers, she had the whole guilt-trip thing down pat. I made a mental note to kill John when I got back to the city. It would be a long, slow death.

"Mom, I'm not dating anyone. The detective and I are working together on a case. You know these things are confidential."

"You can't give me details, but you can give them to John?"

"John only found out when I canceled on him to meet with the detective. Otherwise, he wouldn't know any more than you do."

I was finally able to get her off the phone after I promised to text and snapchat frequently. I wasn't even on

Snapchat, but I'd worry about that later. Thinking more about my mother, I decided to call John.

"You are a dead man," I said as John answered on the first ring.

"You are probably the only person in the world," John replied calmly, "who begins conversations that way."

"I just spent thirty minutes talking to my mother about an app I've never used and a woman who likely thinks I'm crazy for throwing her out of bed last night."

"I hope you didn't tell your mom about the bed part. Regarding you being crazy, I wouldn't worry. I've never tried throwing a woman out of the sack, but foreplay is different for every couple. I could tell you some stories."

"I'm sure you could, but I don't want to hear any of them. I called to let you know I'm going to be out of town for a while. I need to fly to New Orleans for the case I'm working on."

He paused a few seconds before responding. "In all seriousness, buddy, be careful on this one. If this case has you working directly with the Cleveland PD, it sounds like something that could be trouble. Keep your head down. There aren't too many people I can crush so easily on the Xbox. I need you around, if only for my ego."

"We'll pretend you can actually beat me. And about the case, there's no need to worry—it's just starting to get interesting."

CHAPTER ELEVEN

LIKE MOST MIDWESTERNERS, Clevelanders tend to approach life with a certain amount of stoicism. This attitude extends from items as disparate as "lake effect" snow to the fortunes of our Cleveland sports teams. Regarding the former, certain communities on the east side of Lake Erie take pride in the fact that their suburbs typically receive the most winter snowfall. Among those select, snow-deluged locations, civic pride is really on the line for the city that wins that competition.

In the case of sports, Clevelanders understand that the Guardians and Cavaliers will win only occasionally, but tales of those seasons are passed down from father to son like the myths of ancient Greece. Clevelanders also know the Browns will win only in an alternate universe, but similar tales are still told: the time our running back made the Pro Bowl, the year we almost won as many as we lost, etc.

That same stoic attitude extends to the Cleveland airport. Experienced travelers know that airport departure times are only theoretical at best. Certain variables, like the plane actually taking off, might not be visible to the naked eye. Like scientists studying advanced physics, most Clevelanders assume the theory is valid, nonetheless.

Travelers not versed in the scientific method often take a more religious view of their airport delays. Like the Second Coming, those passengers have been told their departure will happen at some point in the future. Like the Second Coming, they just don't know exactly when.

Hannah and I, both far from stoic, were exceptions to the Midwestern norm. We sat impatiently by our departure gate, trying to come up with a diversion as we were now more than forty-five minutes past our scheduled New Orleans departure. For lack of anything better to do, Hannah played Candy Crush. I've never seen the point of any game not involving the bloody slaughter of your opponents, so I spent my time pondering the case and hoping our guns managed to make it to New Orleans at the same time we did.

The State of Louisiana recognized concealed carry permits from Ohio, so Hannah and I decided to take our weapons on this trip. TSA regulations require guns to be stored, unloaded, in lockable hard cases, and checked ahead of the flight. That was usually not an issue except for the extra time involved. The directive included informing the ticketing agent, who then called a TSA employee to ensure your gun was packed according to regulations. If done correctly, the procedure worked just fine.

I did hear of one case where an individual walked up to the desk and announced, "I've got a gun," in a voice loud enough for others to hear. The TSA agent, actually several of them, arrived considerably faster in that instance. Since our guns had already been checked, I was just hoping some other agent didn't decide to cut open the locks on our cases to recheck. I heard that could happen and worried since this was my first time flying with a weapon.

Hannah was nervous for other reasons. She'd warned me ahead of time she didn't like to fly, and I suspected she would have driven to Louisiana if we'd had the extra time. As for myself, I was used to flying next to terrified travelers, having flown several times with my mother. Mom never opened her eyes until the "fasten your seatbelt" light beeped off, preferring to pretend she was still safely on the ground while the plane was taking off.

Our plane started boarding at nine o'clock, an hour past its scheduled departure time, and I managed to get the seat next to Hannah. I offered her the window, but Hannah turned me down, thinking the less she could see, the better.

As the engines began to roar and the plane moved down the runway, I suddenly felt a sharp pain in my right arm. I assumed it was the coach seating until I glanced down and discovered Hannah had my forearm in a death grip. She continued to squeeze harder by the second. Seeing the look in my eyes, Hannah responded with her usual tact.

"Don't be such a baby," she said. "You didn't hear me complain after you tossed me out of bed at 3:30 a.m."

"Actually, you complained quite a bit."

"Then try thinking of this as karma."

I tried to ponder the karmic justice of it all, but my mind

kept wondering how long my hand and lower arm could go without blood. Luckily for me, Hannah gradually released her grip as we reached cruising altitude. With no wish to become permanently left-handed, I made a mental note to sit on her other side for the return trip home.

Once airborne, Hannah and I spent the rest of the flight talking more about our respective childhoods in Greater Cleveland. Outsiders tend to underrate the city, but it boasts a vibrant downtown, beautiful beaches, and a climate that changes from season to season despite our claims of perpetual winter. Overall, it wasn't a bad spot for a kid to grow up.

Hannah also spoke in more detail about her parents. She didn't find out until much later, but her mom and dad almost broke up due to her father's repeated infidelities. Counseling kept her parents together, though Hannah suspected expediency had also been a factor. Her mother's political ambitions benefitted from having a congressman as a spouse, and her husband often cited his wife's law-and-order reputation on the campaign trail.

"Most of all," Hannah said, "it's the hypocrisy I hate. They and their friends pose as champions of the little people, but you wouldn't believe the comments I heard at parties. They're perfectly friendly as long as 'those people' stay in their place. God only knows what they would do if 'one of them' moved next door."

"Do they know how you feel?"

"We had a real falling out when I decided to join the police force, and I threw a lot of this stuff back in their faces. I felt terrible about that later because, in many respects, they weren't terrible parents. We went on a lot of trips, and we flew to Europe at least twice that I can remember. My parents weren't all bad, but they became incredibly hard to take, especially after I got older."

"Do you ever see them since you moved out?"

"They stop by the house occasionally, usually unannounced, and I typically go over to their house for birthdays and Christmas. We have a relationship. It's just not particularly comfortable. To be honest, we probably share the same judgmental streak. As hard as that is to admit, it doesn't make them any easier to take."

The plane began its descent into New Orleans. Fortunately for my arm, Hannah was calmer on the way down than taking off, though she did jump a bit when the wheels touched the ground. After the plane had finished taxiing, she pulled out her cell phone to tell the New Orleans PD we'd arrived. She'd informed them previously of our flight arrangements, and they promised to send a detective to meet us at the gate.

It was there that we met Detective Christopher Robinson, quite possibly the largest man I'd ever seen. The detective was African-American, at least six feet, seven inches tall, and had to weigh well over three hundred pounds. He greeted Hannah warmly as she came into view, then took a long, rather disdainful look at me.

"You must be the private detective. I can't say I've ever met a transgender detective before."

I knew I needed to deal with this quickly. "I was thinking of having *TD* embossed on my business cards, but I thought it'd seem too gaudy. Besides," I continued, looking at his considerable bulk, "I was a little afraid someone would think it stood for 'Tub of Lard Detective.' We couldn't have that, could we...Detective?"

As far as insults went, it wasn't my best. That being said, I was still worried. Detective Robinson didn't need to use his gun to kill me. He could simply fall on me and later claim it was an accident. Luckily, my concern was for nothing.

He looked stunned, and then he burst out laughing. "You've got balls, Detective. Literally or figuratively, you've got balls." He then turned to Hannah, who also seemed relieved. "I like him. He's okay."

"He talks too much," she said, "but he's not a complete idiot."

I remembered why Detective Robinson's name sounded familiar. "Detective, did you play defensive tackle for LSU about twelve or thirteen years ago?"

"I did, but how could you possibly know that?"

"You started on the LSU team that beat Ohio State for the national championship in 2008. I've always been an OSU fan."

Hannah was getting impatient. "If you boys are done bonding, you think maybe we could do some real police work?"

Detective Robinson looked back at me and shook his head. "Women."

"Women," I agreed.

CHAPTER TWELVE

AFTER URGING US to call him Chris, Detective Robinson drove us to our hotel and waited patiently in his car while we dropped off our luggage. After we returned, he then gave us a quick heads-up concerning the organization of the New Orleans PD. As Chris described it, the city of New Orleans was divided into eight police districts. While the murders had occurred in multiple regions, the investigation was centered in the Eighth District, where Dr. Grieve's downtown psychiatric practice was located.

We arrived at the Eighth District around eleven o'clock. Chris first introduced us to his captain, a tall, bespectacled, friendly-looking man with the improbable name of Landry Giacomo.

"My father was Italian," Captain Giacomo explained.

"He met my mother in college at Tulane, and they both decided to stay in New Orleans after graduation."

Unlike Chris, the captain made no comment regarding my appearance. Whether due to discretion or the fact that he didn't look very closely, I was grateful either way. Still, I had one question.

"How did you get the name 'Landry'?"

"I always tell people I was named after the French saint. Saint Landry is one of the parishes in Louisiana, what you Ohioans would call a county. The truth is a little more mundane. My father grew up in Texas, and he was a big Dallas Cowboys fan. He worshipped Tom Landry."

The captain saw Hannah staring at his glasses—he bore an uncanny resemblance to Ben Franklin—and said, "I see you noticed my specs, Detective Page. I only wear them to make people around here think I'm smart."

"No worries, Captain," Chris replied. "We stopped thinking that a long time ago."

Giacomo shook his head. "Why I put up with this guy, I don't know. In any case, Detective Robinson will show you the case files and can answer any questions you might have. If he gives you any crap along the way, just let me know."

We were led to a small conference room with pictures of the Mississippi River lining all four walls. In the room's center, a table was stacked with police notes, witness statements, and medical reports pertaining to the four murders. After taking seats at the table, Hannah and I began the task of reviewing every detail of the investigation. That lasted a little over four hours, but it left us with a much clearer picture of the victims and where the investigation stood so far.

The first victim, Sean Doohan, a nineteen-year-old

student in the Tulane University School of Science and Engineering, had been murdered during finals week on May 8th of the previous year. A maintenance worker discovered his body in a steam tunnel, one of many in a labyrinth that ran underneath the campus. Even though the school locked all entrances to the tunnel network, engineering and science students found creative ways around the bolts, including freezing them with dry ice. Once in the tunnels, students took great delight, particularly during Halloween, in drinking and trying to navigate the system at night.

While Sean Doohan often joined in these excursions, none of his friends were with him the night of the murder. When questioned, none could remember Sean ever going into the tunnels by himself. According to the medical examiner's report, he'd suffered multiple stab wounds to the neck with one additional detail, a small puncture mark on his arm. The medical examiner found traces of a drug called propofol in Sean's blood.

"What is propofol?" I asked. "I've never heard of it."

"Propofol," Hannah answered, "is a short-acting medication that results in decreased consciousness as well as loss of memory."

"It scares me you could just rattle that off."

"While I am brilliant, I also read faster than you. Look down to the next paragraph in the ME's report."

That mystery solved, we continued to piece together the investigation into Sean's death. Like the other victims, our victim was being treated by Dr. Michael Grieve. In his case, the treatment was for anxiety. Sean was in great danger of losing his scholarship due to poor grades, likely a result of too many nights out with his friends. His parents weren't rich, and the loss of his financial aid would force him to leave school and face an uncertain future.

As we continued reading, we discovered Sean's anxiety might also have been related to his sex life. From interviews with his friends, the police learned that Sean had been dating at least three girls in the weeks before he died.

Despite that activity, Sean's roommate suspected he might be gay. The roommate couldn't provide any specific basis for the belief. It was just a general impression from the way Sean spoke about men.

His sexual confusion aside, Sean appeared to be little different than most college students. While he could have hit on the wrong man or woman, the use of propofol pointed to a planned killing rather than a crime of passion.

We moved to our next victim, Melanie Sailes. According to police records, Melanie was a thirty-two-year-old recent divorcee living with her sister, Andrea Tubbs. Two months after Sean Doohan's death, Andrea found Melanie's body after returning home from her job as a receptionist at a local dentist's office.

The ME estimated Melanie's time of death as somewhere between 1:00 and 2:00 p.m. The cause of death was a single stab wound to the throat, almost certainly from behind. Similar to the two cases in Cleveland, there was no indication of forced entry to the home. Unlike the previous murder, there were no signs the victim had been drugged beforehand.

According to her sister, Melanie's personal life had been a significant source of stress. Melanie was divorced six months ago from Brian Sailes, a cook at a local restaurant. The police spoke to the restaurant manager as well as

Andrea's boss at the dental clinic—both were working at the time Melanie was murdered. Melanie herself had been searching for a job since her divorce. Her sister had tried to help without success.

It was Melanie's inability to adjust to the divorce that resulted in her biweekly visits to Dr. Grieve. According to her psychiatric records, she was being treated for depression due to her husband's unexpected abandonment of their marriage. Hoping for a reconciliation, Melanie refused to return to her maiden name despite being encouraged to do so by her sister. For that same reason, she also refused to date. Police confirmed this fact through their interview with her sister supplemented by a review of Melanie's cell phone records.

That brought us to the third victim, Gillian Norman. Ms. Norman, a twenty-six-year-old nursing student at Louisiana State University, was found murdered in her apartment after she didn't answer her parents' daily 10:00 p.m. phone call.

Gillian's mother and father were paying the bills for Gillian's education and her New Orleans apartment. Based on interviews with her parents and a review of her psychiatric records, we learned that Gillian spent her weekdays at the LSU campus attending classes while residing in a dorm populated primarily by nursing students. On weekends, Gillian drove back to New Orleans, an hour and a half drive. Once there, she split her time between her apartment and her parents' home.

"Do you suppose," I asked Hannah, "that her parents were the ones who insisted on the weekend commutes back home?"

"Given they paid for her apartment," Hannah replied, "I would say that's a virtual certainty."

From the ME's report, Gillian's cause of death was a single stab wound to the throat. Similar to the other victims, the perpetrator was likely standing behind Gillian when they killed her. There was no sign that Gillian had been drugged, and the report estimated her time of death at somewhere between 11:00 a.m. and 1:00 p.m.

There were also no signs of forced entry to the apartment. Though they were working, apartment security cameras recorded few faces that weren't noticeably blurred. Building management stated they were in the process of having the cameras replaced.

According to her psychiatric records, Dr. Grieve was treating Gillian for anxiety and depression. Gillian portrayed herself as directionless and felt forced to attend nursing school by her parents. Both parents were physicians, and both had been disappointed when Gillian was turned down for admission to medical school.

Not surprisingly, her fellow nursing students described Gillian as "distant." Her roommate stated she tried without success to get Gillian to attend social events with the other students in their dorm. Despite her issues, Gillian achieved average to above-average grades at Louisiana State, and she was on track to graduate in the coming year.

Gillian's dating history could best be labeled as spotty. According to her patient history, she was involved in an "on-again, off-again" relationship with Bradley Collins, a graduate student attending Tulane University. In a police interview, Mr. Collins stated their relationship's uncertain status was due to the distance between their schools and what

Gillian's parents feared were his questionable job prospects. Mr. Collins was due to graduate in one year with a PhD in anthropology. Both he and Gillian's parents had alibis for the time of Gillian's murder.

Hannah looked at me as we finished going through the reports on Ms. Norman. "This one hits close to home."

"I figured it might, given your familiarity with controlling parents. Where you chose to rebel, she picked a get-along, go-along approach. I think she paid for that in the end, especially if Dr. Grieve had anything to do with her murder."

We moved to the fourth victim, Mr. Edward Sherman. Mr. Sherman was found dead on February 4th of this year. The date was notable for the relatively long lag time between this murder and the previous three, all of which took place the previous year. As Hannah had already noted, Mr. Sherman's killing also occurred two months after Father Samuel had moved to Cleveland. If the New Orleans killer followed Father to Cleveland, he'd waited some time to do so.

Like Sean Doohan, Mr. Sherman was murdered away from home, his body found in the front seat of his 2014 Toyota Camry. The vehicle was parked in the otherwise empty parking lot of Tambor Manufacturing, a small New Orleans firm specializing in children's toys. Mr. Sherman was employed at Tambor as the company's budget director. According to the medical examiner, the cause of death was a stab wound to the throat, likely occurring sometime between ten and 11:00 p.m. the previous night.

In another similarity to the Doohan murder, the ME found signs that Sherman had been drugged. He had an injection mark on his arm, and traces of propofol were found in his blood. The only fingerprints found in the car belonged to Mr. Sherman and his wife.

Edward Sherman had been married for twenty-nine years to Allie Sherman, and the couple had resided in New Orleans for the entirety of their marriage. A happy relationship by all accounts, the Shermans planned to travel to Mexico next year for their thirtieth wedding anniversary. They had two sons, Todd and Seth. Both were married, and both also lived in the New Orleans area.

While Mr. Sherman might not have been an obvious candidate for psychiatric care, his wife encouraged him to seek counseling due to job-related stress. Tambor Manufacturing had undergone a significant downturn in its business over the past two years. The company had hoped two recent new products would stem the red ink, but sales for those items were significantly below forecast.

As the company's budget director, Tambor's leadership tasked Mr. Sherman with developing a downsizing plan to address the company's financial difficulties. According to his wife, the stress and guilt associated with laying off long-term employees had begun to affect Mr. Sherman's sleep as well as his emotional stability.

When asked about his last night, Mrs. Sherman said she had no knowledge her husband was meeting someone at his workplace. He'd had left home at 9:45 p.m., telling his wife he needed to pick up some items at the grocery store. While she questioned the timing, she didn't become genuinely alarmed until her husband didn't return in time for the evening news. Mrs. Sherman called the police after unsuccessfully trying to reach her husband on his cell. The police found Mr. Sherman's body in his car in the Tambor parking lot at 4:00 a.m. the next day.

There was no such thing as a good murder, but this one was particularly depressing. By all accounts, Edward Sherman was a decent man with a family who cared about him deeply. If that wasn't enough, his wife felt guilty for pushing her husband into counseling sessions that might have led to his death. We owed her some sort of closure. The best we could do, stuck in a conference room surrounded by files, was to move on to Dr. Grieve.

Dr. Michael Grieve was born on October 9, 1978, in Springfield, Illinois. His parents, George and Alma Grieve, still lived in Springfield. They claimed to have rarely spoken to their son, at least over the last ten years. Grieve received his bachelor of science degree in Biology in 2001 from the University of Illinois. From there, he'd moved to medical school at Georgetown University, graduating in the upper third of his class in May of 2005.

After completing his Georgetown psychiatric residency, Dr. Grieve moved to New Orleans. Once there, he opened a private practice in a small medical arts building in the city's downtown. His practice was immediately successful, and he began teaching some classes at Tulane Medical School.

Based on student reviews, those classes were not popular. His teaching method was considered overly autocratic, and several students complained about his arbitrary grading system. Dr. Grieve's receptionist reported him missing in February, just three days after police discovered the body of his patient, Edward Sherman.

"I had a friend who went to medical school," Hannah said. "Based on what she said about her teachers, you have to go a long way to be considered overly autocratic in that setting."

In completing their profile of Dr. Grieve, the New Orleans PD interviewed several patients as well as colleagues from Tulane and Georgetown Universities. When asked about Dr. Grieve, the descriptors they deployed most commonly were aloof, arrogant, intelligent, and mysterious.

According to his driver's license, Grieve was six feet one inch tall and weighed 180 pounds. Unlike most license photos, his showed a man with striking good looks. Hannah thought he looked like an older, darker-haired version of Ryan Gosling. Despite his appearance, Grieve didn't appear to be actively dating. In fact, no one interviewed by the police could say if he dated at all.

Most of Grieve's patients stated they'd benefitted from his treatment. Two of his long-term patients said his personality had become even more distant in the last year. One speculated about a broken relationship, but he had no definitive knowledge on which to base the claim.

We'd just finished with Dr. Grieve when Chris reentered the conference room.

"Do you guys have everything you need?"

"We're fine," Hannah said. "We were going over the various victim reports. It looks like your department did a thorough job."

There was one piece of information missing from the file that still bothered me. Looking at Chris, I said, "Is there any way we can find out if he was Catholic? That might help establish a connection to the cases we're investigating in Cleveland. Also, his background info doesn't mention his high school. If he attended Catholic school, I would be curious to know if it was run by the Jesuits. That would give him another reason to attend the Jesuit parish here in town."

"That should be pretty simple," Robinson said. "We can check with Grieve's parents."

"I was also wondering about the files for the two missing patients. I think they might be your best chance to solve this thing."

"Those files should have been in the stack we gave you. I'll make sure you get them, but I'm curious why you think the missing persons' cases are important."

Hannah also gave me a questioning look. Maybe I was overly optimistic, but I thought there was a good chance those two patients were not part of our kill list.

I closed the file in front of me and turned again to Chris. "Did you ever consider the one thing the victims have in common other than they were patients of Dr. Grieve?"

Rather than respond, Chris waited for my answer.

"All four of them were found at or near their homes either the same day or one day after they were killed. The same is true of the Cleveland murders—all three occurred in the victims' homes. One was discovered weeks after her death, but she was a recluse, and no one noticed her missing."

"I guess what I'm saying," I continued, "is our killer made no attempt to hide the bodies of his victims. With that, I don't think we should assume our two missing patients are dead. They may have suspected something was off about Grieve and taken off before anything could happen to them."

Chris looked at Hannah. He was hoping for confirmation from a fellow police officer.

"He's annoying," Hannah said, "but at times, he's actually right."

CHAPTER THIRTEEN

THOUGH HE STILL doubted their importance, Chris returned with the files for the two missing patients. We then returned to the conference table, all three of us this time, and continued our review.

The missing patients, Harold Reed and Mary Dhillon, were different in almost every respect. Forty-five years old, Harold Reed worked as a New Orleans mailman, the latest in a series of five jobs he'd held within the last nine years. Reed had been diagnosed with adult oppositional defiance disorder, and his current supervisor described him as combative and defensive, asserting, "If I weren't so short on staff, I'd have fired his ass a long time ago." Mr. Reed was also divorced and behind on alimony payments to his ex-wife.

"This guy likely ran off on his own," Chris said, "for reasons having nothing to do with our investigation. With everything else I've got to deal with, I'm not going to spend a lot of time chasing after a guy who's just trying to skip out on alimony."

It was a hard point to argue, so we moved to Mary Dhillon. Mary was thirty-six years old and diagnosed as a paranoid schizophrenic. Joseph Heller once wrote, "Just because you're paranoid doesn't mean they aren't after you." I wondered if that might be relevant in this case.

Until her disappearance, Mary had spent most of her life living with her parents in a single-family home on Laurel Street in the Garden District of New Orleans. According to Chris, the district was once home to a number of southern plantations. While many old-style mansions were still in the area, smaller homes like the Dhillon's had become increasingly more common.

Mary's parents, Libby and Ash Dhillon, reported her missing on February 19th. According to her father, Mary had taken her car to run errands that morning and never returned home. Police later found Mary's car, a 2012 Subaru Impreza, in the parking lot of an Alvin's grocery store. There were no groceries in Mary's trunk, and the police couldn't find anyone who'd saw Mary in the store that day.

Mary had been receiving psychiatric care ever since her diagnosis as a paranoid schizophrenic at age twenty-two. The diagnosis had been made shortly after Mary graduated from college. She began psychiatric care with another physician before being referred to Dr. Grieve for continuing treatment.

The police suspected that Mary had run away. Though

she'd never run off before, her parents said she'd become increasingly agitated in the few months before her disappearance. Prior to that period, Mary's parents had been satisfied with her progress. According to her father, Mary was very diligent in sticking to the medication regimen prescribed by Dr. Grieve.

Given her diagnosis, the police began their investigation immediately after Mary's disappearance. Their search took on an increased level of intensity once Dr. Grieve's connection to the four murder cases became known.

Beyond the Dhillon's neighbors and friends, police interviewed staff from the veterinary shelter where Mary volunteered. According to staff at the shelter, Mary was exceptional at caring for their animals. Her ability to interact with clients was limited, but the shelter's sole veterinarian reported improvement in that area as well.

Mary didn't have a paying job, but she did have a credit card under her parent's account, which was still being monitored. The police had tracked no activity since the time of Mary's disappearance.

Her parents, hoping to encourage her independence, also paid Mary a small, fifty-dollar-per-week allowance, contingent on completing certain chores. Mary's mother told police that Mary particularly loved working in the Dhillon's small garden. Gardening was the only activity Mary found truly relaxing, other than her work with animals.

We didn't finish reviewing Mary's file until after four o'clock. Even though reviewing the case notes was a necessary first step, Hannah and I were eager to get back out in the field. We asked Chris if we could speak with Mary's parents.

"I'm okay with that," he said, "but I'm still not sure what that will tell us."

"You have to remember Mary is paranoid," I said. "Paranoids are defensive, always watching for any situation that might present a danger. If we can find Mary, I want her to tell us what made her run off the way she did. It might be a pending alien invasion, but she could have picked up on something very real that spooked her enough she felt running was her only option."

"You can talk to them," Chris said, "as long as I go with you. With you both being new in town, you might want me to drive anyway."

Chris called the Dhillons to make sure they were home. After being told they would be happy to see us, we drove to their residence in the same car Chris had used to pick us up from the airport. On the way to the Garden District, I discovered three key "rules of the road" when driving in New Orleans.

The first involved traffic lights. From what I observed, New Orleans' drivers viewed traffic signals more as annoyances to be bypassed than legal arbiters governing their right of way. In the half-hour trip to the Dhillon's, I counted at least three instances when cars almost clipped our own as we drove through an intersection.

Chris noticed my concern, though he appeared unruffled. "You drive here awhile, and you learn to follow the five-second rule. If you're at an intersection, you wait at least five seconds after the light turns green before pulling out into traffic. I can't tell you how many accidents I've avoided that way."

New Orleans city planners, perhaps after a visit to one

of the city's drive-through daiquiri franchises, had also virtually eliminated left turns on city streets. While driving on one of the city's major thoroughfares, we passed street after street with No Left Turn signs. Hannah asked Chris what a driver should do if he needed to go left.

"This is the Big Easy," Chris said with a laugh. "Sometimes you need to go the wrong way to end up the right way. You'll see in just a second."

A few blocks down, he took a sharp right on a road called, for some unknown reason, Midget Street. Midget Street was actually rather wide, and Chris executed an abrupt U-turn to get us heading back the way we'd come.

He laughed one more time. "That, my friends, is a New Orleans left turn. The trick is finding a street that isn't one-way. As you probably also noticed, that isn't easy in New Orleans."

The last rule, I discovered, was a corollary to the first—there were no true speed limits in New Orleans; there were simply speed suggestions. As we continued to our destination, cars moved at a pace that would have made drivers on the German autobahn quake with fear.

I turned to Hannah and saw something that looked like envy on her face. "The way you drive, you'd fit right in."

"I like moving fast. I won't apologize for that." She noticed my smile and gave me a quick poke.

If Chris saw, he was smart enough not to show it. Instead, he kept on driving, and after a few more narrow, one-way streets, we finally managed to reach our destination.

We pulled into the Dhillon's driveway just as I was promising God I would never again complain about the Cleveland freeways. I knew I'd break that one eventually, but I was sincere at the time.

The Dhillons came out to meet us when we were still in their driveway. Libby Dhillon, Mary's mother, was a short, gray-haired woman who still wore her hair in a ponytail. With her long, hippie dress, I could almost imagine her as an aging den mother in a 1960s commune.

Mary's father, Ash Dhillon, was significantly taller than his wife. He had silver hair, a beard, and the dignified, intellectual look of a college professor. He walked with his arm around his wife's waist, and I couldn't tell if that was for her comfort or his. After introducing themselves, the Dhillons invited us inside

The police report on Mary Dhillon's disappearance described their house as "a small single-family home." While smaller than some of the other homes on Laurel Street, that description didn't do it justice. Two stories high with verandas on both levels, the yard was beautifully maintained. To my non-Southern eye, it resembled a traditional Southern mansion done in miniature. It fit in well with its larger Garden District neighbors.

In contrast to the exterior's old-Southern facade, the home's inside looked like the display floor of an Ikea store—never my favorite furniture, but I probably wasn't the best judge. After apologizing for not having cleaned recently, Libby Dhillon invited us into their living room and asked us to sit. Hannah squeezed in next to Chris on the modern-style leather couch, and I chose the only older piece of furniture in the room, a rocker that reminded me of the Amish-made one my mother used when sewing.

The preliminaries finished, Chris took the lead. After thanking the Dhillons for agreeing to meet with us, he introduced Hannah and me as Cleveland investigators looking into whether the murders tied to Dr. Grieve's practice were related to similar crimes in our city. With that lead-in, Hannah began our questioning.

"Mr. and Mrs. Dhillon, the police report said Mary had never previously run away from home. Did she have any experience living on her own?"

"Shortly after Mary was diagnosed," Libby responded, "we leased her a small apartment in a complex just a few streets from here. Her psychiatrist at the time felt a degree of independence might help Mary with the adjustment process, but in hindsight, it was probably too soon. Mary had several conflicts with her neighbors. After she accused one of stealing her newspaper, things got...violent, and the building manager said he would need to terminate our daughter's lease. Since then, Mary has lived in one of the extra bedrooms in our home."

I asked them to describe Mary's behavior before she disappeared.

"You're talking about two different periods," Mary's father said. "Mary disappeared in February. If you asked me about her behavior six months before that date, I'd have said she was as good as I've seen her in a long time, definitely more relaxed. I even remember looking out the front window in August and seeing her talking to one of our neighbors, an eighty-year-old man who lives across the street. That was unusual because Mary was smiling. That was not her normal reaction when speaking with people she didn't know well."

"Things started to change around Thanksgiving," Libby added. "In late November, Mary started to get testy all over again. She began sniping at Ash and myself, and she refused to run errands. In the past, Mary always liked doing those things. Her mood got even worse in the two or three weeks before she disappeared. Her paranoia was as bad as it's ever been."

"Can you clarify that?" I asked. "What kinds of things was she saying?"

"Mary started to think people were watching her almost everywhere she went. It got to the point where she would hardly go outside. That's why I was happy when she agreed to go to the store the day she disappeared. I thought it was a sign she might be getting better."

"Tell me, Mrs. Dhillon," Hannah said, "about Mary's visits to Dr. Grieve's office. Did she have any specific complaints about him or any of her fellow patients?"

"Mary did criticize Dr. Grieve, but it was an odd complaint. Even when she first started seeing him, she always called him slick. She said Grieve reminded her of one of those televangelists. Before Mary disappeared, she moved from calling him slick to calling him two-faced. She said he never kept his promises. When I asked Mary what promises she meant, she stopped talking altogether. She said a few of the other patients struck her as creepy. I don't remember her mentioning anyone specifically."

"Actually, I do," her husband said. "It was sometime last year, probably September or October. Mary came home and said Dr. Grieve asked if she'd be willing to attend a group session with one of his other patients. Grieve told her the session was about trust. Mary and the other patient were allowed to ask questions about each other's condition. She said the session got too intense, and she complained to Dr.

Grieve when it was over. According to Mary, Grieve said it was just an experiment."

Now we were getting somewhere. I leaned closer. "Did Mary ever give you a name or describe the other patient in any way?"

"Unfortunately, that was as descriptive as she got."

Chris turned to Mrs. Dhillon. "The last time we spoke, you said Mary didn't have any friends. What about the other volunteers at the animal shelter?"

"I don't know if I'd call them friends, exactly. It's not like Mary ever hung around or talked with anyone after work. That being said, she was probably more attached to the people at the shelter than anyone else in her life. You have to understand how much Mary loved those animals. Dogs, cats, you name it. Anyone who helped care for them was at least a little okay in her book. For Mary, that was her version of trust."

None of us had any more questions, so we asked if we could see Mary's room.

Located on the second floor of the Dhillon home, Mary's bedroom was small and notable for its lack of decoration. There were a few pictures of Mary at various stages of her life: her high school graduation, her prom, and two more recent photos likely taken at the animal shelter. Chris and Hannah asked the Dhillons if they could look through Mary's closet and her dresser—other than a queen-sized bed, the dresser was the only piece of furniture in the room.

While the others looked through Mary's closet, I concentrated on the pictures. Mary's police file contained a small photo of her, but it didn't do her justice. The real Mary was tall, very pretty and very blonde—your classic southern belle. Wearing a plain dress with no jewelry, she easily out-shone the other girls in her prom photo. That thought led me back to her picture taken at the animal shelter. It was the only photo in which Mary was wearing jewelry, an unusually colored green-and-orange pendant necklace that appeared to be a golden retriever. Libby Dhillon saw where I was looking and guessed at my thoughts.

"I thought the pendant was unusual, to say the least, but Mary insisted on wearing it. She said she received it as a Christmas gift from one of the people she worked with."

I went back to the pictures and noticed something else. Mary was undoubtedly a beautiful woman, but there was something brittle in her appearance. It was a look you see in some Hollywood actresses, a gaze that said, "I'm beautiful, but you wouldn't want to spend any time with me."

Turning again to Mrs. Dhillon, I said, "Mary is certainly very pretty. Did she go out on dates? I imagine there was no shortage of male suitors."

She smiled, if only briefly. "The South is getting to you, Mr. Luvello. Male suitors? The next thing you know, you'll be talking about gentleman callers. The truth is, Mary didn't go out on many dates. As you guessed, that was not due to a lack of interested men. Mary was just very...clinical when it came to dating."

"What do you mean by clinical?"

"Mary would date if she had a reason to date. If she wanted to see a specific movie or attend a concert, she would then agree to a date. Mary would never go out just because she liked a boy. We encouraged her to date more, but she was never very interested. Unlike most girls, I don't ever remember a time when Mary had a crush or any sort of romantic interest in a boy."

We finished going through Mary's bedroom and thanked the Dhillons for their time. As we were leaving, Libby Dhillon stopped us with a question.

"Detectives, our daughter has been missing for four months. Do you think Mary is still alive?"

"The most honest answer I can give you," Chris responded, "is that we're proceeding as if she is. I know you're aware of the deaths associated with Dr. Grieve's practice. If you're looking for hope, I would think of something I was reminded of earlier today—in every one of those murder cases, the killer made no attempt to hide his crimes. Given that, our assumption is your daughter may have run off. We don't know where, but we're going to keep looking until we find out."

After saying goodbye and promising to keep the Dhillons updated, the three of us went back to Chris's car. It was now six-thirty, so Hannah asked Chris if he would drop us off at our hotel.

En route, we talked about our plans for the next day. We'd arrived in New Orleans on Monday, and our return trip home was scheduled for Wednesday morning. That gave us just one more day to come up with any information linking these murders to the ones in Cleveland. I still thought Mary Dhillon was our best lead, and we agreed to start the following day by talking to the staff at the animal shelter.

Chris let us off in front of the hotel and agreed to pick us up at 8:00 a.m. Now on our own, Hannah and I set off to find someplace to eat. Fortunately, there was a Cajun place just across the street advertising "traditional" jambalaya and cochon de lait, the latter only available on certain days and times.

We weren't too worried about the cochon de lait since neither of us had any idea what that was. The jambalaya, however, was appealing. I had made it out of a box a couple of times and liked it. The real stuff turned out to be even better, and Hannah and I both finished the large helpings the waiter brought to our table.

Despite our lack of progress, I was in an upbeat mood. Before going back to our room, Hannah and I stopped at a religious store next door to our hotel so I could get a gift for Father Lawrence. As the Jesuits were paying for my plane tickets, I figured I owed Father something. I found an item I was sure he wouldn't already have, and we made our way back to the hotel.

My mood changed after we reached our room. As soon as we closed the door, Hannah said we needed to talk.

Everything I knew about male-female interactions had come from John, the equivalent of getting relationship advice in a boy's high school locker room. Despite my inexperience, however, I knew "we need to talk" was female code for "you're in trouble." Even with that, Hannah still managed to catch me by surprise.

"We've only been together for about a week, and I never expected things to move quite this fast. Maybe I've been responsible for that, but you were so unsure of yourself I thought I needed to take the lead. In any case, I think there's something you should know about me before we go any further."

"Let me guess. You've got an ex-husband and five kids you're hiding out somewhere."

At the stricken look on her face, I realized what I'd

stumbled onto.

"I take it you don't have five kids."

"I don't even have one."

"So, you're divorced. A lot of people are. I wouldn't have guessed, but it's not the end of the world."

She continued giving me the same look, which meant confession time wasn't quite done.

"I'm going to stop babbling and let you finish."

"That would be nice. The other thing wrong with your guess was the 'ex' part."

"You're still married?"

"Technically, I guess I am."

"Being technically married is like being technically pregnant. You either are, or you're not."

Now she was annoyed. "I knew you'd react this way. Despite all your jokes about the Church, you're still the good Catholic boy at heart. Here's the situation. The marriage happened three years ago. He was a surgical resident, and I was a beat cop. When I became a detective, we were lucky to see each other for even one hour on any given day.

"We still tried to make it work, or at least I did. About six months ago, just before I received my detective's shield, I found out he was seeing another resident on the side. Can you believe the idiot lived with a cop and had his girlfriend send text messages to his phone? No one that stupid should be anywhere near an operating room. Do you want to know how I knew I was no longer in love? When I found out, I actually felt relieved. All I could think was, 'perfect grounds for a divorce.' I filed the papers almost immediately, and he's not contesting. My lawyer tells me things should be finalized in about a month."

She saw my hesitation and added, "I thought you should know. Are you okay with this?"

"After our first night, you said we need to take things slow and not overthink everything. I don't think this changes that. I am curious about one thing. Do you really think I'm a good Catholic? I should have you repeat that to my brother."

"Out of everything I said, you picked that to ask about? I do think you're a good Catholic in your own weirdly unique way. Trying to corrupt you is half the fun of our relationship."

Over the next two hours, we brought each other much further down that long road to corruption. People say sex in a relationship gets stale over time. That might or might not be true long-term, but I could safely say Hannah and I had yet to reach that point. We started on the queen-sized bed in the center of our room and moved to the hotel shower, a rather cramped area that suited us just fine. After the shower, we moved back to the bed again. It was long; it was glorious, and most of all, it was fun. On more than one occasion, my mother told me I needed to get more enjoyment out of life. While I don't think she pictured a married woman in a hotel room, she couldn't have been more right.

As we lay exhausted on the bed, I brought up an even touchier subject.

"How did your mom and dad react to the news of your divorce?" I knew from her piercing look there'd be no more fun that evening.

"How did they react? My mother tried to get me to stay with the asshole. I told her to screw that. Just because she stayed with my father after he messed around doesn't mean

I'm going to make the same mistake. I couldn't believe she thought I'd have so little self-respect."

I quickly agreed. I did so in part because Hannah was right, but I was also afraid for my life if I even hinted otherwise. That was our last exchange of the evening, and we eventually fell asleep.

I experienced no more traumatic dreams, though I did remember something about a race car. The car was traveling clockwise around an oval racetrack. The speedometer was close to two hundred miles per hour, and Chris, the driver, kept saying, "Don't worry, there are no left turns."

CHAPTER FOURTEEN

THE NEXT MORNING, we learned that New Orleans traffic would be the least of our problems. Chris picked us up promptly at eight and gave us an update.

"I was able to dig up some of the additional background info you requested on Dr. Grieve. After talking with his parents, I found out he was raised a Catholic. Whether Grieve still observes is anyone's guess. Grieve also attended Saint Ignatius Loyola High School in Springfield, Illinois. Unless I'm mistaken, that is a Jesuit school."

"On a different note," he added, "I realized I forgot to give you guys some suggestions for dinner before I dropped you off. Where did you go?"

I told him about the Cajun restaurant across the street and the jambalaya. He asked if the cooking was traditional style and grew strangely silent after my reply. Hannah picked up on that almost immediately.

"Chris, why the concern over our eating habits?"

"You're still walking, so I guess everything's fine. It's just that Louisiana has some unusual laws regarding health inspections. As it happens, the state excuses restaurants preparing certain traditional foods from following the usual health codes. That includes jambalaya."

"Gee, thanks, Chris," I said. "Are there any other quaint, local customs you forgot to tell us about? Concentrate on those that might be deadly."

"I told you New Orleans is an acquired taste. This is one of those times when that's true in more ways than one."

Yesterday, Hannah and I walked past a teenager with a T-shirt that read, "You know you're a Cajun if the Wild Kingdom inspires you to write a cookbook." While drivers all around us were exhibiting the same level of road awareness normally found only in a demolition derby, Hannah and I spent the half-hour trip to the animal shelter contemplating death by food poisoning. I wasn't sure if that was better, but it was certainly a unique way to pass the time.

We forgot our culinary concerns when we arrived at the shelter, a large, single-story brick building at the end of a small one-way street. It looked out of place amid the two-story homes surrounding it. A tall fence enclosed the rear of the property. We pulled into the driveway, and I noticed someone had spray-painted a pornographic image on the side of the backyard fence. Not only was the clinic out of place; it was unpopular as well.

Dogs began barking as soon as we rang the shelter's front doorbell. After a moment, the door was opened by a short, African-American woman in a bright, purple lab coat. By the name on her badge, we'd just met Dr. Treenway.

Standing in front of the entrance, the doctor was clearly not pleased by our presence. "Last month, I called the cops every day for a week, trying to get somebody to do something about the damage to our property. I left messages, but no one would call back. Can you at least write a report while you're here talking to my volunteers?"

"I'm sorry, ma'am," Chris responded. "We're only here about the Mary Dhillon disappearance. We're under something of a time constraint, but I promise I'll have a patrol car come out to address your concerns about property damage. Can we please come in?"

Though still miffed, Dr. Treenway stepped back so we could enter. The barking became more emphatic when we walked into the shelter, and we'd have to speak loudly just to make ourselves heard.

The shelter was cleaner than I anticipated, without the smell I would have expected for this type of facility. Dr. Treenway led us to a small room just big enough for the four of us to sit. Based on the instrumentation on the walls and the pull-out table, the room likely doubled as an examination area when not used for meetings.

As he had done with the Dhillons, Chris introduced Hannah and myself. He then asked Dr. Treenway if she would run through the staff she had at the shelter.

"Even though the shelter is open Monday through Saturday, we still have a relatively small staff," she began. "I am the director of the facility and the only veterinarian. Our full-time employees include two veterinary technicians, Bernice Carson and William Laws. They provide most of the day-to-day care for our animals and even perform some minor procedures. Drew Allen is our maintenance man. He only works four days a week, and much of his time," she added pointedly, "is spent fixing all the property damage caused by the locals around here."

"Because our paid staff is so small," she continued, "we rely a lot on our volunteers. Mary is one of five volunteers working at the shelter. Depending on the individual, they work from one to three days each week. Their duties include cleaning the cages, walking the animals, and some general chores.

"The entire staff will meet with you today, though we are having some logistical issues. Nicky, one of our volunteers, might not be here for another hour due to childcare issues, and Drew just called to say he might be late as well. Someone stole his car a couple of months ago, and he's had to take the bus here ever since."

We decided to finish our interview with Dr. Treenway and talk to the veterinary technicians and volunteers in separate groups. The remaining discussion with Dr. Treenway was short and to the point. The technicians had the primary responsibility for supervising and assigning work to the volunteers. As the sole veterinarian at the shelter, Dr. Treenway concentrated on the animals themselves. Her duties included examining each animal brought to the shelter and performing most of the procedures that were necessary based on the animal's condition.

Dr. Treenway's contacts with Mary Dhillon had been typically brief, usually limited to when Mary helped bring an animal into one of the examining rooms. Her feedback on Mary's behavior was also brief: Mary was punctual, she worked well with the animals, and with one exception, she worked well with the other staff.

We asked about the exception. According to Dr. Treenway, Mary'd had a "dustup" with Bill Laws when she first started working at the shelter. Dr. Treenway didn't remember what the dispute was about, but she'd heard Mary talking loudly to Bill from the next room.

With no more insights to offer, Dr. Treenway left us to perform an examination on a "large black-and-white Siamese cat with an exceedingly angry disposition." It sounded like a few of the nuns I'd known in grade school.

With Dr. Treenway gone, Bill Laws and Bernice Thomas joined us in our makeshift conference room. Bernice was tall and gray-haired, with the same no-nonsense attitude as her boss. Speaking to the three of us was clearly not at the top of her agenda.

Bill Laws, with his blond-hair and easy smile, didn't seem to mind our presence in the slightest. He fixed his eyes on Hannah from the moment he entered the room. For that reason alone, I disliked him on sight. Unlike Dr. Treenway, Bill and Bernice had some interesting insights regarding Mary's personality.

"Let me start by emphasizing," Bernice said, "that Mary was exceptionally good with our animals. More than the other volunteers, she was willing to do the dirty work this place requires. This is a clean and well-run shelter, and we couldn't keep that up without people like Mary. On the negative side, Mary was also a bit odd. Our clients never took to her, and I don't think she ever really took to them. She was judgmental, and people don't react well to that type of attitude. Eventually, Bill and I decided to keep her in the back with the animals."

We asked Bill Laws about the dustup mentioned by Dr. Treenway. He shook his head and laughed.

"That happened very early in Mary's tenure here. It was the first time she saw me scruff a cat. That's when you pick up a cat by the skin and hair on the back of its neck. It's something we do on a daily basis, but Mary thought I was hurting the animal. More than her words, I remember the look she gave me—you'd have thought Mary wanted to rip out my spine. When I first saw her, I couldn't help noticing how pretty she was. After that incident, Mary looked a lot less appealing."

"Was there anyone on staff Mary was friendly with?" Hannah asked him. "Did she talk about any friends outside of the shelter?"

"Not that I know of. I don't think Mary ever felt friendly with anyone. You could say she wasn't a people person, but that didn't go far enough to describe her personality."

Dr. Treenway picked that moment to renter the conference room and tell us the volunteers were now available. Having finished with Bill and Bernice, we moved to a larger exam room so we could speak to all of them at once.

Mary's fellow volunteers were a mixed group. All were female, ranging in age from their midfifties to early seventies. At thirty-six, Mary would have easily been the youngest of the volunteer staff. With the age difference and her personality issues, I wondered how well Mary had fit in.

I didn't have to wait long for an answer because the knives came out quickly. If I've noticed one thing in my twenty-seven years, it's that men and women tend to take a different approach when faced with someone they dislike, particularly if the dislike is intense. While men might not resort to physical violence, that calculation, "can I take this person if I need to?" is always present in their minds.

Women often prefer a surgical approach—they identify a weakness and verbally cut away using every tool at their disposal. With Mary's fellow volunteers, that surgical technique was very much on display.

The remarks concerning Mary's character and personality were quick and pointed. Mary was "cold and calculating." She was "perfectly willing to take advantage of her good looks, and her appearance got her whatever assignment she wanted." All four of the volunteers agreed, "things around here are a lot more pleasant since Mary has been gone." Purely as a matter of strategy, I wasn't sure I'd have made the last statement to police in a discussion regarding a potential kidnap victim. Maybe *Law and Order* reruns didn't run on cable in New Orleans.

After listening for a few minutes, none of us bothered asking whether Mary had built any friendships around the shelter. The answer appeared obvious if somewhat depressing. Remembering something the Dhillons had said, I asked if Mary's behavior had changed in the few months before her disappearance. Denise Evers, one of the older volunteers in the group, spoke up almost immediately.

"I'm not sure if this is what you're looking for, but Mary started talking with herself, somedays almost constantly. I know everybody speaks to themselves occasionally, but with Mary, you'd think another person was in the room. Sometimes it would sound like a conversation, other times an argument. When it first started, I thought she was talking to the animals. Looking back, I think this was something else."

Hannah followed up with, "Two questions—when did this start, and did you ever get a sense of who she might be talking to?"

Denise thought for a minute. "I do remember hearing a name. I think it might have been Michael, or maybe just Mike. As to when it started, I'd say sometime last fall."

Chris, Hannah, and I all looked up when we heard the name. The timing and the behavior change also fit perfectly with what Mrs. Dhillon had relayed in our interview at their home.

We asked the ladies if they had anything else to add, but they were all out of Mary Dhillon stories. And we received word that Drew Allen had just arrived at the shelter. We dismissed the four volunteers and prepared for our last interview of the day.

From the moment he walked in the room, I knew Drew Allen was a moron. It wasn't his appearance that led to that judgment. Drew looked a little like Boyd Crowder, the bad guy on the TV show, *Justified*, John insisted on binge-watching. If you took Boyd and sucked away his intelligence and charisma, you'd be left with Drew Allen.

It wasn't even Drew's clothing, although his old Nirvana T-shirt would have been enough to condemn him in my eyes. Instead, it was what he was wearing with his shirt. Specifically, it was the green-and-orange golden retriever pendant, the same one Mary Dhillon wore in the picture in her bedroom. I wasn't sure Hannah and Chris had noticed, so I figured I'd jump right in.

"That's a nice-looking pendant you have there, Drew. Mary Dillon was wearing one just like it in a picture her parents showed us."

Drew had several different options for his response: "I saw Mary wearing hers, and I decided to buy one for myself," was one option; "I told her how much I liked it, and she gave it to me as a present," would have been another.

Drew picked a different approach—he ran for the conference room door. Unfortunately for him, that doorway was occupied by Detective Chris Robinson, the same Detective Robinson who was large enough to eclipse the sun at certain hours of the day. Drew ran into Chris, bounced off his considerable bulk, and careened backward, almost ending up in the same chair he'd started from.

He was, indeed, a moron.

CHAPTER FIFTEEN

THE REST OF Drew's interview took place at the Eighth District Police Station. Before we began his interrogation, Chris discovered Drew lived with his mother in a house a few miles from the animal shelter. After obtaining a warrant, he sent two detectives to search Drew's home while we talked with him at the station. Drew sat in the interrogation room looking utterly defeated as Chris informed him of his rights.

Despite his legal peril, Drew refused the services of an attorney. That box checked, Chris started the interrogation by telling Drew that other detectives were searching his home, looking for signs of Mary's presence. Drew looked up but remained quiet. Chris then asked a series of questions.

"Did you kidnap Mary Dhillon?"

"No."

"Do you know where she is right now?"

"No."

"How did you end up with her pendant?"

Drew didn't have an answer for that one.

Chris tried a new strategy. He told Drew if the cops found evidence that Mary had stayed at his home, Drew would put his mother in legal jeopardy as well as himself. While I doubt any prosecutor would have tried to make that case, the threat had its desired effect.

"You can't do that!" Drew retorted. "Mary wanted to stay with me. She's an adult. You can't arrest my mom."

Hannah spoke up for the first time. "Drew, you're right. If you and Mary cared for each other, that puts a whole different light on things. You're the only one here who knows the real story. Why don't you tell us what happened, and we can stop imagining the worst." After some hesitation, Drew finally opened up.

"I promised Mary I wouldn't tell anyone, but you guys are going to find some of her things there, so I guess that ship has sailed. Let me start by saying I gave Mary the necklace as a present this past Christmas. She was surprised, but she seemed happy. Some people thought it looked funny, but Mary wore it for everyone to see.

"A few days after the holiday, Mary stopped me as we were leaving work and told me she might need my help in dealing with her parents. She didn't say what kind of help, but I think Mary knew I'd do anything she asked. I gave her my cell phone number and told her to call me anytime.

"I didn't hear anything more until sometime in mid-February. Mary called and asked if I would meet her in the parking lot of an Alvin's grocery store close to where she lived. She said she was finally running away from her parents. I picked her up at the store, and Mary asked if she could stay at my house.

"All the while, I wondered why she needed to be so secretive. Mary was a grown woman in her thirties—it's not like she was only twelve years old. I just told myself she was one of those people who's secretive about everything, and I marked it down to that. The way she looked, I would have taken Mary to my house if she said Martians were following her. A guy like me doesn't get many chances with a woman like her.

"Don't get the wrong idea. I never forced myself on Mary. She brought some clothes, and I let her sleep in the extra bedroom in my house. Mary always insisted on giving me money for food, and she reminded me every day that I could never, ever, tell anyone she was there."

"How did you explain all this to your mom?" I asked.

"My mom has Alzheimer's. I love her, but she wouldn't notice if I brought a herd of monkeys to stay in the house. She has a home health aide who takes care of her when I'm at the shelter."

"How long did Mary stay?" Chris asked.

"I was getting to that. Sometime around mid-April, Mary got a call on the cell phone I bought for her at the drugstore. I remember because that was the first time someone called her on that phone when I was around. She wouldn't even give me the number, and I was disappointed she'd given it to someone else."

"Her parents said she had her own cell phone," Chris said. "Did she say why she needed another one?"

"When I first brought her back to my house, she said she had to destroy her old phone. She was afraid her parents would use it to find out where she was.

"When this call came, we'd just sat down for dinner. Mary excused herself and went to her room to talk. The call lasted close to an hour, and I'd almost finished my food when Mary came back.

"I remember she looked really happy. She said a friend called, a friend who could fix her. Those were the exact words she used. She told me she needed to leave the next morning to stay at the friend's house and asked if she could borrow my car to get there.

"I drive an old Ford Focus, and it's the only car I have. I almost said no, but Mary told me she'd be gone no more than a week. I think she saw how disappointed I was. She told me again how much she cared for me and how she considered us more than just friends. That night, Mary came to my room for the first time. After we finished, Mary reminded me I couldn't ever tell anyone she was there. Once she got settled, she said she would come back for me.

"That's also when she returned the golden retriever necklace. She said I should keep it for her until she came back. Mary left about seven o'clock the next morning. She wouldn't tell me where she was going, but she did say it might take her a couple of days to get there."

"What day did she leave?" Hannah asked.

"It was April 18th. I remember it exactly."

Somehow, I knew he would. "Drew, did Mary have her own computer, a laptop, a tablet, anything like that?" I asked.

"I have an old desktop and a printer. Mary used my

computer whenever she needed to get on the internet."

"Did she use it the night before she left?"

"Yeah, she was on it for a couple of hours before she came to bed."

"Drew," I said, "Mary's been gone for two months now. If she's still alive, she may be in some real danger. If we can get access to your computer, that will make it a lot easier for us to find her."

"I'll give you the password. I just want Mary found."

At this point, Chris, Hannah, and I left the interrogation room to decide on next steps.

Mike was surprisingly sympathetic. "I assume you believe his story? I almost felt sorry for the guy. He seems too stupid to lie."

"What about his car?" I asked.

"I put out an APB on the Ford Focus, but you can bet Mary either changed the plates or ditched the car by now."

With new information and Drew's stated willingness to cooperate, we decided our next move was to re-search Drew's home and perform a thorough forensic autopsy of his computer.

With the latter task in mind, Chris decided to bring in the Eighth District's computer expert. Drew had given us his password, but we feared Mary might have deleted her search history. If that was the case, none of us knew enough about computers to recover the missing information.

Before we left, we felt we should have one more conversation with Drew while he was still in interrogation. We had little to hold him on, but it was looking more likely that Mary wasn't an innocent party in this affair. We couldn't risk Drew contacting her.

Chris took the lead as we reentered the room. "Drew, we're all going to take a ride back to your house so you can show us how to get on your computer. I cannot emphasize enough how serious this is. There is a chance Mary's disappearance is tied to some other cases we're investigating, including several murders. If you cooperate, we'll let you go as soon as we're finished. If you don't, you will risk arrest for obstruction of justice. At that point, we'd be forced to remove your mother from your home since she couldn't take care of herself without you there.

"This is what I mean by cooperation—You will allow us access to your computer; you will allow us to search your home; you will not contact Mary Dhillon in any way, and you will inform us if she should seek to contact you. Now, a lawyer would tell you we need a separate warrant to search your computer. That's true, but giving us your permission right now will save us a lot of time. If you care about Mary's welfare, time is of the absolute essence."

"I know I can force you to go to court," Drew said. "But I don't see the point. I already said I'd let you look at my computer, but the home health aide is due to leave in a couple of hours, and I need to get back before that happens."

We took two cars to the Allen home. Drew and Chris drove ahead in one car while Hannah and I tagged along with Detective April Ross, the department's computer specialist.

I know better than anyone the dangers of stereotyping, but Detective Ross was not the computer expert I expected. To start with, she looked older than my mother. Tall and pretty, the detective's gray hair was stylishly cut, and she wore what appeared to be designer sunglasses. Based on appearance alone, Detective Ross looked like she would be more at home at a high-society dinner than a police investigation. To my surprise, she also spoke with a Midwestern accent.

"Chris tells me you're both from Cleveland," she said. "I grew up in Fairview Park, so I know that area well. My family still lives there."

"Seriously?" Hannah said. "How did you end up in New Orleans?"

"After I got my computer science degree, I spent five years working for the NASA Lewis Research Center. That's also where I met my husband. Shortly after we were married, he got a great job offer from a tech firm headquartered in New Orleans. Computer start-ups were popping up almost everywhere in those days. Luckily, this one took, and he still works at the same company.

"I had a little more trouble finding a job after the move. On a whim, I decided to join the police academy. I figured if I didn't like it, I could always look for something else. Fortunately for me, that took as well."

"Was your husband okay with you joining the force?" I asked.

"He was worried at first, but he settled down when it was clear I'd be working mostly with computers. He tells his friends you can't argue with a woman who carries a gun."

We made it to Drew's house without incident, always a victory in New Orleans' traffic. Chris and Drew had already arrived and waited by the front door. Drew's home was considerably older and smaller than the Dhillon's, but it was well-maintained, particularly when compared to the other houses in his neighborhood.

I noticed Drew whispering to Chris as we walked toward the door and Chris nodding his head. When we finally caught up, Chris said, "Since the home health aide is still with his mother, Drew asked if he could say we're friends coming for a visit. He'll send the aide home as soon as he has a chance to check on his mom."

Chris was agreeable to Drew's proposal, though I wondered what the aide thought about the two policemen who'd searched Drew's house earlier that day.

With Chris's okay, Drew unlocked the front door and led us into the living room. We waited there for several minutes while he went upstairs to check on his mother. The home health aide, a pretty young Hispanic woman, came downstairs with Drew a few moments later. She proceeded out the front door with barely a glance in our direction.

The four of us went to work. With Drew as a guide, Chris and Hannah again searched the house, starting with the upstairs bedrooms. With the two of them occupied, I stayed with Detective Ross as she navigated through Drew's computer.

I'd always thought of myself as reasonably adequate with computers. Watching Detective Ross, I realized how little I really knew. Drew's computer was connected to the internet through a cable modem. Knowing our goal was to find Mary's destination, Detective Ross began by checking the computer's Google, Bing, and Yahoo search history. Following that, she moved to some of the more commonly used online mapping programs. Given that we were searching more than two months after Mary's departure, Ross wasn't surprised to find there was no history going back that far. After a few minutes of typing, she turned back to me.

"It looks like someone cleared Drew's browser the same day Mary left. Fortunately for us, that's all they did. Most people don't know how their search history is stored on their computer. Unless she used some very sophisticated data wiping software, I should have no problem recovering it."

Detective Ross grabbed a disc, one of many stored in a CD folder in her briefcase. She inserted the disc into Drew's computer and again began typing. When a blue screen appeared, she entered a series of pathways. Several minutes later, the process was complete.

"Now is the time to cross your fingers," she said.

She then went through the same routine she'd started with, looking through all the common and some not-so-common search and mapping websites. She found what she was looking for on MapQuest. "You're going to want to see this."

We had our connection. Mary had mapped a route to an address in Cleveland, Ohio.

CHAPTER SIXTEEN

I RETRIEVED HANNAH and Chris from upstairs. Drew remained with his mother, a choice I encouraged since we needed to keep Mary's location as confidential as possible. Once downstairs, I updated Hannah and Chris regarding Mary's MapQuest search. While we were speaking, Detective Ross continued looking through Drew's computer and copying his hard drive for a more thorough review back at the station.

Hannah began making calls as soon as she heard about the Cleveland address. After a quick Google search, we found that the address in Mary's MapQuest history corresponded to the Lakeview, a small hotel on Cleveland's West Side.

Hannah's first call was to her captain. She filled him in

on the latest developments and asked if he could assign someone to speak with the hotel desk staff and verify that our suspects had rented a room. For his part, Chris called the New Orleans Eighth District and faxed pictures and descriptions of Mary and Dr. Grieve to a number Hannah provided.

On her captain's suggestion, Hannah then spoke to Andrew Roberts, a Cleveland detective who had already assisted in what he called the "Confessional Murders." I felt a chill when I heard that name. It was a natural for the media, and the Jesuits would have my head if it were publicized. Once Detective Roberts received the pictures of our two suspects, he agreed to contact the Lakeview and call Hannah with an update.

When Hannah and Chris finished making their calls, we then sat down to discuss our next steps. Hannah and I had a flight back to Cleveland the following day, so we needed to make the best use of our remaining time in New Orleans. I had an idea based on another unanswered question.

"We've established a likely connection between the New Orleans' murders and the ones in Cleveland. Unfortunately, we still haven't figured out what that connection is. Our working hypothesis is that Dr. Grieve committed the murders in this city. Sometime after Father Samuel's transfer to Saint Edmund's, Grieve followed him to Cleveland and committed three additional murders. If that scenario is correct, we still haven't figured out why he followed Father Samuel. If all Grieve wanted was to kill, New Orleans would provide a much larger playground."

"There's also a related question," I continued. "If Samuel is the connection, then why did Grieve commit one more murder in New Orleans before following Samuel back to Cleveland?"

"Don't forget Mary," Hannah said. "We still don't know why Grieve would want her in Cleveland."

"I've been thinking about that. One thing that always bothered me was the lack of forced entry into the victims' homes. Looking at the Cleveland murders, there's no way in this day and age that two housewives and an older widow would open their doors to an unfamiliar male visitor. Common sense and a million TV shows would tell them that was a really terrible idea. Those women wouldn't open their door to a man, but they might open up to a pretty, white woman who looks like she just came from a debutante ball. I think Grieve may have used Mary to gain access to his victims."

"There is some logic to that," Hannah admitted. "The lack of forced entry was bothering me as well."

"Agreed, but where does that leave us?" Chris asked.

"I'd like to call Grieve's parents when we get back to the station," I said. "We know Grieve was Catholic and educated by Jesuits. By themselves, those things prove nothing. There are probably thousands of men in New Orleans and Cleveland, including me, who fall into both of those categories.

"What we need to figure out is how deeply religious Grieve was. His office wasn't far from Father Samuel's church, and that could have been where the connection started. When Detective Page and I get back to Cleveland, I'd also like to have another conversation with Father Samuel and see if he has any memory of Dr. Grieve."

While Detective Ross was still working on his computer, we told Drew that Chris, Hannah, and I would be leaving. After again cautioning Drew about attempting to contact

Mary, Chris drove us back to the station. Once there, we took over the meeting room we'd used the previous day and waited while Chris contacted Grieve's parents.

After some initial reluctance, the parents agreed to speak with all three of us. Chris transferred the call to the conference room phone, and George Grieve, Michael's father, got right to the point.

"The longer this drags on, it seems you're looking at my son more as a potential suspect than a victim. Can you give me one straight answer as to where things stand? Do you have any new information you can give us?"

"Mr. and Mrs. Grieve," Chris responded, "we don't have a definite suspect at this point. We're still leaving ourselves open to all possibilities, and that does include your son. Regarding new information, we believe there might be a religious link to this case. For that reason, we wanted to ask you about your son's connection to the Catholic Church. Would you describe your son as religious? Did Michael attend mass on a regular basis?"

Mrs. Grieve answered, "Michael was raised to be religious. He even considered joining the priesthood. As to what he is now, he rarely talks to us anymore. I couldn't say if he still attends mass or not, though I always assumed he didn't."

My interest perked up when she spoke about the priesthood. "You said Michael considered becoming a priest. Can I ask why he didn't?"

After a notable pause, Mrs. Grieve finally answered. "There was a family issue we would prefer not to discuss. Can I ask why this is important?"

"We can't go into detail," Hannah said, "but this is the

best lead we have right now. It could determine whether or not we find your son and how quickly we do so. I understand how family situations can be delicate. We will try to be as confidential as possible with any information you give us."

After another long hesitation, it was again Mrs. Grieve who spoke. "You've got to understand, Michael was a unique boy. Among other things, he was very handsome—girls always wanted to be around him. Despite that, he never showed any interest. He wasn't gay," she added hastily. "He didn't have any friends of either sex."

"With that and Michael being so religious," she continued, "we weren't at all shocked when he decided to join the priesthood. Michael went to the seminary after high school, but he was forced to leave after just one year. The next part is rather sordid, and I would ask that you keep it as confidential as possible.

"Early on, Michael's cousin, Susan Leads, visited him at the seminary. Susan was my sister's only child, and she was the closest thing to a friend Michael had while growing up. The seminary allowed visitors, so having Susan there was not a problem. The incident I'm referring to occurred when Michael's roommate, Josh, returned to the seminary after visiting his parents. Josh not only found Michael's cousin in their room, he found them together in Michael's bed.

"Michael and Josh never got along, and Josh told the rector in charge of the seminary. The seminary insisted Michael leave immediately. We tried to speak to the rector, but there was no absolution. Michael left the same day."

"What did Michael say when he got home?" Hannah asked.

"He refused to say anything at all. Susan told my sister

the affair had been going on since they were both fifteen. As you can imagine, the whole mess really blew up my family. My sister blamed me, and she even tried going after Michael for statutory rape. Luckily, the two of them were too close in age to fit under the law. My sister, her husband, and Susan eventually moved to another town. We've barely spoken since the whole thing happened."

"Can you describe Susan's appearance?" I was playing a hunch.

"She was quite pretty, tall, blonde, and very graceful in appearance."

She looked, in short, just like Mary Dhillon. Being his patient, Mary was also forbidden. That was another trait she shared with Grieve's cousin, and I wondered if that played a role in the attraction. From Mary's standpoint, Grieve was good-looking and also cold-blooded in his dealings with other people. Mary's mother had described her as "almost clinical" in her approach to dating. With that, it was possible to see how she might view Grieve as a kindred spirit. Together, the two made quite a pair, terrifying but logical as a couple. The case was starting to fall into place, but I had one more question.

"After the incident, I understand that Michael gave up on the idea of being a priest. Did he break from Catholicism altogether, or did he still attend mass and accept the sacraments?"

"As I said, I can't speak to what happened after Michael moved to New Orleans. He did attend mass after the incident while he was still here. Michael may have held a grudge against the priesthood but not against the Church itself. I know that sounds odd, but I think he separated those two things somehow."

"You said he kept up with the sacraments," Chris said. "Did that include confession?"

"I don't remember him going to confession. I think that would have been too close to a priest for his comfort."

"The seminary Michael attended," I said. "Was it a Jesuit seminary?"

"It was. Michael was quite taken with the Jesuits from the time he was in high school."

Before we ended the call, Hannah had one last question.

"Mr. and Mrs. Grieve, we wanted to thank you for your honesty in answering some very difficult questions. I have just one more. You know we are investigating a series of murders tied to your son's psychiatric practice. You know him better than anyone else. Do you think Michael is capable of murder?"

"I love my son," said Mrs. Grieve. "I loved him as a boy, and I love him now as an adult. Still, Michael could justify almost anything, and yes, that does include murder."

CHAPTER SEVENTEEN

CHRIS ENDED THE call after promising to keep the Grieves informed of our progress. That done, we tried to figure out where we stood. We had hoped to find the reason why Dr. Grieve had followed Father Samuel to Cleveland. With Dr. Grieve's animus to the priesthood, his location close to Father Samuel's New Orleans' parish, and Samuel's difficult personality, there was at least some reason to believe the two might have had a negative encounter. Given Grieve's sociopathic nature, that encounter could have driven him to following Father Samuel once Samuel had moved out of town.

Father Samuel said he didn't recognize the voice of our killer while in the confessional. Depending on their previous interaction, he might not have had a reason to. It could have even been a particularly moralistic sermon that pushed Grieve over the edge.

We'd gotten all we could from our time in New Orleans, in fact, considerably more than we'd expected. Most importantly, we now had a prime suspect for our own set of murders, a potential female accomplice, and the name of the hotel where they might be staying. In a perfect world, Detective Roberts might have wrapped the case up before our plane arrived back in Cleveland. Assuming we wouldn't get that lucky, Hannah and I decided we should have a conversation with Father Samuel.

For his part, Chris promised to relook at the available evidence from the cases in New Orleans. While there was considerable circumstantial evidence pointing to Dr. Grieve, there wasn't remotely enough to convince a jury. We needed physical evidence tying him to at least one of the murders. As far as unfinished business, there was also the matter of Harold Reed, the other missing patient from Dr. Grieve's practice. We suspected Reed might have skipped town, but we would certainly feel better knowing if that were true.

Our next steps resolved, Chris offered to take us out to dinner. I don't know if he felt guilty about our dining experience the previous evening, but Hannah and I decided to accept.

We experienced some momentary regret for that decision when we pulled into the parking lot of Joe's Heart Attack Chicken & Ribs. If the name wasn't enough, a smaller sign on the window said: Lick a Chick Today. Apparently, eating in New Orleans always involved the risk of imminent death.

Seeing the looks on our faces, Chris said, "Trust me.

You're in the French Quarter now. They don't allow bad restaurants in the French Quarter. It's a civic pride kind of thing."

Luckily for our stomachs, Chris turned out to be correct. Eating at Joe's also gave me the chance to cross another item off my bucket list—I got to try barbecue ribs for the first time. I made the mistake of mentioning that to Chris, and he was shocked at my limited culinary experience.

"Even the Jewish people in New Orleans eat barbecue," Chris said. "Is this some kind of Catholic thing, like no-meat Fridays?" Looking at Hannah, he added, "We've got to add some spice to this boy's life."

"I know," Hannah said. "After that, we work on his wardrobe."

Looking down at my jeans and T-shirt, I said, "What's the problem with my wardrobe?"

She never responded. Seeing how quickly Chris nodded his head, the answer was apparently obvious. Before they could move on to my hairstyle or other personal traits, the waitress arrived and seated us at our table.

Chris was right. The ribs were excellent—plenty of flavor, but not too hot. Having exhausted ourselves with the case, we spent some time talking about our families and experiences growing up. Those were pleasant memories for Chris and me, for Hannah not so much.

To change the subject, we then talked about our most amusing cases. I told my story about the drunken husband trying to shoot me through a hotel window. Chris almost spit out his beer when I mentioned his ex-wife had a photo of him embossed on a set of coasters. Hannah's story occurred when she was still on patrol. It involved a couple in their fifties who found themselves with way too much time on their hands one Saturday evening.

"For whatever reason," Hannah said, "they decided it would be fun to fake the wife's murder. The wife put on some old pajamas. She then lay down on their bed, and the husband covered her in ketchup. To top things off, he took a picture with his cell phone and sent it to their married daughter with a text saying, 'I warned your mother she better stop snoring.'

"The daughter immediately called the police. My partner and I got the call and rushed into the house, guns drawn, expecting a murder scene. By that time, the supposed victim and the perpetrator had moved on from crime scene photographs and decided to take a shower. Trust me, that's not a picture I will get out of my head anytime soon. The wife was so embarrassed. She called the daughter immediately after putting on some clothes, though I think she left out the part about the shower. Once he realized his home wasn't being invaded, the husband looked rather proud of himself."

"Did he have reason to be?" Chris asked.

"Not based on what I could see, but from what we heard when we came up the stairs, the guy's wife seemed to think he was impressive. In the end, I guess that's what counts."

Chris's story also took place when he was out on patrol. It started with a carjacking and grew progressively more bizarre.

"My partner and I were driving through the old warehouse district, and we came upon this guy waving his arms trying to flag us down. We stopped, and the guy shouted that he'd just been carjacked. He pointed to an old Cadillac that was already some distance down the street and yelled,

'That's my Caddy! That's my Caddy!' So my partner and I go racing off to see if we can catch up to the Cadillac. The car was well ahead of us, and I'm thinking there's no way in the world we're going to make it.

"About ten seconds later, the Caddy veers off into a utility pole, and the carjacker practically levitates out of the car. We caught up with him quickly at that point. While I'm putting the cuffs on, the carjacker's raving in a language I'm pretty sure was French.

"So, I'm dealing with this guy, and my partner walks over to look at the car. All of a sudden, he calls me over and says, 'Chris, you've gotta take a look at this.'

"I start walking over to the car, dragging the suspect along with me as I go. The closer we get, the crazier the perp starts acting, and the more French words pour out of his mouth. Finally, we're right by the side of the Cadillac, and I'm close enough to see a four-foot alligator lying, calm as can be, in the back seat of the car.

"Neither of us wanted to go anywhere near the gator, so we called animal control. They came and took the thing to some alligator preserve outside the city. When we drove back to tell the owner we'd found his car, he told us he'd picked up the alligator along the side of the road. I'm not sure how he got the thing into the car, and I'm not sure I want to know. He did look happy it was gone."

It was right about the time Chris finished his story that Hannah received a call from Cleveland. Armed with pictures of Dr. Grieve and Mary Dhillon, Detective Roberts had questioned the front desk staff at the Lakeview. After a minute's thought, one clerk was able to positively identify the picture of Dr. Grieve. Insisting he would "never forget a woman who looked like that," the clerk was equally positive Mary Dhillon had never arrived at his hotel.

When asked how he remembered Grieve two months after his stay, the clerk mentioned Grieve's behavior as well as his sudden decision to leave the Lakeview. Grieve's attitude stretched from complaints about his hotel bed to the view out his window and the poor condition of the hotel's exercise room.

For us, Grieve's attitude was far less interesting than his change of plans. According to the Lakeview's computer registration system, Grieve, using an alias, arrived at the hotel on April 18th, the same day Mary Dhillon set out from New Orleans. When Grieve checked in, he told the front desk he intended to stay at least one week, and his wife would be arriving two to three days later.

The following day, Grieve called the front desk and informed them he would be leaving before noon. Grieve checked out at 11:48 a.m. and paid his bill in cash. When asked if Grieve had driven or taken a taxi, the clerk was unsure.

"Sometime on April 19th," Hannah said, "Grieve found another place to stay. The questions are where and why. Wherever he went, he likely called Mary Dhillon mid-route and told her about the change in plan."

"A hotel likely seemed too public," Chris said. "There's always someone at the front desk, and that doesn't even account for the people staying on the same floor as you. I have no idea how, but I'm thinking Grieve found an apartment or a house."

"I'm guessing a house," I said. "We know Grieve's responsible for at least three home invasions in the city of

Cleveland. It wouldn't be too big a leap for him to seize a fourth home, kill the resident, and decide to stay. The situation would need to be just right, ideally another shut-in like the first Cleveland murder."

As I finished that thought, I realized the idea of Grieve staying in a home bothered me for reasons beyond the obvious. I was missing something important, but I couldn't put my finger on what that was. I reminded myself to revisit that feeling later on.

Chris asked Hannah about the room where Grieve had been staying. She said Detective Roberts had searched the room but found nothing useful. There were no maps, scraps of paper, or anything else indicating where our missing psychiatrist might have gone.

Our hopes for a quick resolution dashed, we wolfed down the remainder of our Heart Attack chicken and ribs and thanked Chris for taking us out. Before Chris drove us back to our hotel, the three of us exchanged business cards and promised to call should there be any new breaks in the case. Chris volunteered to drive us to the airport the next morning, but Hannah and I felt he'd already been more than accommodating. We decided to take the hotel shuttle instead.

Once we were back in the room, Hannah turned to face me. "You were good out there today. That pendant gave us our one and only lead in this case. You have a gift for this, and I'm not saying that just because we're sleeping together."

I was grateful for the compliment. I've always wondered how my investigative skills looked to someone else in the business. I wasn't sure if Hannah was trying to soften me up because she followed with a question.

"Do you want to hear another confession?"

My honest answer was no, but I tried humor her instead. "I'm okay as long as you don't tell me you're married to someone else. I can put up with a lot, but bigamy would be hard to take."

She ignored me. "After we met in that lousy diner, I had you checked out. I needed to know who I was working with and how much help you could truly be. None of the cops I knew had ever heard of you, but I found your name change in the system and remembered you saying something about your high school."

"Saint Robert Bellarmine."

"I had a girlfriend in college who worked as a teacher at Saint Bellarmine. I reached out and asked if she could talk to one or two teachers who'd been there awhile and might remember you.

"Apparently, you had quite a reputation. My girlfriend spoke to a Father Brady, and he said you could have been class valedictorian, but you only put effort into the classes that interested you."

"Father also mentioned," she continued, "an incident in the chess club. He said you walked in out of the blue one day and said you wanted to join. The club moderator was surprised, but he eventually figured out you only came to play the star of the club, a state chess champion."

"Her name was Tammy Lasky," I said. "She was also the prom queen. She and her little friends used to really piss me off."

"From what I heard, you played a match with Tammy Lasky and crushed the life out of her. You then declared that chess was boring and proceeded to quit the club. By itself, that didn't bother me. I knew you were just playing with the girl's head. I might have done the same if I knew how to play chess.

"In the context of our investigation, however, it did raise a concern. I needed to know this case wasn't the chess club all over again, something you would get bored with if it got too tedious. You partially answered that question when we went to dinner, and I got the full answer here in New Orleans. It wasn't just the necklace. You were just as engaged when we were going through those files to see if the New Orleans' cases were tied in with ours."

She looked up at me intently. "So I checked up on you. Are you pissed?"

"No. You're a cop. That's what cops do. If I had any sources in the Cleveland PD, I probably would have asked questions about you. Now I guess you want me to teach you how to play chess."

"No thanks. Someone I know said it was boring."

"You're clearly no Tammy Lasky. If chess is out, you'll just have to come up with something more interesting."

She had several ideas, and none were remotely boring. We fell asleep a couple of hours later, and I remember feeling a little sad beforehand. It was our last night in New Orleans, and the place I would miss the most was our hotel room.

CHAPTER EIGHTEEN

LIKE THE TRIP out, the trip back from New Orleans had its high and low points. On a pleasant note, the plane boarded on time. We were more familiar with the Cleveland airport, so Hannah and I assumed our flight had been called in error. Once we realized there was no mistake, we gathered our carry-on bags, boarded, and found our seats. Based on the sudden constriction in my arm, that was also the time Hannah's fear of flying set in for real.

"You know," I said, "you could have gotten something to drink like every other red-blooded American who hates to fly."

"That would be completely unprofessional," Hannah replied. "Besides, do you have any idea how much they charge for alcohol in an airport? Not to mention that if I drank too much, you'd have to drive my car. There's no way I'm letting you behind the wheel of my BMW. I'm not even sure the car would let you drive it."

"Trust me, I have a lot of experience being rejected by cars."

Fortunately for the circulation in my arm, a young boy came to my aid. Sitting directly behind Hannah, the boy started to kick the back of her seat the moment we began taxiing down the runway.

Hannah withstood this impact to the limit of her patience—about ten seconds by my count. At that point, she turned around and gave the boy a stare. I'd seen the look before, a gaze that said, "You're dead; you just don't know it yet." Hannah continued to stare, and the kid stared back. Eventually, Hannah wore him down, and the kid sort of shrank back into his seat. He looked more than a little stunned.

She glanced at me and whispered, "I guess he's not going to do that anymore."

I looked back at the boy. He had the dazed stare of a child forced to watch an adult horror movie just before bedtime. "I don't think he's going to be doing much of anything anymore. He appears to be catatonic."

"He's fine. Don't be such a worrywart."

"I don't know. I think you broke him."

Luckily for me, this interaction took place during takeoff, the time when Hannah would have normally been wearing divots in my right arm. I figured I owed the kid. If he showed any signs of consciousness, I should probably give him a tip.

The rest of the flight was more uneventful, although I

wasn't nearly as lucky during landing. With my friend be-hind us now out of commission, Hannah had nothing to dis-tract her from the threat of an imminent crash. I tried to hide my arm, but that didn't deter her in the slightest.

"Remember," she said, "your arm isn't the only thing I could grab."

Despite my lack of what she so sweetly called "guy parts," I still felt a shiver. In fairness, Hannah did try to take it a little easier this time. At least I could still feel my fingers after we set down on the runway.

After we exited the plane and retrieved our weapons, I called Father Lawrence to see if we could schedule a meeting with him and Father Samuel, making sure to mention De-tective Page would be there as well. Hannah's presence prompted a request for more information which I was loath to give in the middle of a crowded airport. We finally com-promised and decided Hannah and I would meet with him alone at three-thirty to summarize our findings. Once that was complete, we would call Father Samuel into the room to fill him in on the status of the investigation and ask our questions.

Our plane had arrived in Cleveland at exactly 12:00 p.m. That gave some happy travelers there the opportunity for an on-time departure, Cleveland's version of winning the lottery. With so much time to spare until our afternoon meeting, Hannah and I decided we'd drop off our bags at our respective homes. She would then go to her station to fill in her captain and speak to Detective Roberts.

I also had a plan for my time alone. I had to speak to an old client, and that conversation needed to take place with-out Hannah in the room.

Tomas O'Malley was one of my first clients and the owner of one of the most unusual names in the city of Cleveland. Like many city residents, he was the product of the ethnic integration that had crossed all Cleveland boundaries over the last two generations.

Fifty years ago, Cleveland's neighborhoods were as diverse as an early pilgrim church meeting. There were separate neighborhoods for the Polish, the Italians, the African-Americans, the Germans, the Irish, and almost every other ethnic and racial group you could think of. These communities had well-defined boundaries, most with their own schools and churches. The inhabitants of each locale knew they should never transgress the boundary of another.

The rigid lines defining these neighborhoods gradually broke down as residents discovered their fellow Clevelanders weren't so different after all. According to family lore, Tomas's parents met when his mother, Maria, wandered into his father's church for the eleven o'clock mass. From the stories Tomas heard as a child, the beautiful, raven-haired Mexican immigrant and the tall, fair-skinned Kevin O'Malley sat in the same pew that day and immediately fell in love.

Tomas didn't find out until he was an adult that his mother's quest for citizenship played a role in his parents' early relationship. Before agreeing to marry Kevin, Maria asked for only one thing—since any children would bear Kevin's last name, she wanted to be the one to grant them their first. Kevin quickly agreed, and that's how the name Tomas O'Malley was unleashed upon the unsuspecting world.

While practical considerations might have contributed to their early romance, no one who met Kevin and Maria today would doubt their deep and abiding love for each other. That devotion was evident the first time I met Tomas's parents at their family's home. After they explained their problem, I realized that love was also mixed with fear.

Tomas's sister, seventeen-year-old Rosa O'Malley, had recently begun living with Leonard "Leo" McDougal, a smooth-talking street hustler who presented himself as a professional photographer. Rosa, beautiful like her mother, wanted to make a living as a model. As she was from a small Cleveland neighborhood, Leo looked like her best shot. The fact that Leo was a drug addict whose picture-taking expertise tended to pornography did not deter Rosa in the slightest.

My involvement in the case came after Tomas spotted his sister on the street outside Leo's home, her beautiful face, now bruised. Rosa barely appeared to recognize her brother.

Alarmed, Tomas decided he needed outside help. He ended up picking my name from the online Yellow Pages with the hope that a lone private investigator would charge less than an agency.

From the moment I stepped into their home, I knew I wasn't what the O'Malley's had been expecting. Kevin's first comment confirmed that impression.

"We thought you would be...bigger. I'm sorry, but the man we're concerned with is at least six foot two."

I understood their reaction, but I promised if they stuck with me, I would bring Rosa back that evening. The O'Malley's agreed, though still with some reluctance. Tomas told me Leo's house was located on a side street off Euclid Avenue just outside Cleveland's downtown.

Euclid Avenue, once home to mansions built by men such as John D. Rockefeller and Samuel Mather, was known to old-time Clevelanders as Millionaire's Row. Unfortunately, that era was more than a hundred years past. Little more than an alley, Leo's Euclid side street now looked like an abandoned neighborhood from some post-apocalyptic horror movie. I drove there at about 1:00 a.m. and parked a few houses away until I was reasonably sure Leo and Rosa were asleep.

For most visitors, parking in that neighborhood would be an open invitation to car thieves, the majority of whom wouldn't care if the owner was still in the car. For me, they weren't a concern. No self-respecting thief would consider my car worthy of even a joy ride.

To get into Leo's house, I'd brought along the set of lockpicks John had given me to celebrate my detective's license. Amazingly, he'd ordered them through Amazon. After some practice, I'd become pretty good at picking locks, a skill that has served me well in the years since.

I was helped by the fact that Leo had only one lock on his back door, a significant oversight for that neighborhood. That lock took about twenty seconds to pick, and I needed just two more minutes to find Leo and Rosa asleep in Leo's bedroom. Not surprisingly for a pornographer, the room also included most, if not all, of Leo's photography and projection equipment. Closer to the bed, I found a case of homemade DVDs.

I woke them both up. While Rosa screamed, Leo, ever the hustler, sized up the short, skinny guy standing by his bed and decided a fight was his best option. He stood up and started to move forward. It was the second time in the space of a few hours that someone had questioned my abilities. I was beginning to get annoyed.

To deal with my irritation, I fired two bullets into the large camera by the bed before shifting my aim to Leo's head. Reassessing the situation, he decided his bed was a perfectly comfortable place to stay. Before Leo could change his mind, I decided to press my advantage.

"Leo, you are one ugly shithead. I should shoot you for that alone, but here's how things will go. I'm taking Rosa back to her parents. If you try to stop me, I will shoot you; if you so much as talk to Rosa ever again, I will shoot you; if I see a picture of Rosa on the internet, I will shoot you; if you bother anyone in her family, you guessed it—I will shoot you.

"I have to be honest, though, Leo. Even if you don't do any of those things, I might shoot you anyway just because you're such a fucking stupid piece of shit."

Having no wish to argue further with the crazy person in his bedroom, Leo remained mute and seated.

I told Rosa to put on her clothes. While she dressed, I collected Leo's homemade DVD collection, putting all of them in an empty shopping bag I'd found in Leo's kitchen. Once dressed, Rosa came with me willingly. I drove her back to her parents' house, earning the eternal gratitude of Tomas and the entire O'Malley family.

I don't think Kevin and Maria ever understood some of my life choices, but they were fiercely loyal. From that day on, they treated me like a stepson. I kept the existence of the DVDs to myself, destroying them after I went back home. For his part, Leo McDougal never attempted to contact Rosa. In a wonderful example of addition by subtraction, he was killed six months later in a drug deal gone bad.

All of this came back to me as I thought about Tomas and his particular expertise. With a name like Tomas O'Malley, you might expect an exotic occupation like a movie star or a llama farmer. Instead, Tomas spent his days working as an accountant with a large Cleveland accounting firm.

For this case, I was more interested in Tomas's nighttime occupation. I was one of a small circle of friends who knew Tomas for what he really was, one of the Midwest's most accomplished computer hackers. I called him as soon as I got back to my apartment, and he picked up almost immediately.

"Hola, Terry. How's my favorite private investigator these days?"

"I would be more impressed, Tomas, if that wasn't the only word of Spanish you knew. By the way, how's your sister doing?"

"Rosa's doing well. It's hard to believe she's in her second year of college. She also started dating an engineering major. It's nice to see her with someone who doesn't have a criminal record, and don't think I didn't check. While we're talking about family, Mom mentioned she hasn't seen you in a while. She wanted me to invite you over for dinner, and she said you could bring a friend if you wanted."

Like my own mother, Maria lived in fear that I would die a bachelor. "I wish I could, but I'm in the middle of a case right now. I really called to ask you for a favor. It involves hacking into the records of a Jesuit priest."

"Sounds good. Why don't you send me straight to hell while you're at it? Also, how many times have I told you not to use that word over the telephone?"

I've heard that most hackers hate the term, and Tomas was no exception. His preferred title was computer consultant. Compared to "hacker," I thought that was boring as hell. Like all people in his profession, Tomas was also paranoid when it came to discussing his craft.

Fortunately for me, he was also innately curious. I asked him to look for any and all information he could find on Father Samuel Dennert, starting with school records and progressing through his Jesuit career. I then asked him to cross-check anything he found against the academic and professional records for Dr. Michael Grieve. If there was a connection, I intended to find it. I probably wasn't being fair, given our meeting had yet to take place, but I didn't trust Father Samuel to tell me the full truth on the subject. Tomas agreed to what I asked, and I told him to call my cell immediately if he found anything worth reporting.

After we ended our call, I once again considered and rejected the idea of telling Hannah. I'd be putting her at risk, and I knew she'd tell me to stop. I didn't want to hazard either outcome, convincing myself I could apologize later if she ever found out.

I still had a couple of hours left before the meeting at Saint Edmund's, so I took a quick nap after calling John and my mother to let them know I was home. After the past week, it felt odd to sleep alone. Whether that was good or bad, I really wasn't sure.

CHAPTER NINETEEN

OTHER CITIES USE speed bumps, traffic cameras, and other modern means to reduce speeds on their roadways. Not able to rely year-round on orange barrels, Cleveland traffic engineers chose a more homegrown approach. Large winter snowfalls necessitated enormous amounts of road salt, and the resulting potholes were a low-cost yet effective means of regulating traffic flow. Unless they were insane—or my detective girlfriend—few drivers choose to risk their hubcaps by exceeding the speed limit on Cleveland's major streets.

Traffic aside, I arrived at Saint Edmund's in time for our three-thirty meeting with Father Lawrence. Hannah met me in the parking lot, and we walked into the main office where Hannah met Miss Lambert, the ever-present church receptionist. Seated behind her oversized desk, Miss Lambert greeted me with the warm, friendly look one would typically only display when they're about to back over you with a car.

"You're looking bright and cheery this afternoon, Miss Lambert. You need to stop flirting with me though. This is a church, after all."

"I'll tell him you're here."

Hannah smirked, no doubt landing her on Miss Lambert's ever-growing list of undesirable characters. Along with my notebook, I was also carrying the gift I'd purchased for Father in New Orleans. Despite the box's small size, Miss Lambert regarded it with suspicion. I half-expected her to call out the bomb-sniffing dogs. I wouldn't have been surprised if she had a pair behind the oversized boat she called a desk.

Luckily, Father Lawrence arrived, saving us from whatever carnage Miss Lambert had in mind. He led Hannah and me back to his office.

Once he shut the door, I said, "Your secretary hates me."

"Not a new experience for you, I'm sure. What do you two have for me?"

Before we started, I gave him the gift I bought in New Orleans. Father appeared genuinely touched until he opened the box. Removing the contents, he asked, "What the hell is this?"

"I found it at a religious store. It's a Saint Ignatius bobblehead doll—for the Jesuit who has everything. I figured you could put it on your desk. The head moves up and down. I thought it was very affirming."

Shaking his head, he said, "I may have to hide it from Miss Lambert. This might scare her. To be honest, it almost scares me."

Finished with the gift, we moved into the case summary. I took the lead with Hannah filling in the gaps. We started by reviewing the murders in New Orleans and the similarities between those killings and the murders in Cleveland. We then moved to Dr. Grieve, the evidence linking him to the New Orleans' murders, his religious background including the incident with his cousin at the seminary, and his positive ID at the Lakeview Hotel. Lastly, we talked about Mary Dhillon, the MapQuest route to Cleveland, and Mary's assumed role in the Cleveland killings.

Given Grieve's issues with religion and his proximity to Father Samuel's church, we felt there was a strong if circumstantial case for Grieve following Father Samuel to Cleveland.

Father Lawrence was less than convinced. "It's still pretty thin. You're basing your whole theory on this doctor having a grudge against the Catholic Church and an office near Father Samuel's parish. If Dr. Grieve truly had that many issues with religion, I'm not sure how he and Father Samuel would ever come in contact."

"With all due respect, Father," Hannah said. "There's considerably more than that. In our conversation with Dr. Grieve's parents, they indicated their son continued to attend mass even after the incident at the seminary. If he kept up that practice in New Orleans, the logical church to visit would be the one closest to him, Father Samuel's parish. And why would Dr. Grieve and Mary move to Cleveland a few months after Father Samuel? I have trouble believing that's a coincidence, and I suspect you do as well."

Not certain I was being entirely truthful, I said, "This isn't about giving Father Samuel a hard time. We're just looking for any information he can provide that would help catch the two most likely suspects in these murders."

Father finally agreed and called to have Samuel come to his office. While we were waiting, I promised myself to be on my best behavior. The nuns were always lecturing me about my "smart mouth" and poor attitude. While I hated to admit it, every so often they wandered into a point. I resolved not to let my feelings toward Father Samuel get between us and what we needed to know.

Father Samuel walked into the office in timing with that thought, his eyes displaying the same intensity I remembered from our first encounter. He hadn't yet met Hannah, so Father Lawrence performed the introduction. I then reiterated the current status of our investigation and why we wished to speak with him, detailing point by point our reasons for believing Dr. Grieve had followed him to Cleveland. When I finished, Hannah handed Father Samuel the police file photos of Dr. Grieve and Mary Dhillon.

He took his time scanning each one. Finally, pointing to the Mary Dhillon picture, he said, "I don't remember this one at all, but I think I might remember the man in the other photo."

"Can you give us some context, Father?" I asked. "Where was he? What was he doing?"

He looked at me reluctantly, as though he'd just remembered I was in the room. "I am a priest. If I remember an individual, it is going to be from the church, not the local grocery store. If I'm correct, this person sat in the front pew during many of my masses. I remember because he always left right after receiving communion. He never stayed around for the final hymn."

"Do you remember any conversations with Dr. Grieve?" Hannah asked.

"Not that I recall. He came to mass, and he left. Like I mentioned, he didn't stay after church like other parishioners."

"Father, you must have an awfully good memory," I said. "To remember one face among the hundreds of people who attended mass at that parish is pretty remarkable."

"It was a small parish, and he sat in the same seat every week. Do you doubt my word, Mr. Luvello?"

"Not at all, Father. I'm impressed. I'm good with faces, but I don't think I could remember a single individual based on where he was sitting in a church full of people. Are you sure you didn't have any other contact with Dr. Grieve?" Despite my earlier vow, I was trying to strike a nerve. I wanted to see how he reacted when I questioned his credibility. I wanted to know if he was lying.

"I can understand why you wouldn't be used to the social dynamic of a parish, Mr. Luvello, but a priest must be familiar with all of his parishioners. That is true if they sit in the first row or the last. To the matter at hand, you asked me if I remembered the faces in these pictures, and I told you my answer. I don't know how much more I can do."

"You have been helpful, Father," Hannah said, "and we appreciate your time. You're free to go unless you have anything more for us."

He stood and started walking toward the door. Before leaving, he turned to face me.

"I actually thought you might stay in New Orleans, Mr. Luvello. The people there are very tolerant of those who are...different."

I was about to reply, but Hannah beat me to it.

"Is that why you left?"

Samuel left the room, not bothering to reply.

CHAPTER TWENTY

WITH SOME ANNOYANCE, Father Lawrence asked if we'd gotten what we came for. Taking that as our cue to leave, we thanked him for his time and exited his office. I noticed Miss Lambert didn't even look up when we passed her desk.

With the door safely closed behind us, Hannah asked, "Do you think Samuel was lying?"

"Whether you call it lying or withholding information, I don't think he told us everything he knew."

"For what it's worth, I think the prick was lying through his teeth. What do we do about it?"

At that moment, Hannah got a call on her cell phone from New Orleans. "Chris," she said, "I'm here with Terry. We're standing in a church parking lot, and I can hardly hear you with all the street noise. We're going to move to my car so that I can put you on speaker."

It was my first time in the sainted BMW. To be honest, it was my first time in any BMW. I felt like I should bow. In the passenger seat, I was careful not to leave anything approaching a mark. Hannah put Chris on speaker. His booming voice came through loud and clear.

"How are my two favorite Clevelanders? You guys miss the Big Easy yet?"

"Sure, Chris," Hannah said. "I'm still trying to adjust to food not associated with a death wish."

"I always say if your food can't kill you, you aren't really eating. I called with some news regarding our mutual psychiatrist friend. We've finally got some real evidence linking Grieve to the crimes down here."

"To start with," he continued, "we did another search on Grieve's apartment. I told the CSI boys to tear everything apart, and this time they really did. What they found was one of those fake, hollowed-out books mixed in with the other books in his library. Inside the opening, they found several vials of propofol, the same drug our killer used on a couple of his victims. I had someone check with the Behavioral Health Department at Tulane, and they couldn't think of a single legitimate reason a psychiatrist or any other physician should have that drug in their home."

"That would help with a jury," Hannah said. "But you said 'to start with.' What else did you find?"

"We found two more things that should help. One is an additional piece of direct evidence tying Grieve to one of the crimes. The other might help us find where he's hiding. Concerning the first, one of our detectives reinterviewed residents in Sean Doohan's dorm, hoping to find something new about the night he died. We're into the summer session, and the detective wasn't expecting much.

"But this time, we got lucky. A girlfriend of one of the summer residents looked at pictures of Doohan and Grieve and remembered seeing Dr. Grieve on the night of the killing. She couldn't recall the specific date, but she did remember it was in the dorm where she'd gone to study for her biology final the next day. We checked, and the date of her test was May 9th, the day after John was killed."

"In my day," Hannah said, "going to your boyfriend's room to study for a biology final would have had an entirely different meaning."

"Yeah, well, kids these days are a lot more studious than we were. In any case, she didn't just recollect seeing Grieve; he and Sean were walking out of the dorm together, talking and laughing. She remembered thinking all the best-looking guys were gay."

"I'm sure her boyfriend appreciated that comment," I said. "But it does give us a possible explanation for why Sean was killed in the steam tunnels. His roommate thought John was confused about his sexuality. Grieve was his therapist, so if Sean were bisexual, Grieve would certainly know. As the handsome, older man, Grieve could have used his feelings to lure him someplace private. Sean might have even mentioned the tunnels in one of their sessions."

"Choosing to have sex in a steam tunnel sounds like a stretch," Hannah said.

"Think about it from Sean's perspective," I said. "He's bisexual but probably enjoys his reputation as a lady's man. That rules out the dorm or any of the usual hook-up places on campus. Grieve and John could have gone to a motel, but even that might have seemed too public. The steam tunnels would be the perfect place—private but with a forbidden feel."

"I agree with Terry on this one," Chris said. "I'm sure they wouldn't have been the only couple to have sex in those tunnels. At the very least, this gives us another piece of direct evidence linking Grieve to one of the murders."

"You might want to talk to John's girlfriends," I suggested. "Ask if he brought any of them down to the tunnels. If so, that would establish a pattern."

"I'll follow up, but there's one other thing I need to fill you in on. Detective Ross has done some more work analyzing Drew's hard drive. She thinks she figured out how Mary and Grieve were communicating while Mary was at Drew's house. She found an account on Drew's computer and some suspicious-looking message activity posted on the Private Matters website. That's the online site competing with Ashley Madison as a place for married people to hook up with other partners."

Hannah asked if we could get copies of the messages, and Chris promised to send them within an hour. I then asked if the messages were traceable. Chris pulled in Detective Ross for that part of the call.

"So far," she said, "I haven't had any luck with a trace. I found the IP address, but given how far back we're looking, all that does is give you a general radius. I can tell you that Grieve sent the message from somewhere in the Cleveland area, but that's a pretty wide range. I am working to pin it down further, but even that might not tell you much. If it were me, I'd have gone to the nearest public library and sent the message from there. Unless Grieve is a lot dumber than we think, this is not going to be a magic bullet."

I started thinking about Tomas. While I had no doubt Detective Ross was correct about the old messages, I was considering another possibility.

"Is there any chance we can get an electronic copy of the hard drive?" I asked. "Not for the old messages, though that would save you the trouble of copying them. I was wondering if Grieve might still be monitoring the site. Don't some services send you an e-mail prompt if someone leaves you a message? I know Facebook does that."

"I wouldn't be surprised if there was an e-mail prompt," Detective Ross replied, "but I can check to make sure. Are you thinking about sending Grieve a message?"

"I was wondering if we could send an e-mail that might bait him into responding from his real location. He is smart, and I have no doubt he sent his messages to Mary from another site. That being said, he's also arrogant. I'm hoping the right message might goad Grieve into replying from wherever he's hiding out."

"It'd be nice," Hannah said, "to play offense for a change."

Chris promised to have a copy of the drive sent by courier no later than tomorrow afternoon. After he ended the call, I turned to Hannah.

"I know a computer expert who's worked with me in the past. Any chance you could let me have the copy of the drive when it comes in?"

"Do I want to know this person's name and what they do for a living?"

"He has a perfectly legitimate job. He just happens to have a knack with computers." I was understating Tomas's abilities dramatically, but my statement was still technically true.

"I'm going to trust you. I'll have our computer guy make a copy. Your guy can review the drive, but no message gets sent without my approval."

"Agreed. Now for the question I've been waiting to ask—how many biology finals did you study for in college?"

"It was actually one of my best subjects."

I noticed she avoided the "how many" part of the question.

My next step was to talk to Tomas. I needed his opinion on the hard drive and whether my idea was even possible. I exited Hannah's car and walked back to Hannibal. I was sure he was disgusted with me for parking him so close to a BMW. Hannibal hated expensive cars on principle alone. The fact that I'd sat in the BMW would only compound the insult. I expected a revenge breakdown or a failure to start, but before I could turn the key, Hannah waved me back to her car.

Tomas would have to wait. Detective Roberts had called while we were on the phone with Chris. The police had found Drew Allen's car in the Cleveland airport parking lot.

CHAPTER TWENTY-ONE

HANNAH ASKED IF I could follow her back to the Twelfth District. As if eager to prove me wrong, Hannibal trailed Hannah's BMW back to the station without incident. Hannah and I walked in together, and she introduced me to Detective Andrew Roberts.

Roberts was tall and mildly overweight with brownish-gray hair. Only six months from reaching his thirty years, he'd told Hannah he had no intention of serving even a minute past that date. He was the only detective who volunteered to assist Hannah with this case, however, and for that she was grateful. Hannah introduced me as the private investigator who was working on the church aspect of the investigation.

The detective's look was a mixture of cynicism and

disdain. I didn't take offense. That look was standard with most cops and not just in my presence. I held out my hand, but Detective Roberts only stared and grunted. His first words were to Hannah.

"This afternoon at about three o'clock, a husband and wife parked their car in the 'Red' long-term lot at the Cleveland Airport. After they parked, they noticed the car next to theirs—a Ford Focus with a broken window on its front driver's side. Thinking someone had tried to steal the car, the couple reported it to airport security. Security checked the Focus and called the Cleveland PD to file a report. When the cop on duty checked the license plate, it matched the BOLO on Drew Allen's car. We impounded the vehicle, and the crime scene guys are going over it now. So far, it looks like it was wiped pretty thoroughly."

"I know the lot has security cameras. How widespread are they?" Hannah asked.

"You can see the license plates of the cars coming in. The coverage throughout the rest of the lot is a mixed bag. Not bad, but it could be better. The real problem is the sheer volume of traffic coming through that lot. It's open 24-7, and we don't even know what day to look at. We'd need a lot of man-hours to review those tapes, and we already know Mary Dhillon or her boyfriend likely dropped the car off."

I knew my input might not be welcome, but I'd stopped caring about those things a long time ago. "The tapes might be able to tell us quite a bit. Whoever drove the car had to get back to wherever they were hiding. If it was Mary, Grieve might have followed her in another vehicle, and we might see that other car's license plates. If Mary took a taxi back, she'd likely walk toward the airport itself. If we know when she arrived, we could check with the cab company and see who was picking up fares from the airport at that time."

"The long-term lot is credit-card entry only," Hannah added. "If we knew her arrival time, we should also be able to get a record of the card Mary used to enter the lot. We know she didn't use her personal card. That account has been dormant since the time Mary disappeared. Whatever card she swiped, it's possible they're still using it today."

"It's not perfect," I said, "but we can probably even narrow the window of the time they abandoned the car. We know Mary left New Orleans on the morning of April 18th. Given the driving distance, she couldn't have reached Cleveland until the 19th and, more likely, April 20th. If you add an extra day on the back end of that estimate, we should be checking the tapes for April 19th through April 21st, with the first two days being our most likely."

"That assumes they abandoned the car right away." Detective Roberts was looking at Hannah when he spoke—he still hadn't tossed a word in my direction. But before Hannah could answer, their captain called her into his office for an update. Once she was out of earshot, Roberts turned to me.

"She's a nice kid when you get beyond all the sass, smart too. Now you, I don't like. Don't get all pissed off; I don't like any PIs. In my experience, most of them are assholes who couldn't make it through the police academy if their lives depended on it. Detective Page, however, thinks very highly of you, so don't fuck that up. I'd hate to have to shoot you. It might mess up my retirement."

"I promise you, Detective, I will do my best. Just so you know, I also think highly of Detective Page. Before I met her,

I figured most cops were dickheads who couldn't solve a homicide even with the murder weapon and a signed confession."

I thought I saw his lips curl. It could have been a smile; it could have been a snarl. Luckily Hannah returned before I had a chance to find out.

"I hope you boys played nice when I was gone."

"Sure, Mom," I said. "We're best buds now."

We talked about next steps. Hannah felt she and I should go to the airport to speak with the security staff and get the tapes for the long-term lot. While we were doing that, Detective Roberts would reinterview residents from the neighborhoods of our three murder victims.

Because it was now past six-thirty, Hannah called the airport and spoke to the second shift supervisor for airport security. To gain access to the tapes, we'd have to meet with Caitlyn Grivens, the department director. After a bit of wrangling, the supervisor agreed to give us Ms. Grivens' cell phone number. Hannah called her, explained what we were looking for, and Grivens agreed to meet with us at eight-thirty the next morning. While the delay was inconvenient, I was secretly happy for the excuse to go back to my apartment. We'd been running around nonstop since we left New Orleans. All I wanted to do was sleep, and I suspected Hannah felt the same.

Before leaving for home, I told Hannah I also wanted to have my computer expert perform a background check on Susan Leads, the cousin whose visit to the seminary resulted in Grieve's expulsion. I was still thinking about a potential message through the Private Matters website, and I wanted to see if there was a weakness we could exploit. With

Grieve's likely embarrassment over the seminary incident, his cousin seemed the best place to start.

Hannah agreed, and I called Tomas as soon as I got back to my apartment. Given his usual routine, I was sure I'd catch him in the middle of some attempted, high-level system incursion. To my surprise, he was with a girl. At least I had the incursion part right.

"Terry, you asshole," he whispered. "You need to call back tomorrow. I might get lucky tonight, and you are not going to screw this up for me."

Tomas's record with girls was the equivalent of my own before I met Hannah. Maybe both of our fortunes were changing.

"I just need five minutes of your time, Tomas."

"Come on. This woman is interested in what I do. That's a rare thing."

"If she finds accounting interesting, I would send her home right now."

"Nice, very nice. You know what I mean."

"I thought you were obsessive about keeping the computer thing a secret. You would drop that on the chance you might get laid?"

"Terry, I'm an accountant by day, and I play with computers at night. I'd be willing to do a lot more than that if it would end up with me getting laid."

"Fair enough, but I still need five minutes."

"Someday, you are going to open your bank statement and find a zero balance."

"That would be frightening if only it wasn't my usual monthly experience."

He was silent. For his sake and mine, I needed to cut

through the bullshit.

I decided to go nuclear. "If you don't listen to what I need, I'll not only tell your mother you refused, I'll tell her you had a girl in your apartment."

"Bastard. Go ahead, but I'm cutting you off after five minutes."

In our previous conversation, I'd asked Tomas to check the backgrounds of Father Samuel and Dr. Grieve to see if he could discover any links between the two. After swearing him to secrecy, I told him the rest of the story, or at least what I could summarize in five minutes. Beginning with the confessions that had started this case, I gave Tomas a bullet-point version of the Cleveland and New Orleans murders and the details regarding our two prime suspects. I also covered the discovery of the computer in Drew's home and the messages sent through the Private Matters website.

"By tomorrow," I continued. "I should have a copy of the hard drive from Drew's computer. The New Orleans IT expert would only say the messages sent to the hard drive came from the Cleveland area. We suspect he might have sent the original messages from a library computer to avoid a trace. Grieve is careful, but he's also arrogant. If I can send him a message, I believe I can bait him into replying from his actual location.

"I know Grieve is probably no longer monitoring the site directly, but don't those services send an e-mail prompt when a person sends a message? If that's true, I'm hoping we might still be able to get his attention. If he notices my message and replies, can you pin down his location if you catch his answer quickly enough?"

"I'll give you a qualified yes to the last one," Tomas said.

"Depending on certain variables, I should be able to give you a location no more than an hour after Grieve sends his message. More likely, I could have it in fifteen to thirty minutes. I'd like to look at the site and see how their system works, and then I can tell you for sure. Regarding the e-mail prompt, I'd guess the site does have that as an option. Whether Grieve set it up and left it operational is anyone's guess."

Knowing I was pushing my luck, I asked for one more thing. "I promise I'll only take one more minute of your time. I mentioned Grieve's cousin, Susan Leads. I think she might be his weak point. Can you look into her history? Find out if she's married, where she works, does she have an arrest record, or anything else I might be able to use to poke Grieve a bit."

"You aren't giving me much besides a name, but I'll see what I can find. Now I am returning to my date."

"Go with my blessing. By the way, what excuse did you give her for taking this call?"

"I told her I have a friend who is manic-depressive, and he always calls me during his down periods. She's a social worker. She was surprisingly sympathetic."

"Good to know in case I ever meet this girl. Now go and show her your hard drive."

Tomas hung up without replying.

CHAPTER TWENTY-TWO

AFTER TOMAS ENDED our call, I had an unexpected visitor. John stopped by, and he came bearing Chinese food.

In any long-term friendship, you start to develop certain habits that allow the other person to know what is really going on in your life. With John, it was his choice of food. Thai food meant his parents had pissed him off; nachos meant the Browns had lost; and Chinese meant he'd broken up with a girl. We eat nachos and Chinese a lot, sometimes together.

John saw me looking at the food and figured he would preempt my question. "Carol and I broke up."

"Was this blonde Carol or brunette Carol?"

"This was brunette Carol. I broke up with blonde Carol about six months ago."

"I thought you liked this one."

"I did, but Carol broke up with me. She said I wasn't serious enough about the relationship."

"Are you okay?"

"I'll survive. I know it sounds funny coming from me, but I would like to find someone to finally settle down with. I'm in my late twenties, and I don't want to become one of those guys in their forties always trying to hit on women. Don't tell me you haven't worried about the same thing."

"To tell you the truth, I'm having trouble seeing anything beyond the case I'm on right now."

"I was wondering about that. How are things going?"

As we sat down to eat the Chinese, I gave him the complete rundown. I usually tried to keep my cases confidential, but this one was different. I really needed an outside opinion, and I couldn't exactly ask my mother. I told John everything from my first conversation with Father Lawrence through our attempt to lure Dr. Grieve and Mary Dhillon through the Private Matters website. The only thing I didn't tell him was Tomas's name. I owed him that.

When I mentioned my conversation with Father Lawrence regarding confession, John said, "That doesn't sound like you. It almost seems like you're coming back to the Church."

"I'm not coming back. I just feel like I need to understand it better. Didn't you always wonder about confession when we were growing up?"

"I tried not to think about it. My only goal was to get through penance as quickly as possible so that I could be free for another week."

When I finished my summary, John looked genuinely

impressed. He thought all my cases involved peering through hotel windows. This case sounded like something on TV, involving several cities and its own serial killer. He asked me how I liked working with Hannah.

"I never thought I'd say this, but it's been fun. Hannah's annoying, and she questions everything I do. With this case, that's actually been helpful."

"Don't take this the wrong way, but I'm amazed the Cleveland PD is letting her work with you."

"I was surprised myself. When we started, Hannah told me she didn't have any real friends in the department. That being said, I spoke to her partner, and he seems to think of her like a daughter."

I took a quick bite of kung pau chicken. "She also has relationship issues with her parents. Her mother is a Cleveland district attorney, and her father is a congressman. Neither of them ever liked that she became a cop. From the way she describes them, their personal relationships are as political as their professional lives. Overall, I think she just wants them to accept her for what she is."

"And what do you think she is?"

"To start, I think she's a hell of a detective. Hannah's smart, tough, fun to be around, and yes, we've been sleeping together since day one. She was the one who first asked me to spend the night. Since then, she's also slept over at my place. To this day, I'm still not sure why she's interested."

"Stop overthinking everything. Maybe she just likes you and wants to have sex."

"That's just it. Why me? She's good-looking, has a great body, and loves sex. She was, and technically still is, married. Be warned—if you tell her I said that, I will shoot you and hide your body somewhere in the Chagrin Reservation."

"She's technically married. Is that like being technically pregnant?"

"Now you stole my line."

"So you being transgender was never an issue?"

"The first time we slept together, she asked if I'd considered the surgery."

"Good for her. Did you tell her I called you a wimp for backing out?"

"Somehow, that didn't come up. I guess I'm still wondering why she likes me. Is this just to torment her parents?"

"You're the smartest guy I know," John said, "and you're also the biggest idiot. You're questioning whether this woman likes you. She invited you back to her place, and she also came over here and slept on that little thing you call a bed. To add to that, she asked you to go on a trip to New Orleans."

John leaned back in his chair before continuing. "You're going to hate me for saying this, but when it comes to relationships, you still sound like a teenager. You said Hannah doesn't have any friends in the police department. You also said she feels alienated from her parents but still hopes to win their approval. You pride yourself on being logical. On the one hand, you can believe she's dating you as part of an agenda. This smart lady has decided that dating a transgender guy will somehow help gain the approval of her parents and her fellow cops. Does that sound logical to you? Conversely, you could believe she's dating you because she likes you. Why does she like you? Who the hell cares? Quit overanalyzing everything. Just grow a pair and be glad she does."

"Looking at it that way, I guess I do sound like a teen-ager."

"Don't let it interfere with your relationship. You'll re-gret it if you do."

"John, can I ask you something? I know you have other friends. Have any of them ever given you shit about hanging out with me?"

"I can think of two."

"What happened?"

"Not much. I haven't talked to either of them since then."

I didn't know how to reply, so I just said thank you. We've known each other most of our lives, and I was begin-ning to wonder what other sacrifices John had made to keep our friendship going.

John knew I was thanking him for more than just get-ting rid of two friends. Emotions were running high, and we did what most guys do in those moments—we changed the subject. Video games are perfect for those situations, so we settled in to play Mortal Kombat.

About twenty minutes into our game, I had another vis-itor. To my surprise, it was Hannah. I hadn't expected to see her that evening. When we'd parted ways, she'd complained of jet lag and said she needed some rest.

I let Hannah in and introduced her to John.

"It's good to meet another friend of Terry's; it's a pretty exclusive club," John said, his usual charming self. "If he ever gets on your nerves, just call me. I know all his embar-rassing secrets."

"That's okay. I'm having fun learning them myself."

John offered to leave and let us discuss the case. By that

time, Hannah had spotted the Mortal Kombat game in progress on my TV.

"You should stay," she said. "I'll watch while you guys kill each other."

"You sure you don't want to play?" I asked. "I have a third controller."

"Aren't you afraid I might beat you?"

"Beating me is an awfully low bar. The only one lower," I said, pointing to John, "is beating him."

John responded by throwing the third controller in an arc that would have reached my head if I hadn't caught it in time. The three of us settled down to play for the next hour, and Hannah beat us both quite handily.

"I thought you owned a gun," she said to me. "Have you ever bothered to fire it?"

John also conceded defeat and stood to leave. As he and I walked to the door, he whispered, "I like her. Don't fuck this up."

After John left, Hannah stood to face me. "He seems to fit you as a friend."

"Better than I could ever tell you."

"I know you're probably wondering why I came over tonight. I need to ask you a favor."

"Anything I can do, I will."

"Don't say yes until you hear me out. Tomorrow is my birthday."

"That's great! You should have told me sooner."

"Not so great. My parents want to take me out to dinner. The idea of spending an evening alone with them gives me hives."

"So where do I come in?"

Hannah hesitated, suddenly taking great interest in the color of my carpeting. Finally, she spoke. "I want you to come with me. They told me I could invite a guest. I think they were hoping I'd bring my ex. You were the first person I considered."

"Are you sure you thought this through? I'm not exactly the kind of guy you invite to meet Mom and Dad."

"We're not getting married; we're going out to dinner. I need someone with me who's halfway normal, or my parents will drive me insane. Every time I see them, I feel like they're trying to bring me over to the dark side. Since I know you're going to ask, I did tell them about you."

"How did they react?"

"I think they were torn. My mother looked appalled and asked if I knew what I was doing. My father was excited about meeting you. He always wanted an inroad to the LGBTQ community."

"I'm not part of any community. I hate communities."

"I told him. He still thinks you can help."

"That raises the question of how you want me to play this. Do you want the real me, or do you want the sanitized version of me?"

"I didn't know there was a sanitized version of you. Be yourself. I'm not trying to play up to my parents."

"I hear you say that, but I have to ask—are you sure part of you isn't still seeking their approval? That wouldn't exactly be unusual. I do the same with my mom."

I could see by her face that she was furious. This was the look she'd given the kid on the airplane coming back to Cleveland, only dialed up by a factor of ten.

"Do you think any of this is easy? You grew up with

parents who liked you. You may have been different than they expected, but they liked you anyway. Do you know how damned lucky you are?"

Hannah said all this while smiling. For someone who didn't know her, that might seem incongruous. I did know her, and I knew she had two smiles. The first, not-scary one brightened her entire face. It was, for lack of a better word, joyful.

This was the second one. Upon seeing it, a wiser man would have backed down. Since I was now also pissed, I kept plowing forward.

"You're right. My relationship with my parents is totally different than yours, or at least it was in the case of my father. That doesn't mean I haven't experienced rejection. Do you want to know about my friends growing up? You just met the only one. Did that bother me? Absolutely it did, but I got over it, and you need to do the same. If you don't, it's going to eat you up inside.

"You are a bright, beautiful woman who's exceptionally good at what you do. If your parents don't like that, then screw them. It's their problem, not yours, and you need to keep reminding yourself of that. If you do, these dinners will be a lot easier to take."

She looked up at me with tears in her eyes. She stepped forward, and for a second, I thought she might slap me. Maybe she considered it, but she put her head on my shoulder instead. Having no idea what to say, I let her cry it out.

I could tell she was exhausted, so I eventually moved her to my bed. She lay down without prompting and fell asleep almost immediately. There was no way I could move her, so I laid a blanket on the floor and grabbed an extra pillow for myself. I watched her for a while before I fell asleep. That was as close as we'd get that night.

I woke up at seven and attempted to fix breakfast. Given the state of my pantry, that pretty much limited us to Captain Crunch. Hannah woke up about ten minutes after me. I wished her happy birthday, and she apologized for being so melodramatic.

"I thought about it," she said, "and you were right. I spend too much time worrying about my parents. I've told myself that before, so you're going to have to keep reminding me."

"The funny thing is," I said, "John gave me essentially the same advice last night. I've never been great at relationships, and he's worried I'm going to drive you away."

"For now, I'm inclined to put up with you. That being said, will you still come to dinner tonight?"

"Tell me when and where."

It occurred to me that I'd just agreed to go to dinner with a cop, a prosecutor, and a politician. It sounded like a bad joke, and Hannah sensed my hesitation.

"I said it yesterday, but I want to say it again—you should feel free to be yourself. That's why I like hanging out with you."

"I thought it was my dashing good looks."

She didn't respond—so much for my good looks.

Luckily, Hannah had anticipated staying over last night and had brought over a change of clothes. After joining me for a healthy breakfast of sugar-infused cereal, she excused herself to use my shower. We had a morning appointment at the airport, but it still took an act of will not to go in there with her.

About fifteen minutes later, she came out of the bathroom, wet and undressed, to ask if I had an extra towel. We were going to be late for our eight-thirty appointment. My willpower only went so far.

CHAPTER TWENTY-THREE

HANNAH DROVE US to the airport. We made the trip in record time, arriving just a half hour past our eight-thirty appointment and parking in the same long-term lot where the police had found Drew Allen's car. As we exited Hannah's BMW, I looked for security cameras but saw none. Hopefully, they were well-hidden, or this trip would be a waste.

To get to the airport concourse, we walked through a long tunnel before arriving at an escalator that led to the ticketing entrance. There, Hannah showed her badge to a security officer, and he directed us to the administrative suite on the airport's third floor. Caitlyn Grivens' office was near the front.

Caitlyn wasn't the older, grizzled security director one

met in most organizations. In her late thirties, she had long blonde hair and wore a plain gray business suit that failed to hide her strikingly full figure—if I had walked past her on the street, I'd have pegged her as a retired swimsuit model. Given that she worked primarily with men, I could only imagine the difficulty they had walking out of her office.

Hannah shot me a look and not a very pleasant one. We introduced ourselves to Caitlyn and apologized for being late. Without going into every detail of the case, Hannah summarized our interest in Drew's car, its abandonment in the long-term lot, and our need to view the security tapes from April 19th through April 21st.

Caitlyn asked if we were interested in the tapes from the entire parking lot or just the entrance camera. After looking at Hannah for confirmation, I said we'd only need the entrance tapes. Once we determined the date and time Drew's car had entered the lot, we could request the feed from the other cameras.

Caitlyn then called her assistant and told him what we were looking for. Fifteen minutes later, he returned with a stack of surveillance DVDs covering all the dates in question.

"I want to show you what you're going to be looking at." Caitlyn put one of the DVDs into the drive on her computer. After about two minutes, a Ford Explorer pulled up to the automated entryway. The driver slid his credit card into the machine and quickly pulled it back. After about five seconds, the security arm lifted, and the driver proceeded into the lot. From the time the driver first came into view, the whole transaction took about thirty seconds. Most importantly, we were able to see his face and the car's license plate before it drove in.

I commented on the clarity of the picture. The video timestamp showed it at just after midnight on April 19th, yet the car and the plate appeared as clear as day.

"If you had come here last year," Caitlyn said, "you'd have noticed a huge difference. With the video quality we had then, the images were pretty much useless after dark. We replaced the cameras in all our lots about ten months ago."

"On average," I asked, "how many cars enter the long-term lot each day?"

"Vehicle turnover is pretty consistent in all the lots. There are about twelve hundred spaces in the Red Lot. Assuming the normal turnover, that means about two hundred and fifty new cars per day. I wish we had the manpower to help you run through these, but we're pretty short-staffed at present."

Looking at me, she added, "If you want, I could set you up here with a computer. That way I could get you any additional tapes you might need if you find the car you're looking for."

"That's okay," Hannah said quickly. "We'll take them back to the department."

I thought of one more question. "I know you can't get into the long-term lot without a credit card, but the charge isn't entered into the system until you leave. If someone leaves their car in the lot and never exits, how long would the system retain their credit card information?"

"There's no time limit built into the system. This is a long-term lot. We've had people park for well over thirty days."

We thanked Caitlyn for her time and left her office. Walking back to the parking lot, I said, "I noticed you were pretty quiet in there today."

"It was pretty apparent the lady only had eyes for you. I may not like that, but I'm not above using it to my advantage."

"I didn't notice her paying attention to me."

"Maybe you were too busy drooling. Oh, Terry," she said, imitating Caitlyn's voice, "do you want to watch those tapes from my private office? It may take all night, but I'm sure it will be worth your while."

"I thought women in positions of authority tried to support one another."

"Then you're more naïve than I realized."

CHAPTER TWENTY-FOUR

HANNAH DROVE US back to the police station, where we appropriated a small conference room with two computers. We divided up the tapes and began looking for Drew's car.

There were three days of tapes to review. If each car took thirty seconds at the entrance gate and two hundred and fifty cars entered the lot per day, we were hoping to finish in less than four hours. However long it took, neither one of us was looking forward to what promised to be a long and tedious process.

To our surprise, the video proved unexpectedly amusing. A half hour into our review, Hannah called me over to her computer screen. She backed up the disk to an old Cadillac pulling up to the entryway. The recording showed the driver, a gray-haired gentleman in his midfifties, as well as the make and license plate of his vehicle. Once at the entrance, the driver put his hand to his side and struggled to reach his wallet.

A few seconds later, the reason for his fumbling became clear. A female form rose slowly from the man's lap. From her gray hair, she looked almost as old as her companion.

"I wonder if it was his birthday," Hannah said.

"I wonder if it was his wife."

"I was wrong. You really are a cynic."

"I have to give him credit. I would have driven into the parking barrier."

"I'll try to remember that."

After watching a young woman's attempt to drive through the parking barrier—a unique if less effective way of avoiding the lot fee—we finally hit paydirt when Hannah spotted Drew's Ford Focus pulling in at 9:54 p.m. on April 20th. The security camera image was clear. The driver was Mary Dhillon.

Hannah and I felt a certain amount of relief. We'd considered the possibility that Grieve had simply paid someone to drop off the vehicle. Mary's image on the camera provided some confirmation that we were finally on the right track.

To be certain Grieve did not follow Mary into the lot, we reran the security footage for the cars coming in thirty minutes before Mary and thirty minutes after. A total of six vehicles drove into the lot during that timeframe, and Grieve was not in any of them.

"It would have been nice if he had followed her," Hannah said, "but it still leaves us with our other possibilities. We know Mary entered with a credit card. Even if Grieve had stolen it, I'd love to know what else they purchased on that card and where. Now that we know when Mary came into the lot, we should also be able to figure out how she got back to wherever they're staying. Grieve didn't follow her, so it's likely she either grabbed a taxi, or he picked her up in front of the terminal. The security footage from the other cameras should tell us which one."

Hannah assigned me the task of contacting Caitlyn Grivens and asking her for the other tapes from the time Drew's car was abandoned. If that assignment was based on my perceived sex appeal, I thought it best not to ask. Obtaining Mary's credit card information was a little more complicated and would require a warrant. As the police officer in our little partnership, Hannah left to find a judge.

I contacted Caitlyn on the phone without a problem. She agreed to copy all the tapes from the long-term lot and the walkway to the airport terminal based on the time of Mary's arrival. She asked if I'd be picking them up, but I requested they be messengered instead.

Caitlyn sounded disappointed, though that might have been my imagination. After ending our conversation, I got a call from Tomas.

"Tomas, how was your date?"

"It ended successfully, no thanks to you."

"I am genuinely sorry for the interruption. I do owe you one."

"You owe me two. Remember how you asked me to find any connections between the priest and the psychiatrist? I don't know if this fits what you're looking for, but I found a reference to a court appearance that could indicate a juvenile arrest record."

"Dr. Grieve had a juvenile record?"

"Not Dr. Grieve. It was the Jesuit you told me to look up, Father Dennert."

"A priest with a record? What did he do?"

"That's where it gets interesting. First, this was a juvenile case. Samuel was seventeen when it happened, and you know those records are sealed."

"I'm sure you didn't let that stop you."

"I didn't. Sealed or not, juvenile records are remarkably easy to break into. That's what I meant about it being interesting. Dennert doesn't have a juvenile record."

"Now I'm confused. You said he had one."

"No, I found a reference to a court appearance. That reference was in the local newspaper, the *Manhattan Mercury*. They have a small local crime section, and this somehow made it in despite the juvenile seal. The article mentioned an upcoming court appearance and not much more."

"If he had a court appearance, wouldn't it show on his record?"

"I wondered the same thing. I suspect the court dropped the charges before the appearance took place—no appearance, no juvenile record. I do have two other bits of information, however. The first is the name of the detective involved in the case, Jason Aldean."

"Like the country singer?"

"Terry, I'm Irish-Hispanic. We don't do country."

"Fair enough. Were you able to get any contact information for Detective Aldean?"

"I called the Manhattan Police Department. They told me he retired five years ago. I asked them for contact information, and they gave me the name of a local tavern, the Drunken Cow. Come to think of it, that does sound like a country bar."

"You said you had two pieces of information. What's the other one?"

"I don't know how important this is, but it could explain why the juvenile case never came to trial. While I was only able to find one reference to Samuel Dennert, I found multiple references to his parents. It appears they are what passes for high society in Manhattan. The father owns a chain of furniture stores, and the parents have been involved in fundraising efforts for local charities as well as Kansas State University. I know it's an assumption, but that might give them the clout to get a juvenile charge dropped."

"It probably has nothing to do with my case, but I'd dearly love to find out what he was accused of. That's probably spite on my part, but it would be interesting."

"Unless you can locate the detective, you might need to physically go to Manhattan if you want to hunt this down. I don't think I'll be able to find any more. I also figured any further searching on my part might alert the parents, and they could contact their son. I assumed that was the last thing you'd want."

"You're right. I'll try to follow up with Detective Aldean."

"Any word on Drew Allen's hard drive? You were supposed to get me a copy."

"Let me check with Detective Page; I thought it was coming in today. Seriously, Tomas, I want to thank you for all this. I won't forget it."

"You remember what my parents said when you brought Rosa back? We will always be in your debt. Anything you need, call me."

Hannah returned as I was finishing up with Tomas. I filled her in on the news about Father Samuel, but she was unimpressed.

"He probably got caught joyriding a car or vandalizing a cemetery. This is Kansas. He may have even tipped a cow. In any case, I don't see how it affects us."

"It probably doesn't, but I want to follow up. I need the contact information for the Manhattan detective, Jason Aldean. Any chance you could call the Manhattan PD for me? They've got to be sending his pension check some-where."

"I owe you for dinner tonight. I'll call and see what I can do."

The warrant for Mary Dhillon's airport credit card was still in process. I asked Hannah about the copy of Drew's hard drive, but it had yet to arrive from Louisiana. Interest-ingly, the security tapes from the airport had already reached the station. It'd been a little over an hour since I'd hung up with Caitlyn Grivens. Her assistant must have been flying to get them copied and sent here that fast.

It was nearly four o'clock, and Hannah and I decided to review the airport video before getting ready for dinner with her parents. The six tapes came marked "Long-term Lot, April 20th." After fast-forwarding to the time Mary Dhillon entered the lot, we eventually found Drew's car as it made its way down the first aisle of parked cars. Though there were several openings, Mary continued to the last aisle, where she chose a space at the north end of the parking lot. Following Mary's progress meant switching between foot-age from the three different security cameras monitoring the lot. Once we got the hang of which camera surveyed which sector, that process became much more straightforward.

Eventually, Mary parked and exited Drew's car. For someone presumably new to Cleveland, she appeared to know exactly where she was headed. She walked through the lot to the tunnel leading to the main airport concourse. That path led her through the airport's short-term parking lot as well as a long, windowed skyway. Four additional cameras monitored those areas, and we followed Mary's progress until she entered the airport terminal, where the crowd grew so large we could no longer locate her. Before that happened, however, we did see Mary turn in the direction leading to ground transportation.

"We're still in good shape," Hannah said. "We know no one picked her up in front of the terminal, and that almost certainly means she took a taxi. We can check with the taxi company to see who was picking up fares that evening. We also have the advantage of Mary's appearance. Where a lot of passengers wouldn't have stood out, I'm betting most drivers would remember Mary if we showed them a picture."

It was almost five-thirty. Hannah and I wanted to leave the station no later than six o'clock so we could change and be at the restaurant by seven. Before we left, Hannah called the Manhattan Police Department and obtained the contact information for Detective Aldean. In the evening mail delivery, she also discovered the copy of the hard drive messengered from New Orleans. Hannah wouldn't give that to me until the department's own computer expert could make a second copy.

I'd hitched a ride with Hannah to the station, so she dropped me off at my apartment. On the way, she said we'd be eating at Le Chateau Franklin, one of Cleveland's most exclusive downtown restaurants. For the second time in this case, I would be wearing one of my mom-purchased gray suits. Part of me thought I should mention this to my mother, but I knew that would buy me a return trip to the suit store. Feeling guilty, I decided to hold off for now.

I asked Hannah about the restaurant. I'd never heard her say anything about liking French food.

"I don't," she said, "but my parents do. They picked out the restaurant."

"Isn't it your birthday?"

Hannah gave me a long, flat look and said absolutely nothing in reply. Taking the hint, I figured it was safer discussing the case. I asked her about tomorrow's schedule.

"I'll pick you up at ten o'clock. By that time, we'll have a warrant and the credit card records. I want to see those before we talk to the taxi company."

Hannah dropped me off in front of my apartment building with a warning to be on time. Luckily, my downtown apartment was within walking distance of the Chateau Franklin. I took a quick shower, picked out a suit, and put on my best power tie. Impressing Hannah's parents was pretty much out of the question. Acknowledging that, I didn't want my wardrobe to be an issue.

I figured it was bad form to arrive at a birthday dinner without a gift. On my way over to the restaurant, I stopped at Samantha's, a small shop on Euclid Avenue. Samantha's sold every type of present, from the raunchy to the sweet, and I chose a small crystal globe. I had no idea what Hannah would like, but I figured the globe might catch the sunlight coming through her front bay window. It would probably look cheap next to whatever her parents gave her, but at least it was something.

I arrived at the restaurant at precisely seven o'clock, my first assignment accomplished. After checking with the front desk, I found I was the only one there from our party of four. The maître d' gave me a skeptical look and asked if I was sure I had the right restaurant.

I ignored the question and told him I would wait. Luckily for me, Hannah and her parents arrived just ten minutes later. From the looks I received from the restaurant staff, that was right about the time they were considering calling the police.

Hannah's father, David Page, was tall and handsome with graying, well-styled hair and a bright smile, the stereotypical image of a successful politician. He shook hands with me as Hannah performed the introductions.

"It's good to meet you, son. Hannah told us you two have been working together."

Maybe I was overly sensitive, but I hated people who called me "son." It always sounded presumptuous, like the speaker was trying to usurp my father. I wanted to call him Dad in reply but held back for Hannah's sake.

"Thank you, sir. Your daughter is an excellent detective. I couldn't ask for a better partner."

One parent out of the way, I turned to Hannah's mother. Amanda Patterson-Page resembled her daughter. She was roughly the same height and shared Hannah's curly, brown hair, though hers was beginning to gray. She gazed at me closely as we shook hands—I felt like one of those exotic animals you see at the zoo. I figured I should break the ice.

"It's a pleasure to meet you, ma'am."

"I'm pleased to meet you as well, Mr. Luvello."

The suddenly solicitous maître d' escorted us to our table. I glanced at Hannah as we walked through the restaurant, and she gave me a quick shake of her head. I wasn't sure if it was a commentary on my performance or her parents. It was turning into a long evening.

The service was prompt, and I managed to order my meal without incident. My knowledge of French was nonexistent. As a defensive measure, I ordered the item that was the closest thing to English I could find on the menu. That turned out to be the porc dijonaisse, basically a pork tenderloin with orange sauce. It was nothing I would have requested at a more ordinary restaurant, but it seemed less dangerous than my other options.

The staff was clearly aware there were two VIPs in their midst. They served our food within fifteen minutes of our order, well before any of the other people seated around us. With our entrees in place, the interrogation began. It started with Hannah's father.

"Mr. Luvello, I wanted to let you know I am a big supporter of the LGBTQ community. Hannah tells me you are not politically active. Is that true?"

"I'm afraid it is, sir. I read the front page the same way I read the sports section. I'm just interested in who won the latest game."

He laughed like it was the funniest comment he'd heard that day. Coming from the political world, maybe it was. He tried again to raise my social awareness.

"With your rather unusual profession, I thought you could be a symbol to others in the community. They might view you as an example of a transgender person who successfully broke down barriers."

"I'm not sure I can do that, sir. Private investigators operate in the background of life. It's how we survive. Other than Sherlock Holmes and Bruce Wayne, I don't know of any famous detectives."

He looked confused. "Bruce who?"

"Batman, sir."

"Oh, yes, Batman."

It was fortunate Hannah had inherited her mother's intelligence. Right on cue with that thought, Mom picked up the conversational slack. I hoped she might steer things to safer ground, but I couldn't have been more wrong.

"There's been a lot of talk about transgender people being forced to use certain public restrooms," Amanda said. "How do you feel about that issue?"

Hannah looked like she was suffering a migraine. "Mom, why don't you let Terry eat his dinner?"

"Your mother's just asking, dear," replied her father. "I've been pushing this for some time. Terry, don't you think transgender people should be allowed to use any public restroom they choose?"

"To be honest, sir, I don't think about it much. I usually avoid public restrooms like the plague, primarily because that's what I'm afraid of catching if I walk into one."

"On those rare occasions, which restroom do you use?"

"I use the male restroom. That isn't a social statement. I've just found one area where men and women differ the most is in restroom etiquette. If you walk into a lady's room, everyone expects you to hold a conversation. If you walk into a men's room, other men suddenly develop a fascination with the tile on the wall in front of them. No one says a word in a men's room, and that suits me just fine."

Hannah's migraine looked like it was degenerating into a stroke. If she survived the evening, Mrs. Page might soon be prosecuting her daughter for attempted murder. For my part, I was beginning to enjoy myself. I hadn't expected the dinner to get this absurd this quickly. John knew I was going out tonight. Describing this conversation would be fun.

Hannah finally found her voice. "If we're done discussing Terry's bathroom habits, maybe we could get back to the part about this being my birthday."

Her father sounded miffed. "I wanted Terry to know we are on his side of these issues."

"I appreciate that, sir. While I don't often use public restrooms, I'll think of you when I do."

Hannah smiled for the first time that evening. Her parents seemed uncertain if I was joking. I guess they didn't want to upset the transgender guy—I was, after all, holding a knife. I smiled to reassure them I was okay. That done, I tried to resurrect the evening. Remembering the gift in my pocket, I handed it to Hannah before her parents could think of any other inappropriate topics.

"I wanted to get you something for your birthday. Mr. and Mrs. Page, your daughter is an exceptional investigator. I've never worked with a partner before. With this case, I don't think we would have accomplished nearly as much if we hadn't been working together."

"Thank you," her mother said. "We don't say it often enough, but we're proud of the path our daughter has chosen."

The words sounded fine; her perfunctory tone did not.

Forgetting my previous reticence, I resolved to call my mother and thank her for everything she'd done for me, including the suits.

Hannah had been silent through this part of the discussion as she concentrated on opening my gift. I wasn't sure about my choice, but she looked genuinely touched as she held the globe up to the restaurant lights. I restrained myself from mentioning that it might reflect the sun from her bay window. It wouldn't do to let her parents know I'd been to her home.

For the rest of the meal, we transitioned to topics that seemed less contentious. Hannah's father talked about the new crime bill now before Congress. I asked Hannah's mother if she'd ever been the prosecutor for one of Hannah's cases—your basic small talk with the Page family. At least we managed to finish the meal without Hannah pulling out her gun. From a culinary standpoint, I also learned that orange sauce should never come anywhere near an otherwise decent cut of meat.

Hannah's mother made one more attempt at a personal connection. "Terry, you mentioned a few policy matters that don't interest you. Is there anything you do want on a policy level?"

"Not to sound rude, ma'am, but what I want most is to be left alone. I am a private investigator. I'm good at my job, and it's all I ever wanted to do. What would get me upset? If someone tried to keep me from doing that job because I'm transgender.

"With that in mind, I'd choose workplace discrimination laws. Those have a far more significant impact on people like me, though I understand that effort would likely come at the state level.

"My philosophy about issues like this goes back to what my dad told us growing up. He said you need to decide the four or five things that are the most important in your life and protect them with everything you've got. Beyond those four or five things, everything else is just an annoyance.

"Would it be an inconvenience if the government said I could no longer use a men's bathroom? Absolutely, but I have the advantage of looking male, and I would use the men's room anyway. Call it civil disobedience for the sake of convenience. To me, the whole bathroom controversy is no worse than when the government insists we take off our shoes in an airport TSA line. Both are annoying, but I can live with either one."

"Not to pry," Hannah's mother said, "but can I ask what are your four or five things?"

"My job, my mother, and my friends. I have three friends, so that comes to five."

After my little soliloquy on current affairs, Hannah's parents grew quiet. We finished our meals and left the table. I thanked the Pages for dinner and again wished Hannah a happy birthday. I'd walked to the restaurant, but I went out to the parking lot with Hannah. She looked more stunned than angry, and I wanted to make sure that wasn't on my behalf.

When we reached her BMW, she said, "I know I owe you big time for this. Do you see why I wanted you along?"

"It was a little more theater of the absurd than I'm used to, but I still had fun. Did you like your gift? I thought it might reflect some of the light coming in from your front window."

"The gift was special. It's the first real gift anyone's ever given me for my birthday. My parents just give money."

Paul and I always got gifts for our birthdays. They weren't huge, but they were fun to open, and I assumed everyone else did the same. I never thought of myself as screwed up. If I was, it was due solely to my own choices. Hannah's issues started with her parents.

"If your parents aren't stopping by," I said, "I could come over tonight."

"I'd love to have you over, but I'm exhausted from the effort of not killing them. Let's go with the original plan. I'll pick you up about ten o'clock, and we'll review the credit card records."

I stood in the parking lot and watched her pull away. After a short distance, she stopped and rolled down her window. I hoped she'd changed her mind about me spending the night. Instead, she had a question.

"Am I one of your three friends?"

"I hope so."

"Good."

With that, she rolled up her window and drove away. I stood and watched until she reached the street. I'm not sure I would ever understand her, but I was certainly having fun trying.

CHAPTER TWENTY-FIVE

FEELING EXHAUSTED, I decided to sleep in the next morning. Factoring in the one-hour time difference between Cleveland and Kansas, my plan was to call Detective Aldean at nine o'clock. I was skeptical that he could provide anything of importance, but I figured I should at least follow up.

As it turned out, I should have called later. Detective Aldean picked up on the sixth ring, and he was clearly not happy. A hangover will do that for you.

"Whoever the hell this is better have a damned good reason for calling me at this hour."

I explained who I was, where I was calling from, and my interest in Samuel Dennert. I expected him to claim lack of memory or just hang up. Instead, the line went silent for a full minute.

Finally, he spoke. "Explain to me in more detail your interest in that cocksucker. Be warned, your answer will determine mine."

This was getting interesting. Giving as few details as possible and remembering this guy used to be a cop, I gave him a quick summary of the case. I included the link to the priesthood, the murders in New Orleans, and our belief the prime suspects might have followed Father Dennert to Cleveland.

"Right now," I said, "I'm looking for anything that might link the suspects to Samuel Dennert. When I discovered Dennert was involved in a juvenile incident, I figured I should at least find out what that incident was. Even if he only lifted a car, it would still help me know who I'm dealing with. I know the records are under seal, but I figured with you being retired..."

"You figured with me being retired, I might not give a fuck. Normally, I wouldn't give you a goddamned thing. You woke me up, and I have a splitting headache—I've shot men for less. It just so happens, though, you struck a nerve. You want to find out about Samuel Dennert? I'd be happy to tell you everything I know.

"Let me start by saying Samuel Dennert was a punk. All the Dennerts were. Except for the college, this town ain't much. What it does have, the Dennerts own most of it."

"I heard they owned a chain of furniture stores."

"They own a lot more than that. People around here call them the Dennert F's, and you can imagine the fun we all have with that name. The Dennerts started with fertilizer and farm equipment and then branched out to fireworks and furniture stores. Just for fun, they later bought two funeral homes. With ownership comes power, and with power comes arrogance. The Dennerts are as arrogant as they come.

"The case looked routine at first," he continued. "I got called to the home of Jill Donahue. Jill was the divorced mother of two girls. Sandra Donahue was seventeen at the time of the case, and Grace Donahue was fourteen. Both were students at the local high school.

"Jill met me at the front door crying. Sandra had gone to the prom the previous evening with a boy named Bobby Hurt. Bobby was a moron, but Sandra had gone out with him a few times in the past, and Jill had no real worries about the evening. That changed when Sandra came home at 3:00 a.m. with a black eye and a torn dress. She also smelled of alcohol.

"After repeated questioning from her mother, Sandra broke down and admitted what happened. From what Jill told me, the couple never made it to the dance. Bobby drove them directly from her house to one of the Dennert furniture stores. He told Sandra they were going there to meet Sammy Dennert and his date. Bobby needed to pay Sammy back some money he borrowed, and the four of them would go to the prom together.

"Sandra wasn't totally naïve. She asked Bobby why they were meeting in a furniture store after closing hours instead of at Sammy's house. Bobby told her Sammy had full access to his father's store keys, and he liked to party there after hours.

"They arrived at the store, and Bobby asked Sandra to come in with him while he met with Sammy. Once they were inside, Sammy was waiting for them alone next to one of the furniture displays. That's when Sandra found out she was the payment for Bobby's debt.

"Sammy had some whiskey he stole from his father. The two boys forced Sandra to drink from the bottle until she almost passed out. They then taped Sandra's mouth and tied her spread-eagled to the posts on one of the display beds.

"They took turns after that, with Sammy going first. They penetrated Sandra vaginally and anally, always being sure to wear condoms. Sometime during the evening, they tried to force her to have oral sex, but Sandra told them if either one of them put their thing in her mouth, she would bite it off. That's when Sammy gave her the black eye.

"Throughout the night, they kept making jokes about prom. Whenever one boy would finish, the other would take over and ask 'if he could have this dance.' When they were done, the boys untied Sandra, and Sammy gave her what he described laughingly as 'the lay of the land.'

"It turned out Sammy had put a lot of thought into the evening, and his plan included their choice of victim. Sammy knew Sandra's mom was divorced and worked in one of the Dennert stores. He assumed that would give them leverage.

"The alcohol was also not a whim. Sammy told Sandra if she brought this to the cops, the police would insist she go to a hospital for a rape test. Once there, the fact she had alcohol in her system would be sure to come out.

"If questioned, Sammy and Bobby would claim that Sandra agreed to have sex. In fact, they would say she suggested it when she saw all the store beds. Sandra's blood-alcohol level would only support that claim. When you add all that with the fact that she'd voluntarily walked into the store, Sammy told her there was no way anyone would believe she was raped.

"Sandra repeated the entire story at her mother's urging. I believed her. If you had been there, you would have too. All the while Sandra was talking to me, her mother looked more and more furious. That was one area where Sammy had miscalculated. Jill Donahue was devoted to her two children, something I can't blame her for one bit. Losing her job wouldn't keep Jill from pursuing Sammy Dennert and Bobby Hurt. What really worried me was Jill owned a gun. I had to do a lot of talking to convince her that we would take this seriously. That turned out to be a lie, even if I didn't know it at the time.

"Manhattan had a female officer who handled most of our rape cases. Fortunately, that number was small. She and I drove Sandra and her mother to the local hospital. The boys had used condoms, so there was no semen to analyze, but the trauma around her vagina and anus was consistent with rape. As Sammy had guessed, they also tested Sandra's blood-alcohol level. It was high, around .20.

"Any illusion this case would be normal ended after we got back to the station. As soon as I walked in the door, I was told my captain wanted to see me. I walked into his office and found he wasn't alone. He and the district attorney had been waiting for almost an hour.

"They asked me to run through the details of the case, so I gave them the same summary I just gave you. They then asked me if this was something we could win. Think about that for a second. We hadn't called in Bobby or Sammy. We hadn't examined a single piece of forensic evidence. At that time, we didn't even have the rape test results. The investigation hadn't started yet, and they wanted to give up.

"I deliberately didn't answer their question. I told them I wanted to bring in Bobby and Sammy for questioning. They really couldn't say no at that point. They reminded me, however, that I would be interviewing two minors.

"The other officer and I went to pick up Bobby and Sammy, and you couldn't imagine a bigger contrast. Bobby looked confused. Granted, he had an IQ lower than most trees, but I was amazed he was so unprepared for us to show up at his door. His parents were furious, as much at their son as at us. From the beers in their hands, I think we interrupted their afternoon drunk. They followed us to the station, and we stuck them all in an interview room.

"We then went to pick up Sammy. I'm not sure who at the station tipped them off, but Sammy's parents were waiting for us at the door along with their lawyer. The lawyer started by telling us he'd just gotten off the phone with Bobby's parents. The parents agreed he would represent Sammy while his partner would do the honors for Bobby Hurt. That wasn't shocking, but it meant our odds of splitting the two had gone down considerably. The second problem came right after that. Two uniforms and our crime scene investigator went to the furniture store. There was no bed in the display area that matched the description Sandra gave us.

"I won't go over the rest of the gory details. Suffice it to say, Bobby and Sammy consulted with their respective lawyers before they would let us in the room. After that, their stories matched exactly. Bobby went to the furniture store expecting to pick up Sammy and head to the prom. Sammy was going solo since he'd split up with his girlfriend. Once

Bobby and Sandra arrived at the store, the three of them passed around a bottle until Sandra noticed all the beds. As Sandra warned us, the boys said it was she who suggested they take advantage of their surroundings. They also said the more the night went on, the rougher Sandra liked it. They both denied tying her hands.

"As I mentioned, all the beds on display at the furniture store had standard headboards. None had the type of bedposts that Sandra had described. Now, Sammy's father'd had plenty of time to change the beds on display, but no one who worked in the store would acknowledge a switch had taken place.

"The district attorney said he looked at the inconsistency about the bed, the alcohol in Sandra's system, and her acknowledgment that Bobby had told her they partied in the furniture store when making the decision not to bring the boys to trial. With another case, I might have accepted his judgment. When you were a cop as long as I was, you realize prosecutors toss good arrests all the time.

"Knowing that, this case still gnawed at my gut. Everyone knew the fix was in. Someone from the police department called Sammy's father and warned him we were coming after his son. That gave him plenty of time to move or destroy any evidence before we arrived at the store."

"Couldn't Sammy have told his father?" I asked.

"I wondered about that myself. All the people I talked to said Sammy hated his father with a passion, and the two barely spoke. One family member even suggested Sammy might have hoped the story would get out. The newspaper ran an article about a potential court appearance for Sammy and Bobby. The same family member suspected it was

Sammy who'd tipped them off. It would have been the perfect way to embarrass his father.

"Throughout the case, it seemed like the entire police department and prosecutor's office were mobilized on behalf of those two boys. Nobody cared about the victim. The hardest thing I ever did was drive out to the Donahue house and tell Jill her daughter's case wouldn't be going to trial. Jill was furious. She slapped me, and I didn't even think of trying to stop her. She threatened to get her gun and hunt those two boys down, but I talked her out of it. I told her the girls would need her now more than ever.

"Jill quit her job and moved her family out of town. About ten years later, I heard Sandra had hooked up with some guy in a trailer park and tried to commit suicide. Two days after her attempt, someone took two shots at Sammy when he walked home from one of his father's fertilizer stores. We never found out who did it, but I don't think anyone tried very hard.

"Sammy left town soon after the shooting. That was when I quit the force, though you might say I really quit right after the Dennert case. I was never part of the in-crowd after that.

"So that's the whole sad story. Now you tell me Sammy Dennert became a priest, and some psychopath is trying to hunt him down. I don't care if Dennert is reformed. Given what he did to that girl, all I can do is wish the other guy luck."

Detective Aldean hung up the phone, and now I was the one with a headache. He'd given me way more than I expected, and I didn't have a clue where to go from here. I took out my case notes and tried to summarize what he'd told me:

1. Possible link between Grieve and Father Dennert
    a. Both had sex with young girls. In Grieve's case, the sex appeared to be consensual.
    b. Could Grieve have found out about Father Dennert's past? Both of their professions offered possibilities.
        i. Through confession—would Dennert have used his past sin to forge a connection after hearing Grieve's history? Highly unlikely.
        ii. Through counseling—was Dennert one of Grieve's patients? A little more likely, but why didn't Dennert's name come up in Grieve's patient records?
    c. Could be no link at all—don't assume a connection
    d. Follow-up
        i. Call Chris in New Orleans
            • Request new review of Grieve's patient database. Any names similar to Samuel Dennert?
            • Dennert might have used an alias. Ask Chris to show Dennert's picture to Grieve's secretary. She might remember Dennert even if he used a different name.
    e. Talk to Father Lawrence
        i. Did he know about the rape?
        ii. How will he react if he didn't?
            • Might wish to confront Father Dennert himself

- Plus—Dennert might confess link
- Minuses?

As promised, Hannah came to pick me up at ten o'clock. I shared my conversation with Detective Aldean and how I thought we should proceed. Not surprisingly, she had her own opinion.

"I admit, this is more than I expected. Given that, what do you think you're going to accomplish?"

"Remember how we talked about communicating with Grieve through the Private Matters website? If we can come up with the connection between Dennert and Grieve, that gives us one more vulnerability. We already know about Grieve's fifteen-year-old girlfriend. While not involving Grieve directly, this is another case of sex with an underage girl."

"To be honest, the connection to this case sounds sketchy at best. Be careful you aren't pursuing this just because you don't like the man."

"A fair point, but I'd still like to know what inspired Grieve to come to Cleveland. He may be a psychopath, but he's a logical one. He doesn't strike me as the kind of killer who would come here on a whim. There's something we're missing, and I want to find out what that is."

"I have no issues with you following up with Chris, but we still need to look at Mary's credit card records and check with the cab company. Let's deal with those first, and then we can go back to the Dennert thing."

"I can live with that. By the way, did your parents say anything about me?"

"Yeah, my mother said you reminded her of me. Be

warned, that was probably not a compliment."

"It is to me. Now if she'd said I reminded her of your father…"

CHAPTER TWENTY-SIX

WE DROVE TO Twelfth District, where we finally got a look at Mary's credit card records. Not surprisingly, they weren't, in the strictest sense, Mary's records. The card Mary used belonged to Mrs. Isabella Supinsky, and Detective Roberts had already tracked her down. Seventy-years-old and living in North Olmsted, Mrs. Supinsky had had her wallet stolen while walking through the mall in the early afternoon of April 17th.

A frequent visitor to North Olmsted's Great Northern Mall, Mrs. Supinsky noticed her wallet was missing when she attempted to pay for some clothing items at Target. Alarmed, her husband suggested they stop at the mall lost and found. When they did so, the Supinskys were relieved to find someone had brought the wallet back. More shockingly, her billfold still contained all of the cash Mrs. Supinsky had brought with her to the mall.

While marveling at the virtue of their fellow shoppers, the Supinskys failed to notice one of Mrs. Supinsky's five credit cards was missing. The stolen MasterCard, stuffed well behind the first four, was not one she typically used. Mrs. Supinsky didn't notice it was missing until ten days later when the credit card bill arrived in her mailbox. The location of the theft was notable. North Olmsted was an upper-class Cleveland suburb within a few minutes' drive of Westlake, the home of Saint Edmund's Church.

The charges on the credit card were a revealing mix. They included a two-hundred-forty-dollar expense for a Hertz car rental as well as a fifty-three-dollar charge from the Greater Cleveland Cab Company. The car rental charge had occurred on April 18th, the cab charge on the day Mary arrived in Cleveland.

The other items on the bill were a more eclectic mix. Most were gardening tools and cleaning supplies, though there were two additional items relating to a prescription and deodorant.

I wondered about the absence of an airport parking charge; then I remembered Mary had abandoned Drew's car and never checked out through the parking lot exit. I also noted there were no charges after April 23rd. Grieve likely had discontinued using the card under the assumption Mrs. Supinsky would notice its absence much sooner than she did.

"We know which cab company they used," Hannah said, "and we also know how much it cost. Allowing for a tip, that should give us a pretty good idea of mileage from the airport."

"This also might tell us something else," I said. "The New Orleans police report said Mary liked to garden. Other than working with animals, gardening was her only form of relaxation. Mary's not the most mentally stable person. With her whole world turned upside-down, it's natural she might return to her favorite hobby."

"Agreed, but what's your point?"

"Look what she bought—a hoe as well as some general gardening tools. My mother is a gardener. A hoe isn't the kind of tool you'd buy for an indoor or terrace garden. Wherever they're hiding, I think it's in a house."

Our discussion was interrupted by a package delivered to Hannah's desk, the promised second copy of Drew's hard drive. Hannah gave it to me with a reminder she was going out on a limb by handing me police evidence. She again made me promise not to take any action without her approval. I agreed, and Hannah returned to looking at the credit card statement.

"Do you wonder about the car rental?" she asked. "We need to check with Hertz, but renting a car in Grieve's situation was taking quite a risk. After everything else they've done, why not simply steal one? The dollar amount for the rental is also odd. Depending on the type of car Hertz gave them, two hundred forty dollars will get you two to three days tops. Why rent a car for such a short period of time?"

"For all Grieve's intelligence," I replied, "maybe he simply didn't know how to steal one. We're dealing with a psychotic educated in psychiatry and a schizophrenic Southern woman who, before this episode, hardly stepped out of her parents' home. That might qualify them to kill, but car theft demands more technical expertise. You or I could steal a car because we know how. I'm not sure either of them could.

"As to the length of the rental," I continued, "if they're living in someone's house, they could now be using the homeowner's car. Why hotwire or continue renting a car when you can simply force your captive to hand you the keys?"

We'd gone as far as we could with the credit card statement. We decided to try to find the cabbie who'd driven Mary from the airport that evening.

The Greater Cleveland Cab Company was located on West 140th Street, a section of Cleveland dominated by older manufacturing firms. Even in the age of Uber, the ninety-year-old company still provided most of the city's taxi services. Whether that was due to the efficiency of its operation or the old-school nature of most Cleveland residents depended on whom you asked. That aside, the GCCC building was more modern than I expected, particularly when compared to its more industrial neighbors.

Hannah flashed her badge at the entrance, and we were taken to the office of Jack Tatum, manager for the daytime 10:00 to 6:00 p.m. shift. Jack, a gray-haired, African-American gentleman, greeted us with a surly hello. His mood changed when he learned Hannah's last name.

"Any chance you're related to David Page, the congressman?"

Hannah, immediately guarded, said, "Yes, he's my father."

Jack laughed, rose from his chair, and extended his hand. "You tell the old SOB Jack Tatum said hello. Your dad and I went to high school and college together. I would never have made it through either one if your father hadn't pulled me along with him."

Hannah was speechless. I think she'd always assumed her father was the one who needed pulling along in school. The thought of him helping someone else seemed beyond belief.

After some hesitation, she said, "I'll tell my father we met. You two were friends in school?"

"We met at Saint Bellarmine's. It was the mid-1970s, and I was the only Black kid there at that time. The way they looked at me, teachers as well as students, you'd have thought I had two heads. The people there weren't particularly prejudiced; I just don't think they'd ever run into a Black kid before. Your father was the only one who took the time to be friendly and help me with some of my classes. I went to public grade school before coming to Saint Bellarmine's, and the transition wasn't easy. Without his help, I never would have made it through."

Hannah still looked astonished. As kids, we secretly assumed our parents appeared in this world the same time we were born. The notion that her father had a pre-asshole life seemed difficult for Hannah to process. While she was collecting her thoughts, I introduced myself and explained what we were looking for. I also mentioned I went to Saint Bellarmine's.

Jack gave me a closer look. "You went to Saint Bellarmine's? I thought I had it bad being Black."

"It wasn't as terrible as you think; I hadn't transitioned back then."

"Fair enough. So, you two are looking for the cabbie

who picked up a blonde on April 20th sometime after 10:00 p.m. and paid fifty-three dollars by credit card. That should be easy enough to check. Is the cabbie in any trouble?"

"Not at all." Hannah had finally found her voice. "We want to see what he or she remembers about the woman and her destination."

Jack checked his computer and found the driver of Mary's taxi was Lisa Estevez.

"You're lucky," Jack said. "Lisa switched from the evening to the afternoon shift about three weeks ago, so she's on duty now. Let me see where she is."

Jack contacted Lisa through the company's dispatching system and found she had just dropped off two customers at the Cleveland casino. Jack asked us if we needed her to come into the office or if we'd be okay communicating by phone. While the phone option would have been faster, we figured Lisa might need to see Mary's picture to jog her memory.

Lisa arrived at the company headquarters in thirty minutes. She seemed a little intimidated speaking to the police, so Hannah assured her she'd done nothing wrong. Without going into detail about the case, Hannah then showed her Mary's picture and asked if she remembered picking her up from the airport in late April. The odds of her placing a customer from two months ago were slim. To my surprise, Lisa did just that.

"I remember that face and the blonde hair. Most of all, I remember she was in a real hurry. That's not unusual for a customer, but she said she was in a hurry because someone was after her. That made me nervous because I half expected an angry ex-husband to come running after my cab. When that didn't happen, I thought the lady would relax.

"If anything, she got even worse. She spent the whole trip looking all around and saying, 'They're coming. They're coming.' The way she talked, I started to think of my cousin, Tina. She was always jumpy when she was off her meds."

"Do you remember where you dropped her off?" Hannah asked.

"I dropped her off at the Great Northern Mall. I asked if she was sure—except for the cinema, the mall closes after ten o'clock. She told me to mind my own business, so I let her off in front of the theater."

"Do you remember anything else she said while she was in your car?"

"Yeah, she asked me how far Elfin Street was from the mall. I told her I'd never heard of it, but I offered to look it up. She told me not to bother. She said she'd find it on her own."

"Are you sure Elfin was the street name she mentioned?"

"I'm sure. The name stuck with me because of the commercial—the one about the cookies."

I looked at Hannah. "Before parking Drew's car at the airport, Mary must have met Grieve to pick up the stolen credit card. Mary originally assumed they were staying at the Lakeview, and that meeting may have been the first time she heard there was a change in plan. With everything else going on, she never bothered to plot out the new address."

Hannah nodded, and I looked up Elfin Street on my phone. It was a small residential street in North Olmsted, about five minutes from the mall by car and twenty minutes by foot. If Elfin was Mary's current location, we needed to find the specific house. I needed Tomas, but I couldn't speak to him in front of Hannah.

We thanked Jack and Lisa for their time, and Jack made Hannah promise she would give his regards to her father. Hannah looked thoughtful as we walked to the parking lot. I asked if she was starting to reevaluate her dad.

"My father is still an asshole. I just always assumed he was born that way. I wonder what changed him?"

"The Manhattan cop I spoke to this morning said power brings arrogance. That's not exactly an original thought, but it is true. I think most politicians enter the field for the right reasons. Sadly, most of them stay in it for the wrong ones."

"Do you suppose there's any good left?"

"There could be. Maybe that's why he and your mother asked me so many questions about what I wanted from life. Maybe he does want to help. It could be the Catholic in him."

"You noticed he went to your high school? My mother did too. As to whether there's any good left in him, I guess stranger things have happened. That being said, how much do you want to bet he doesn't even remember the guy?"

Our next trip was to the car rental agency. The Hertz office listed on the stolen credit card record was located in the suburb of Avon. Beyond being the location for the second Cleveland-area murder, Avon was only one freeway exit west of Saint Edmund's. If you exclude the New Orleans' murders, almost all of our activity in this case involved a small, three-suburb area in Greater Cleveland.

Like many car rental outlets, the one used by Michael Grieve operated out of a hotel. The agent on duty at the rental desk introduced herself as Karen, and Hannah went through the routine of presenting her badge and explaining what we were looking for.

Karen was clearly new at her job and eager not to make any mistakes. Never having faced this situation before, she told us she couldn't provide any information without a warrant. Hannah, impatient in the best of circumstances, did not react well.

"Are you insane? I'm not asking for medical records or to search their home. I'm asking for information on a car rental. Are you going to give me what I need, or do I have to shut this whole goddamned place down?"

Completely nonplussed, Karen looked at me for support. Not finding any and unsure of her legal ground, she wisely chose to look up the information we requested.

All in all, we didn't get much. Isabella Supinsky, or whoever was playing Isabella Supinsky, had rented a panel van on April 18th at nine o'clock. This brought another question.

"I assume Mrs. Supinsky had to show her driver's license," I said. "Do you have a copy?"

Karen looked in her files and eventually came up with a copy. The picture was of a woman in her early seventies who I could only assume was the real Mrs. Supinsky.

Hannah looked at me. "Why didn't Mrs. Supinsky tell us her license was missing?"

"Maybe she never uses it and didn't realize it was gone. A lot of people that age just renew their licenses for identification purposes. I bet her husband does all the driving." I turned to Karen. "Were you working the desk for this rental?"

"No. We're all part-timers, and I wasn't on duty that day. Someone else processed this request."

"When someone rents a car, do you look at their license picture to verify it's truly theirs?"

"We're supposed to, but no one really looks like their driver's license photo. Sometimes, you take it on faith."

I looked at Hannah. "Do you suppose Grieve paid or coerced someone else to come in and fill out the paperwork, someone old enough to fit the picture on the license?"

"It wouldn't be hard to do. There are a lot of elderly homeless walking around downtown. For the right price, I bet one of them would do it. About the car," Hannah said to Karen, "did the woman request a van, or was that the only car available?"

"It looks like it was the only one we had. There's a note here that says Mrs. Supinsky's nephew wasn't thrilled with that option."

I had a feeling I knew the identity of that nephew. I had one more question for Karen. "What was the address she gave for the rental?"

I expected a phony location, and I wasn't disappointed. The address listed was 2401 Ontario Street in Cleveland, Ohio.

"She must have a difficult time sleeping with all the noise," I said, and now both Hannah and Karen looked confused.

"We're in the middle of baseball season," I explained. "That's the address for Progressive Field."

CHAPTER TWENTY-SEVEN

BEFORE HANNAH AND I left the rental agency, I excused myself to call Tomas. When I checked my phone earlier, I found he'd left me a message. He answered on the first ring.

"Terry, I've got news you're going to want to hear."

"Go ahead, and then I need to ask you something."

"Remember you asked me to come up with whatever I could about Grieve's cousin, Susan Leads? It turns out she's dead, murdered actually."

Now we were getting somewhere. "Did you find out how Susan died? Any chance it was a stab wound to the throat?"

"You are correct—just like the murders you're investigating. In Susan's case, they already caught the killer. I'm going to read you the newspaper article. This is from the March 31st edition of last year's *Cicero, Illinois News*.

"'Susan Monroe, a forty-one-year-old Cicero resident, was killed yesterday at a local McDonald's restaurant. Ms. Monroe, a teacher at Cicero Middle School, attempted to intervene in a dispute between two other customers at the Lincoln Street McDonald's. One of those customers, Mr. Daniel Stedman, is in police custody. According to witness reports, Mr. Stedman stabbed Ms. Monroe in the throat after she tried to step between Mr. Stedman and his eighteen-year-old girlfriend, Jacqueline Towns. Mr. Stedman is confined at the Cicero jail until his arraignment on charges of assault and second-degree murder. A wake for Ms. Monroe will be held Wednesday at the Midland Funeral Home.'"

"How did you figure out Susan Monroe was Susan Leads?"

"That's an interesting story, and it's also why it took me so long to dig this up. Susan Leads never formally changed her name from Leads to Monroe. There was no marriage, no divorce, nothing that would normally lead a woman to change her name. It appears Susan Leads assumed the identity of Susan Monroe ten years ago, just before she moved to Cicero. I would never have found her if she hadn't filled out a post office change of address card under Leads when she moved from her old apartment. When I checked the Cicero address, I noticed Leads had suddenly become Monroe.

"I wanted to be sure," he continued, "so I checked the website for the Cicero Middle School. They have pictures of all their teachers, including a memorial for Susan. When you compare Susan Monroe's picture to Susan Leads's last driver's license photo, they are definitely the same woman."

"Thanks, Tomas. Once again, you went above and beyond. Any chance you can get the contact information for

Susan's parents? Like you said, most women only change their name when they're getting married or divorced. Short of that, they're usually trying to escape a bad relationship."

As I was speaking, I noticed Hannah had already gone to her car. Before following her, I added, "I'm wondering if Dr. Grieve wasn't behind Susan's own name change. I'm betting he continued to contact her after they broke off their relationship. Her parents would know—if they're willing to talk with me."

"I have the parents' number in my records, and I'll text it to you as soon as we're done. If you get through, you'll be talking to just the mother. Susan's father died of cancer last year."

"Unfortunately," I said, "I have another favor to ask. Do you remember the copy of the hard drive I talked about? I finally have it, and if you're going to be at home, I can bring it by tonight. I told you my goal was to send Dr. Grieve a message from the website, one that would goad him into replying and giving us his location. We now believe he's hiding out in a house on or near Elfin Street in North Olmsted, but we still don't know the exact address. That's what I'm hoping you can help us find out."

"Once you get me the hard drive," Tomas replied, "I should be able to send a message. If Grieve answers, I can get you an address if I catch it quickly enough. That assumes Grieve replies from the house and doesn't go back to the same library you said he used previously. It also assumes I can run the trace as soon as he sends his reply.

"The trick to tracing an e-mail message," Tomas continued, "is to identify the IP address. I know you hate tech stuff, so I'll give you the short version. An IP address is an identifier assigned to any device on a computer network. The IP address from your computer goes out every time you send an e-mail. Finding the address is easy. I could even show you how to do it."

"Your faith in my computer skills is astounding. The New Orleans computer expert mentioned an IP address, but she could only track it to a general area. How are you going to go further than that?"

"IP addresses are dynamic. They change every time you access the internet, and that's why we need to catch his reply right away. If you delay your trace, the IP address used by your murderer might shift to somewhere else in the same geographic area. I want to help, but I can't be watching this 24-7. You need to hope he's still monitoring his e-mail and responds quickly. That'll require the right message and a lot of luck."

"I need to speak with my partner, and I also want to talk with Susan Leads's mother. If my assumption about Susan is correct, you may have already given me the perfect message. In any case, I'll drop the hard drive off at your apartment this evening. You sure I won't be interrupting anything?"

"This is just the kind of thing she might find interesting."

"Very funny. This stays between us, okay?"

"I am the soul of discretion. Just be sure you are the same—no mentioning my name to your partner."

Finally reaching Hannah's BMW, I filled her in while making sure to keep my source confidential. I told her about Susan Leads's murder, her name change, and the potential for an e-mail trace. I also told her I wanted to contact

Susan's mother.

"What do you think the mother can tell us?" Hannah asked. "And why do you suppose Grieve's parents neglected to mention Susan's death?"

"Grieve's parents may not even know. If they were aware, you heard how touchy a subject Susan's relationship with Michael was to them. They may have decided to keep her death to themselves.

"I think Susan's murder set everything else in motion. Think of the timing. Daniel Stedman killed Susan in March of last year by stabbing her in the throat. Our first murder took place just two months later, also by a stab wound to the throat. Every other murder used the same technique. Now add in the fact that Susan likely changed her name to get away from someone. I'm betting that person was Grieve.

"I'm also betting Grieve found out about her murder. The knowledge he indirectly caused Susan's death may have been too much for him to bear. Where do Catholics go when they're feeling guilty? They go to confession."

As Hannah began to drive, I continued, "I know I'm reaching, but that might be the Father Samuel connection. I'm betting Grieve went to see Samuel and didn't get the absolution he was looking for. If that's true, then chasing Samuel to Cleveland and confessing to future murders might be Grieve's way of transferring some of his guilt."

"As theories go," Hannah said, "I guess it's the best one we've got right now. You still didn't answer my question about the mother."

"She can confirm a couple of things. Was Grieve still contacting Susan, and is that why she changed her name? I'd also like to know if Susan's mother contacted her sister—

Grieve's mother—about her daughter's murder. If Susan's mother considered Grieve to be indirectly responsible for her daughter's death, she might have unloaded some of that anger on her sister. Even though he is her son, Grieve's mother might have blamed him as well. Think of all the humiliation the original incident must have caused her, not to mention the estrangement from her sister. While she may not have told us, it would be natural for his mom to tell him about the murder."

"If Susan's mother confirms your theory, I assume that will be the basis of our message to Dr. Grieve?"

"Exactly. We need something that'll get Grieve to react quickly without thinking of the consequences. Assuming Grieve is still monitoring the Private Matters site, this is the best we can do."

"You're right about the strategy, though part of me hates taking advantage of a girl's death." Hannah looked like she was seeing me for the first time. "You have a cold side I never noticed before."

"Serial murderers bring that out in me."

CHAPTER TWENTY-EIGHT

AS PROMISED, TOMAS texted me the contact information for Susan Leads's mother. Hannah and I called Mrs. Leads from Hannah's BMW.

Hannah performed the introductions and explained the purpose of our call. In doing so, she made sure to mention we were pursuing Mrs. Leads's nephew as a person of interest in a murder investigation. That was more detail than we'd given others regarding the investigation, but if Susan's mother was still bitter toward her nephew, we hoped that information might inspire her to talk. As it happened, we might have underestimated just how hostile she was.

"Every night I go to bed and wish Michael a slow, painful death. I know this isn't the kind of thing you're supposed to pray for, but I've become very Old Testament since my daughter was killed."

"Mrs. Leads," Hannah said, "was Michael the reason your daughter moved and changed her name?"

"You're damn right he was. Right after she and Michael were caught together, we moved out of town, and I sent my daughter to a psychiatrist. With the doctor's help and Michael out of her life, it looked like Susan was getting her life back together. She even applied to a few colleges to get her education degree.

"It was after Susan started going to college and living away from home that Michael started contacting her again. At first, it was phone calls. Michael began by calling Susan a few times each week, and he eventually moved to every day. Susan told us what was going on, so I called my sister, Alma. She promised Michael would stop, and for a while, that's precisely what happened.

"Six months later, Susan began seeing Michael around campus. I figured she was imagining things, but Susan insisted it was him. I called my sister, and Alma again promised that Michael would stop. Whatever Alma said to him, Susan didn't hear from Michael again for another five or six years. By that time, she was in her first teaching job, and it looked like Susan had found her calling. Unfortunately, Michael graduated from medical school around that same time.

"Maybe graduation made him feel less restricted by parental interference. Whatever the reason, the calls began all over again. Just like the first time, they started on a periodic basis but eventually became every day. We tried to talk Susan into applying for a restraining order, but there was nothing about the calls that sounded threatening or hostile. Susan thought if she refused to answer, Michael would eventually give up and forget about her.

"She was wrong. Michael was in the middle of his residency, but he still found time for daily phone calls. Susan didn't talk about it much, but I could tell she was frustrated. I tried calling my sister, but Alma said Michael no longer took her calls."

"Did Susan try changing her number?" I asked.

"Only six or seven times, but Michael managed to find her regardless. No one ever said he wasn't smart. Then Susan got the idea of moving to Cicero and changing her name. After some research, she decided she couldn't do it through the court system. Unless you're getting married or divorced, Illinois insists you advertise a name change through your local newspaper. If Susan did that, she was afraid Michael would find out."

"Did it work?" I asked. "Did Susan have any more contact with Michael after the name change?"

"To my knowledge, Michael never contacted her in Cicero. When we spoke after her move, it was the first time in years that Susan sounded happy. She liked her job at the middle school and began dating one of the teachers. We missed having her close to home, but it was worth it to know she was in such a good place emotionally."

Hannah and I exchanged glances. "Mrs. Leads, after Susan was killed, did you contact your sister and let her know what happened?"

"I called her the day after the murder. I told Alma if it wasn't for her son, Susan would be alive today. Thinking back, I'm not sure any of that was fair. Murders take place everywhere, and the same thing could have happened if

Susan had stayed. I needed someone to blame, however, and my sister was an easy target."

"Have you spoken to your sister since then?" Hannah asked.

"No, and that's another relationship Michael managed to ruin. That boy was like cancer. He spoiled everything he touched. If he is guilty of the murder you're looking into, just shoot him. He doesn't deserve the chance to get away."

We thanked Mrs. Leads for her time and ended the call. While there was still no direct evidence, it felt like a near certainty: Michael knew of Susan's death, and his guilt was driving him to kill.

We needed to flush him out. I mentioned this to Hannah, and she pointed out the logistical challenges.

"You send him a message, and he replies. If you're lucky, you get his address. Then what do you do? Keep in mind this guy's not stupid. He might realize his mistake immediately and choose to abandon whatever house he's in. We need a team ready to roll as soon as his location becomes available. The team should be small, so we don't alert the neighbors, but it can't be just you and me. Once I tell my captain all this, I'd be amazed if he lets you go at all."

Seeing my face and realizing I was disappointed, she added, "This is a good plan. It's certainly the closest we've come since we started with this thing. We just need to make sure we have a strategy in place before we get moving."

I knew she was right, so I swallowed my frustration. We drove back to the Twelfth District to flesh out our plan.

CHAPTER TWENTY-NINE

BACK AT THE Twelfth, Hannah and I met with Detective Roberts. Once the three of us agreed on an operational strategy, Hannah called her captain to seek his approval. To my surprise, I was allowed into that meeting. It was my first-time face-to-face with Captain Slovitz.

Captain Jeffrey Slovitz was tall, nearly six feet, six inches, though he weighed no more than180 pounds. My mother once said a woman she knew was so skinny you could touch her and get a paper cut. I wondered what my mother would say about the rail-thin Captain Slovitz.

Since the captain was always eating, his weight was the subject of much speculation for those under his command. According to Hannah, half his officers assumed he purged while the other half credited his temper. Based on his scowl when we walked into the room, I was betting on the latter.

The attendees at the meeting were Hannah, Captain Slovitz, Detective Roberts, and myself. Hannah began by summarizing our visits to the taxi company and the rental agency. She then laid out our plan going forward. The captain was, to put it mildly, skeptical.

"You're basing this plan on an offhand comment made by one suspect in a taxi and the hope the other suspect will respond to a taunt. Do you realize how half-assed that sounds?"

"We do, sir," Hannah replied. "As you noted, the key is whether the second suspect replies to our message. If he is monitoring his e-mail, we believe that he will."

"And I understand you're working with a computer expert outside of the department?"

"We are, sir," Hannah said. "This man is an expert used by Mr. Luvello in the past, and he has proven to be reliable."

"Not good enough," the captain replied. "You realize we're going to have to get a warrant to enter the house, correct? No judge will take the word of some anonymous computer expert." He then looked directly at me. "We can use your expert, but he needs to work with the computer geek from our department. Unless our department guy signs off, we won't even think about moving forward."

Wanting to sound agreeable, I said, "That's fair. He'll have no problem working with your guy."

The captain's disdain was obvious. "I am so grateful I strike you as fair, Mr. Luvello." He turned back to Hannah. "Let's assume this guy does respond, and let's also assume the two computer geeks can pin down his location. What's the plan from that point?"

Hannah gestured to Detective Roberts. "Andy and I worked out the details. You want to show him the map?"

Detective Roberts—I couldn't think of him as Andy—opened a large street map. Elfin Street was part of the Countryside Estates, a small housing development in the center of North Olmsted. The development consisted of three blocks with five separate streets. All five had storybook names. Besides Elfin, those included Faerie, Merlin, Arthur, and Troll.

Elfin, Faerie, and Merlin ran east-west between the three blocks in the development, while Arthur and Troll ran north-south at the east and west ends of those three streets. Anyone entering or leaving the neighborhood via car had to do so using Elfin. The street names were a little too cutesy for my taste, but the residents clearly didn't mind. The development looked to be full, based on the satellite photos we saw, and no homes were listed for sale.

"We initially considered staking out Elfin Street," Hannah explained. "That changed when we studied the map. While Elfin is the street Mary Dhillon mentioned in the cab, it's also the entryway to the entire development. That means Grieve and Mary could be hiding on any of these five streets. We could try to watch all five of them, but we'd have the entire neighborhood talking within hours. Our two suspects would likely run, and I can't guarantee we could catch them."

As Hannah described it, the arrest team would be small. Hannah, Detective Roberts, and I would be in the lead car along with a third, yet unassigned, detective. Three other unmarked vehicles would join us, stationed by the entrance to the development and behind the suspects' home, to cut off any avenues to escape.

As the lead vehicle in the arrest, we would park a few houses down from whatever address Tomas identified. I would be in the lead car as an observer responsible for communicating with the other three vehicles while the operation was in progress.

The three detectives involved in the arrest would have their own personal radios, so my job was essentially meaningless. I also knew if I complained, Captain Slovitz would be more than happy to leave me behind at the station. I wanted to be involved, so I chose to keep quiet.

During a phone call from the captain, we were told Detective Franklin Aimes would be joining our meeting. Aimes was the department's computer expert, the person who would be working directly with Tomas to identify Grieve's location. Regarding Aimes and Tomas, Captain Slovitz reiterated, "Our decision to get a warrant will be based entirely on their input. If they don't agree, we don't go in. If we break into the wrong house, we will have a fucking disaster on our hands."

"What happens if they identify a house in a different development?" I asked.

"Then we arrange for surveillance on that street until we can put together a new plan. We need to move quickly, but we're not going to move stupidly."

Then Captain Slovitz asked the question I was hoping he wouldn't. "What message are we going to send?"

I looked at Hannah. I hadn't shown her the text, and I wasn't sure she'd agree to it. She shrugged, so I handed the message to Captain Slovitz.

He looked it over slowly, his eyes growing wider as he

read. "Remind me never to get on your bad side, Mr. Luvello." He handed the paper to Hannah. She read it quickly and also looked surprised. Detective Roberts read over her shoulder and turned back to me when he finished. It was the first time I had ever seen him smile.

The message read:

> Michael: I heard about your slut girlfriend. It's your fault Susan died. You sent her to her death, and then you ran away. You killed others, but you never had the balls to murder the one who killed your woman.
>
> He was in jail. It would have been so easy—any real man would have done it already. Now you're with another blonde slut. Should we slit her throat and let her bleed all over you? Apparently, it's the only thing that turns you on. God is vengeance. You are weak and a failure. How do you live with yourself?

I felt like I needed to explain. "We're dealing with an intelligent psychopath. He's not going to respond if we ask him to be Facebook friends. This message hits all his weak points. As shitty as it made me feel to write it, I think this is the way to go."

You don't get to be a captain without avoiding political minefields. Captain Slovitz agreed with the message and my rationale. But given the content, he decreed, "your geek, not mine" would be the one sending it. The captain asked Hannah her opinion, and she said the message was "dark, but effective." The reluctance was clear in her voice.

Detective Aimes picked that moment to enter the meeting room. Tall and slender like his captain, if he heard the "geek" comment, he showed no reaction. With Aimes now present, Hannah filled him in on his role in the case. Once our message was sent, he and "an outside computer consultant" would be observing Grieve's Private Matters mailbox for a response. Assuming there was a reply, they'd use their separate resources to narrow down a location, and the planned operation would not take place unless the two experts agreed. For Tomas's sake, I made clear that my consultant would be working from a separate location and communicating via telephone. Detective Aimes gave me his direct number, and we agreed Tomas would call thirty minutes before the message was delivered.

We then discussed the timing of the operation. None of us could see a point in waiting. There was also the issue of Tomas. He'd agreed to help me entirely out of friendship. I knew from our previous conversation he would be free tonight, but that wouldn't last forever.

After some further discussion, we decided to send the message at nine o'clock. That seemed like the latest we could go and ensure that Grieve would read it the same evening. Captain Slovitz spoke about the warrant via conference call to a prosecutor from the Cleveland district attorney's office. The prosecutor, a colleague of Hannah's mother, promised to have a judge on call for an immediate response.

The timing set, those of us directly involved in the operation planned to meet at the North Olmsted police station at 8:00 p.m. Captain Slovitz would brief his North Olmsted counterpart, and North Olmsted detectives would provide backup support during the operation.

"Is the North Olmsted chief going to be upset with us taking the lead on his turf?" Hannah asked.

"Are you joking?" Captain Slovitz responded. "They'll be only too happy to hang back in case this is all turns to shit. Now, if your plan works, you can also bet their chief will be on the podium with me to take his share of the credit. That's just how these things play out. Remember that if you ever again get involved in a joint task force."

Hannah brought up the possibility of hostages. All the homes on Elfin Street were occupied. If Grieve and Mary were hiding there, the likelihood was they'd taken over a house by force. While they could have broken in while the occupants were away, the two-month timeframe made that possibility unlikely. Alive or dead, we had to anticipate there were other occupants in the house. We finished discussing the hostage issue without any definite resolution.

I didn't have my car, so Hannah drove me back to my apartment. Once home, I planned to deliver the hard drive to Tomas and make sure he'd found nothing affecting our ability to send the message. After that, I would tell him about the need for a joint arrangement with Detective Aimes. Despite what I'd told the captain, convincing Tomas to work with a partner would be tricky, to say the least.

It turned out tricky was an understatement. Before looking at the hard drive, Tomas wanted to know the details of my arrangement with the Cleveland PD. I preferred working alone, but Tomas guarded his private life with a fanaticism that made me look like a social butterfly. I understood his desire for secrecy better than most. Now I needed to talk him out of it.

"Let me get this straight," Tomas said. "You want me to share information with a guy whose computer experience probably amounts to a community college course. Then, to top it all off, you're going to let him sign off on my work?"

"Tomas, I'm not going to lie. While I have no clue about the detective's experience, that's what this thing comes down to. The truth is, I need you on this. The cops would have been just as happy to let their computer guy try to find the source of the message and let it go at that. I want you involved because I trust you. This may be our best chance to solve this case before these two decide to kill someone else. I don't want some hack to screw up the location and send us off to God knows where."

"You forget something—the hack will be signing off on my work. Unless he agrees I'm right, you're going to be screwed."

"Then I need you to convince him you're right. You're good at this, Tomas. That's not bullshit. My knowledge of computers begins and ends at Microsoft Office, and yet I know you're good at this. Convince him like you convinced me."

He reluctantly agreed based on my absolute assurance of his anonymity. When he asked me for the hard drive, however, I knew he was in for sure. Tomas and I were alike in our desire for privacy, but like me, he also loved puzzles. There was no way he was putting down the drive until he figured out what was on it and how it could be used.

Detective Ross in New Orleans had already cracked Mary's password to the Private Matters website. That task accomplished, our first break came a half hour after Tomas opened the drive. He called me over to look, excitement in his voice. He then spent the next two minutes silently working on his keyboard.

"I'm still waiting, Tomas." I couldn't help it. I got impatient when I was on a case.

"Sorry. While I can't pull it back up, I found activity on the message board the two of them were using. I jumped into the site directly from the hard drive, so the website thought it recognized my computer. From what I could see, it looks like there were some messages deleted. The thing is, they were removed much later than I expected."

"How much later are we talking about?"

"The last deletion took place toward the end of May, the 29th to be exact. Weren't they already in Cleveland by that time?"

"They were indeed. Could Grieve have been cleaning up other messages on the board? I imagine there's spam on this site, maybe a lot given it's designed for hookups."

"I have no doubt there was spam, some of it from the site itself. What this tells you is that Grieve or Mary Dhillon is still keeping tabs on it. I'm assuming it was Grieve. That means there's a real chance he might read your message once it's sent."

"I wonder how consistently he checks it."

"I can't say, though I will keep looking to see if I can find the deleted messages. Here's another question—If Grieve was in the habit of scrubbing e-mails, why did he leave the original correspondence, the messages between him and Mary Dhillon, up on the site?"

"I don't know. Maybe Grieve deleted the spam messages and left anything he thought might be important. They still have no idea we found Drew's computer. Drew could have communicated with Mary, but New Orleans has a tap on his landline and his cell, and they're watching his computer. They would have noticed any communication between Drew and Mary after we left his home."

We talked about timing. The plan was to send the message at nine o'clock, and we agreed Tomas would call Detective Aimes thirty minutes before that to discuss the technical details behind the trace. I gave Tomas the detective's contact information and assured him his own contact info would be private. Not believing me in the slightest, he planned to call from a burner phone.

Tomas then asked about the message. I handed it to him, and he read it slowly. His reaction was similar to Captain Slovitz.

"You are one dark detective. I feel like I should go to confession just for reading this. Remind me to never turn my back on you."

"Don't worry, Tomas. You're a friend."

CHAPTER THIRTY

I DROVE BACK to my apartment and prepared for the evening's assault. I'd be an observer only, but I intended to bring both my Glock and my Colt Mustang. A small pistol, the Colt fit perfectly in an ankle holster. I hadn't fired it except at the range, and this was a perfect time for its maiden voyage.

I also considered a knife. John had bought me one when I first became a detective. It was small, perfect for concealment, and included a sheath. After some thought, I decided to leave it at home. Knives and I have never gotten along. Most days, I could barely pick one up without hurting myself. After a particularly embarrassing incident in a steakhouse, John asked me if I wanted him to cut my meat. I got back at him later, but the last thing I needed tonight was a self-inflicted wound.

My weaponry chosen, I left early for the North Olmsted police station. Hannibal had been fine on our last several trips, which usually meant he was gearing up for a major mechanical failure.

Hannibal surprised me once again, however, and I pulled into the station a good half hour before our eight o'clock briefing. Rather than going right in, I waited in the lot until I saw Hannah's car. She arrived ten minutes after me, and we walked into the station together.

North Olmsted was a suburban community with an affluent tax base. Their police station was brighter and more modern than most, certainly when compared to those in Cleveland. The officer at the desk directed us to a large conference room lined with computers. The room was well designed except for the oddly colored carpeting on the floor. While it might have been initially dark blue, it was now stained to the point where that was uncertain.

We were early, but a number of cops had arrived before us. Captain Slovitz stood at the front with another officer I assumed was the North Olmsted police chief. Hannah and I took seats in the back next to Detective Roberts. Based on the looks I got coming in, you'd have thought a unicorn had entered the briefing—a five-foot-seven inch, very unwelcome unicorn.

I leaned over and whispered to Hannah, "They love me. I can tell."

"They don't have to love you," she whispered back. "You're coming in our car. Just avoid being a smart-ass, and you'll be fine."

Detective Roberts was speaking with a tall African-American detective in his early thirties. Hannah introduced him as Detective Malcolm Davis, an eight-year veteran of the Cleveland PD. Detective Davis would be joining us in the lead strike car. He, Hannah, and Detective Roberts would be the arrest team. Unlike the other detectives in the room, Detective Davis appeared intrigued by my presence.

"The captain said this operation was your idea," he said.

I could feel the bus as it drove over my body. "The captain has a way with words."

"Relax. If it works, you'll have two city police departments that owe you, big time."

"What if things go south?"

"Then you'll have two city police departments that owe you, big time."

He was joking. I think. The briefing started precisely at eight, led by Captain Slovitz, representing the Cleveland PD, and Captain Ronald Lester, representing North Olmsted. As per our original plan, there would be four unmarked cars involved in the arrest. Three were for backup and would be manned by North Olmsted detectives. Two of the backup vehicles would be parked on Faerie and Merlin, the two streets in the development that ran parallel to Elfin. The third North Olmsted vehicle would sit at the end of Elfin Street to cut off traffic should Grieve and Mary attempt to escape.

The lead vehicle, manned by Roberts, Davis, Hannah, and myself, would park on Elfin a few houses from whatever residence Tomas determined our suspects were occupying. The entire plan would be contingent on obtaining a proper warrant as well as the level of certainty expressed by Tomas and Detective Aimes. The potential for hostages was made clear to all participants. Both captains also emphasized the importance of staying in radio contact.

Maybe it was nerves, but I was starting to lose faith in my own strategy. The variables almost boggled the mind. Would Grieve see the message? If he saw it, would he reply? If he didn't, this whole escapade was a waste. I also worried about how well armed our suspects might be. I remembered the handgun someone had used to take a shot at me outside the Moore home. I wondered what other weapons they possessed.

At nine o'clock, Detective Aimes called into the conference room. He'd chosen to work from his Cleveland office and interface with the operations team via phone. His stated reason was his desire to use his own computer, but Hannah told me the detective never appeared comfortable in large groups. At the same time, I got a text from Tomas confirming he'd sent my message. He'd added, *Aimes not a total moron.* For Tomas, that was high praise. When it came to computers, my moron status had never been revoked.

With the message now sent, we'd reached our first inflection point. Anticipating a long wait, the two captains set their men to other tasks with a reminder they should remain glued to their radios. Hannah and I chose to remain in the conference room, a fortunate decision given the wait lasted only fifteen minutes.

The call from Detective Aimes was a surprise to all of us. After telling us there was a return message, Aimes paused a solid minute and simply said, "Wow."

Captain Slovitz was not amused. "By all means, Aimes, keep the entire room in suspense. What the hell did he say?"

"I am reading this verbatim," Aimes replied. "'You ugly shit. How dare you bring her into this? Do you think only God delivers vengeance? I am going to cut off your cock and make you eat it for breakfast. You will never see me coming, but I will find you. If it takes the rest of my life, I will find you.'"

Captain Lester looked at me. "It looks like you struck a nerve, Mr. Luvello."

One of the North Olmsted cops added, "Though he may have trouble with the 'cock' part."

Both captains glared, and the offending detective did not speak again. I was just happy the idea had worked, though part of me feared it might have succeeded too well and cause Grieve to storm out of the house before the message trace. After thinking it through, I realized that was unlikely. Grieve might be angry, but he was also methodical. He wouldn't go anywhere without a plan.

I didn't receive any more texts from Tomas. I figured he was too busy tracking the message to bother confirming what I already knew. His trace was the part of the plan in which I was most confident. I guessed it would take another fifteen minutes, twenty on the outside.

My confidence was not misplaced. It took Tomas ten minutes, then another five for Detective Aimes to confirm his information. Aimes called the conference room at 9:32. The address he identified was 1427 Elfin Street.

We moved on to phase three of our plan, which involved obtaining a warrant from a Cleveland judge. A prosecutor from the DA's office and a judge were waiting in chambers for our call to confirm the location of the suspects. Once Aimes verified the Elfin Street address, Captain Slovitz made that call. That was when things got interesting.

Under most situations, cops executing a warrant are required to announce their presence before entering a home. The courts implemented the knock-and-announce requirement to ensure the physical safety of the home's occupants and comply with the Fourth Amendment's prohibition against unreasonable searches and seizures.

The courts did institute a no-knock warrant exception to this requirement. If officers had reason to believe suspects were destroying evidence or the threat of violence existed, they might enter a home without an announcement. No-knock warrants were most commonly issued in drug cases where evidence-destruction often occurred. Given the perceived threat from Dr. Grieve and Mary Dhillon, that was the type of warrant the prosecutor was seeking for our case.

Based on the uncertainty over the home's identification and believing evidence-destruction wasn't an issue, the judge was reluctant to forgo standard procedure. The fact that all the murders had occurred with knives and not guns was also a factor. It was a justifiable decision on the judge's part, but it meant the arresting officers would be at greater risk.

Hannah and Detective Roberts flipped a coin to see who would serve the warrant, and Roberts won. He would present the warrant at the front door with Davis as backup. That left Hannah to cover the back of the house. If there were any signs of trouble, she would enter the home from that side.

While the legal wrangling was taking place, the rest of us looked at a map of Elfin Street. The address in question was at the end of the block, and records indicated the home belonged to Mrs. Claudia Place, a widow, seventy-nine years old.

Based on property records, Mrs. Place had been a resident of the development for the last forty-nine of those years. Her cell phone was not emitting a signal, an indication it was either turned off or destroyed. We had to presume Mrs. Place was still alive, one additional factor to be considered by the arresting officers.

The location of the house was another complication. As the last home on the street, the front of 1427 bordered on Elfin Street while the right side bordered on Troll, one of the two north-south streets in the development. After some discussion, the North Olmsted cops decided to shift one of their backup vehicles to Troll to ensure our targets were effectively boxed in. I then looked down at my phone and noticed Tomas had sent another message.

Be careful. This guy is scary as hell.

CHAPTER THIRTY-ONE

FOUR UNMARKED CARS exited the police department parking lot at precisely ten o'clock. North Olmsted was a geographically small suburb, and the trip to Elfin Street took less than ten minutes. Once we turned onto Elfin, the other three vehicles continued to their assigned locations. As the lead car, we were now on our own.

As planned, Detective Roberts parked our car four houses down from 1427 Elfin. Despite the distance, I had a good view of our target residence from the backseat. A walkway led from the right side of the driveway to the front porch and the house's wooden front door. Well-tended flower gardens bordered the porch steps. I wondered briefly if that was Mary Dhillon's handiwork, then pushed that thought out of my mind. Although my duties were minimal, I needed to keep my head in the here and now.

I wasn't able to see the rear of the house, but Google Maps showed a wooden fence surrounding it. Hannah would have to either open or scale the fence to cover a potential back exit. The plans also showed a deck door opening to the yard. This was the route Hannah would use to gain entrance to the house should things go south in front.

Hannah, Roberts, and Davis checked their weaponry and exited our car. The detectives moved quickly to the house, and I saw Hannah walk to the back while the other two stepped onto the porch. Once there, Roberts rang the bell.

He was greeted by chaos. The world, or at least our world, picked that moment to explode. The sound was deafening, like the noise from a gun range amplified by a factor of ten. Simultaneous with the blast, the front door collapsed backward, shards of wood flying in all directions.

Standing directly in front of the door, Davis was thrown backward like a six-foot rag doll. Roberts, standing to the side of the doorbell, crumpled to his knees. I didn't think he'd be getting back up anytime soon.

I sprinted to the porch and found Detective Roberts groaning and holding his leg. I couldn't see Davis; then I realized the force of the explosion had thrown him into one of the front yard flower beds. He was still and bleeding from the numerous wooden shards sticking out from his chest, face, and neck. I wasn't a medical examiner, but I knew a dead body when I saw one.

I turned my attention back to Roberts, who quickly waved me away.

"It was some kind of shotgun, likely a ten- or twelve-gauge," he hissed. "I'm fine. Get the fuck in that house. She'd have gone in there by now, and you need to get her the hell out."

I knew who he was referring to and needed no further urging. Drawing my Glock, I ran past the collapsed door and into 1427 Elfin.

In TV shows, detectives running into unfamiliar homes are invariably greeted by near-total darkness. In my case, the first thing I noticed was the light. It seemed like every bulb in the house was illuminated, to the point where my eyes had trouble adjusting from the nighttime gloom outside.

Once I adapted to the light, the second thing I noticed was the staircase directly in front of me. The stairs led to a hallway and what appeared to be four bedrooms. A small balcony on the left-hand side of the staircase directly overlooked the front door.

Just as the words "high ground" came screaming in my brain, a figure appeared over that balcony holding what I assumed was the same shotgun that had killed Detective Davis. I dived to my left as the gun went off, managing to fire my Glock at the same time. Not expecting to hit anything, I was surprised to hear a woman scream. I'd seemingly found Mary Dhillon. Now, where the hell was Hannah?

Back on my feet, I raced up the steps. While I'd never fired or even held a shotgun, I knew most were single- or double-barreled, allowing up to two shots without reloading. I was betting my life that Mary's was one of those. If I was right, I would have time to reach the balcony before she reloaded. If her gun was a pump-action model with eight or nine shells, I would be dead before I reached the top of the stairs.

Luckily for me, I never had cause to find out. Still screaming, Mary dropped the gun and retreated into one of the second-floor bedrooms, slamming the door as she entered. I was facing that room and considering my options when I heard footsteps from downstairs. It was Hannah coming up the stairs on the run.

"Terry, I'm right behind you. Don't shoot me."

As Hannah reached the top of the stairs, another voice, cold and mocking, came from the second-floor hallway.

"I would appreciate if you wouldn't shoot me either."

I turned quickly. Hannah, feeling the gun at her head, did not. Emerging from his bedroom hiding place next to where Hannah was standing, I had finally come face-to-face with Dr. Michael Grieve.

Holding the gun in his right hand, Grieve shifted to Hannah's left side. Though this provided me with a better view, I still didn't have a clean shot. I figured his next step would be to tell me to drop my gun, and I didn't have to be a detective to know that would not end well. I needed a way to take control of the situation, and my only chance was what had worked once before.

I burst out laughing. It was clearly not what Grieve was expecting, and he gave me the same look he likely used with his more insane patients. Not surprisingly, Hannah's look was essentially the same.

"Unbelievable," I said. "You're doing it again. Some guy murders your girlfriend in Illinois. You didn't have the spine to kill him, so you decide to knife some poor, defenseless housewives. Now I shoot your new girlfriend, and you've got your gun aimed at somebody else. The message I sent was dead-on. You are a gutless wonder. I bet if I put my gun down right now, you still wouldn't have the balls to shoot me."

I started to put my gun down as slowly as possible. I was betting on three things. The first was that Grieve would move his own gun in my direction. The second was Hannah would notice the movement and seek cover in the open room directly to her right. As for the third bet, I wasn't quite sure what that one was yet. I was just hoping I'd think of something before Grieve put a bullet in my head.

Fortunately, Hannah solved the problem for me. With a sound of pure rage, Grieve started to point his gun toward me. Sensing his shift, Hannah pivoted directly into Grieve and shoved hard.

With his attention on me, Grieve had almost forgotten Hannah's presence. Her shove caused him to stagger and fall down the stairway, though he somehow managed to hold on to his gun on the way down. Now lying on his back at the base of the stairs, he tried to aim it in Hannah's direction.

He never had a chance. Standing at the top of the stairs, Hannah fired three quick shots. Dr. Michael Grieve, noted psychiatrist and part-time serial killer, had finally joined his victims.

Hannah and I looked at each other, both too shaken to speak. That lasted until we heard groaning from beyond a closed bedroom door and remembered Mary Dhillon was still alive. Drawing our guns, we shoved open the door to the room where Mary had fled and found her rolling on the floor, holding her right shoulder. I realized then that I hadn't shot Mary—she'd been injured by the recoil from her own shotgun.

Hannah searched Mary and determined she had no other weapon. Mary said nothing through this process, though the look on her face was one of pure hatred. That look turned even more venomous when Hannah pulled out her handcuffs. Whether it was from her injured shoulder or an overall sense of hopelessness, Mary's howl of pain was something I would remember whenever I thought back to that night.

Hearing a noise from the bedroom at the far end of the hallway, I left Hannah with Mary and moved to investigate. I entered the room and was shocked to find an older woman lying in bed with one arm tied to a bedpost.

The woman began gesturing as soon as she saw me standing by the doorway. Assuming she was Claudia Place, I wondered about the minimal restraints. As I drew closer, the glassy, drugged look in her eyes provided a likely explanation. I untied Mrs. Place and asked her to stay in the bedroom until the EMTs showed up.

Despite her general confusion, Mrs. Place insisted on coming with me. Thankfully, she could walk with only moderate assistance, so I took her down the stairs while Hannah escorted Mary Dhillon. For her part, Mary now looked catatonic. She would need significant time with a psychiatrist— a nonpsychotic one this time—before she could give the police anything useful.

Outside, the North Olmsted police and emergency responders had arrived at the scene. I glanced at my watch and was astonished to find we'd been in the house for just under five minutes. We exited through the demolished front doorway and handed Mary to the North Olmsted cops and Mrs. Place to the EMTs.

Hannah and I then went to check on the injured Detective Roberts. Luckily, his leg had only been grazed, and he was already hurling expletives at the medical personnel providing treatment.

He saw us watching and relief flooded his stubbled face. "You did okay in there. The North Olmsted cops said you caught the bad guys."

Hannah and I looked toward the body of Detective Davis, still being tended by a cluster of EMTs.

"We could have done better," she said bleakly.

"Not your fault. It sucks, but it's not on you. You got the hostage out alive, and that's what counts."

We started to walk away, but Roberts called me back.

"You never hesitated. You went right in there, and you brought her back. That counts for something in my book. You ever need anything from me, don't hesitate to ask. Also, call me Andy. My friends call me Andy."

The "friends" part made me feel good. I would have said more, but the reporters and news vans had started to arrive. I asked Hannah if she could get me a ride back with one of the North Olmsted beat cops. I told her I'd call tomorrow. I knew she would spend all night at the scene.

Some of the cops who'd responded to the call had started to filter back to the station. With Hannah's prodding, one of them agreed to let me hitch a ride. Before I left, I asked Hannah if it bothered her that we'd never know Grieve's reason for coming to Cleveland.

"Are you joking? I don't care if it was space aliens or a secret message he heard in a sermon. Like Andy said, we caught the bad guys. Enjoy that and stop overthinking things. Get some sleep, and thank you for what you did in there. You really did save my life."

I was too tired for a witty comeback, not that I had one anyway. I accepted the ride from the officer and was soon back at the parking lot and next to my car. Before driving home, I decided to call Father Lawrence. I wanted him to hear the news from me before reading it on the internet. It was already midnight, but Father had told me he usually stayed up until well past that.

He answered on the second ring, and I gave him a quick summary of the events on Elfin Street, ending with Dr. Grieve's death and Mary Dhillon's arrest. I didn't have the energy to go into more detail, but I promised him a more thorough report tomorrow.

Father was grateful for the news and said he'd inform Father Samuel. He also said he'd been on Elfin Street. He thought it was the most insipid street name in all of Greater Cleveland.

"I also want to apologize," I said. "When you hired me, you asked me to keep everything low-key. I failed in that rather spectacularly."

"You didn't fail. You caught the killers before they could hurt anyone else. The fact that it reached the newspapers was not your fault. For now, go get some sleep."

That was the third time tonight someone had told me things were not my fault. I wasn't sure I felt any better, but the sleep idea sounded good. I drove back to my apartment and deliberately did not set the alarm.

CHAPTER THIRTY-TWO

I WOKE UP at ten the next morning and checked the internet. Cleveland.com ran a full report of the events on Elfin Street with pictures of the house and the blown-out door.

Hannah was one of the detectives interviewed. Knowing my desire for anonymity, she referred to me only as a "private consultant" who provided critical assistance during the investigation. She also mentioned I was in the house at the time of the arrest. The article didn't mention Mrs. Place by name. It said a hostage was rescued from the home and was now undergoing treatment at a local hospital.

I took my time writing the report for Father Lawrence. Some of the unanswered questions about the case still bothered me, but Hannah was right. There were questions after any case, and sometimes you just needed to be happy with the answers you did find. I also hesitated over Father Samuel and the rape allegation. I ended up copying my notes from my conversation with the Manhattan police detective. I included no comments of my own, figuring it was up to Father Lawrence to take it from there.

John called me from his office to see if I was okay. Because he was in advertising, he complained that my name never showed up in the article on the shootings. I told him I was fine with that, but John reminded me I would eventually need more cases. He was right, but I couldn't summon the energy to care. I wanted at least one anxiety-free day before I got back to work.

My day of leisure was interrupted by a visitor shortly before supper. To my surprise, it was Paul. My brother had never visited my apartment, and he looked uncertain but determined nonetheless. My indecision over seeing him melted away when I realized he was carrying takeout.

"I decided to take a chance you were here," Paul said. "Father Lawrence told me what happened, so I figured I'd stop by to see if you were all right. I even brought food in case you hadn't eaten."

My feelings about Paul aside, I needed some company. John was on a date, and Hannah was still completing her case report. This whole thing had started with a conversation between Paul and me. It was fitting it would end that way as well.

Father Lawrence had already confided many of the specifics to Paul, so I thought he might as well hear the rest. When I came to the events on Elfin, I spared no details. I told him about the shotgun blasts, my run up the stairs, and the final confrontation with Dr. Grieve. Paul listened without interruption, his expression alternating between fascination and horror.

I wasn't looking for validation, but I wanted someone in the family to understand what I did for a living. Paul could be self-righteous and annoying, but he was my big brother. After I finished, he looked a little stunned.

"Jesus, Terry, you could have been killed. I guess I never realized what you went through with this thing."

After we finished discussing the case, we started talking about the old days—Dad's crazy stories, Mom's reaction to Dad's crazy stories, our grade school, and the nuns. On a more serious note, Paul reminisced about our dad's death and its impact on the family.

"You and Dad were always close," Paul said, "and I know his death hit you hard. I'm not sure you knew this, but I went into a bit of a depression back then myself. That's partly why I became so involved with the church at the same time you were headed in a different direction. I know there was more involved in your decision than Dad's death, but I wish I'd been there for you more than I was back then."

He continued with a chuckle, "On a lighter note, even you were a true believer in your early days. I remember in kindergarten, you told us a priest spoke to your class regarding the sacraments. When he talked about confession, the priest said God would be with you when you stepped into the confessional booth. You came home convinced God was going to be sitting right next to you, and Mom had to yell at me to stop laughing. You were quite the naïve kid back then."

Paul was still talking, but I could no longer hear his voice. LSD users speak of moments of perfect clarity, moments when their perception became so acute they could actually see God. I was experiencing my own such moment now. Unlike theirs, mine came without the aid of illegal drugs.

And unlike theirs, I saw the devil.

CHAPTER THIRTY-THREE

I STOOD UP suddenly, almost knocking over my chair. Paul, seeing my face, assumed I was angry. Given our past history, he thought I was angry at him.

"I only said you were naïve!"

"The only thing wrong was your verb tense. I am naïve; I am incredibly, fucking naïve. I have been since this case started."

He was now totally bewildered. Hoping to get things straight in my head, I started to pace. With the sequence of events finally clear, I turned again to face Paul. I needed him to tell me I was not insane.

"Imagine you have an acquaintance, not a priest, who said a person came to him and declared his intent to commit murder. The person not only told your acquaintance about the murder, he told him exactly how he intended to pull it off. This supposed conversation occurred in a public place. You investigate; you ask questions, but you can't find anyone else who saw this other individual. A few days later, a murder takes place exactly the way your acquaintance said it would.

"About a week later, the whole thing happens again. Your acquaintance tells you that the same individual spoke to him a second time and once more declared his intent to kill. Just like before, the second murder takes place exactly as advertised, with no one noticing the individual making the confession. That latter fact seems especially odd given the room was full of women and this theoretical other person was said to be notably handsome. What do you start to wonder?"

"I guess I start to wonder," Paul said, "if my acquaintance committed the murders all along. But I still don't see what this has to do with your case. The other person wasn't a myth. You know Grieve was the killer."

"I believe that Grieve committed two of the three murders in Cleveland. What I've never known is why. Not why he committed the murders, but why he followed Father Samuel to Cleveland. I made up all sorts of scenarios in my head. I thought he might be angry over a sermon or mad over something Samuel said during a confession. None of that made sense, given we're talking about a cold, methodical killer."

Finally taking a seat, I said, "All along, I ignored the obvious. What if Grieve was invited? What if Father Samuel and Grieve had a relationship back in New Orleans, but what if that relationship was mentor-student rather than priest-penitent? If Samuel had been anyone but a priest, I would have questioned his story from the beginning. Instead, I accepted the whole thing, just like the naïve Catholic kid I was educated to be. Knowing my personal history, I bet Samuel found that hilarious."

In Paul's mind I was well into blasphemy, and he was getting angry. "That's a nice theory, but you're talking about a priest. Do you have a reason for thinking this other than pure speculation?"

"I'll give you several. What if I told you this priest raped a classmate when he was a teenager? I spoke to a detective in Father Samuel's hometown who was dead certain that he did. After he laid out the evidence, I believed him—I think you would have as well. The other aspect of the rape was that Samuel talked his friend into joining him. I'm wondering if he didn't enjoy that part the most.

"Imagine Dr. Grieve, a devout Catholic, coming to Father Samuel for confession after his cousin-girlfriend was killed back in Illinois. This woman was Grieve's obsession. He felt guilty about her death, and he was angry. What if Samuel sensed that and saw an opportunity to up his game, only this time with murder?"

My question aside, Paul was still fixated on the rape. "Father Samuel raped somebody? Does Father Lawrence know?"

"I don't think so. The conversation with the detective was going to be part of my final report."

"That does make Samuel a shit, but it still doesn't prove he was involved with murder."

"True, but there's also the shooting outside Olivia Moore's home. I assumed the shooter followed me there.

Several people were aware I was hired for this job, so that didn't implicate anyone in particular. While that's still true, the only people who knew the four names on my parishioner list were Father Lawrence and Father Samuel. Knowing where I was going would have made it doubly easy to set me up.

"I've also been thinking about the houses where the murders took place. The killings that occurred after the reported confessions involved housewives from Cleveland and Avon. I think those were random murders, both almost certainly committed by Dr. Grieve and Mary Dhillon. The murder that didn't fit the pattern was Nancy Losano, the woman from Westlake. She was the first murder, a shut-in in her seventies, and the police didn't find her body until much later. Nancy also had a connection to Saint Edmund's in that she was once a parishioner.

"She was a convenient target, don't you think? There was no way Grieve could know that unless he had information from someone inside the church. There was also no faux confession related to Mrs. Losano's murder. What if it wasn't Grieve who killed her, but someone else who wanted to try out killing on his own?"

"You're saying Father Samuel killed Mrs. Losano?"

"Think about it. There was never any sign of forced entry, and I always wondered how the killer got these women to open their doors. As the case moved forward, I assumed Mary Dhillon played the critical role. She's blonde, white, very pretty, and in her thirties. To a housewife in a predominantly white neighborhood, Mary might appear completely harmless.

"I still believe that's what happened in Cleveland and

Avon. With Mrs. Losano, I think it might have been different. I'm not sure the Mary Dhillon scenario fits with an older
shut-in. Who else could talk an older, Catholic woman into
opening her door?"

"A priest." While reluctant, Paul didn't hide from the
implication.

"My last reason also involves a house, the one in North
Olmsted where Mary and Dr. Grieve were hiding. The owner
of the home, Claudia Place, was also an older woman and a
shut-in. Isn't it convenient Dr. Grieve and Mary picked her
house for a hideout? Like Mrs. Losano, her neighbors would
be far less likely to notice her absence.

"I'm betting Mrs. Place also had a connection to Saint
Edmund's. When I last spoke with Father Lawrence, he
mentioned he was familiar with Elfin Street. I never mentioned Mrs. Place, but I think she might be the reason he
recognized the name. We can find out for sure, but I need
you to call Lydia."

"Lydia, my wife? How can she help?"

"As hyperinvolved as Lydia is with church, you once
said she knew almost everyone who attended Saint Edmund's. If Mrs. Place was connected to the parish, I'm hoping Lydia would know. I need you to call her and find out."

He was still reluctant, but he agreed to call. When he
hung up, his face was white.

"Claudia Place's husband grew up in Westlake. He and
Claudia were married at Saint Edmund's, and they continued to attend church even though they lived in North
Olmsted. Lydia also told me something else. Claudia hasn't
been able to drive to church for the last year due to her fail-
ing eyesight. Father Lawrence used to take her communion

every week, but lately, she's been taking a senior bus to a North Olmsted church."

His look was almost plaintive. "My God, Terry, we need to call the police."

"First," I said, "we need to call Father Lawrence. I spoke to him last night and told him what happened on Elfin. After I finished, Father Lawrence said he would let Father Samuel know. Once they have that conversation, Samuel will realize his time is short. I need to get Father Lawrence out of that church."

I dialed Father Lawrence's cell phone. The voice that answered was friendly, almost kind. It was the voice of Father Samuel.

"Terry, it's great to hear from you. I just finished talking with Father Lawrence. You saved me a phone call."

"Can I ask why you have his cell?"

"Don't ask questions when you already know the answer. I knew you would eventually figure things out. Who better to catch a deviant than another deviant? That being said, you and I have some unfinished business. If you want Lawrence to get through this night alive, I need you to come to the parish in the next forty minutes. You'll find the two of us in the church. It's usually locked at this time, but I'll make sure the front doors are open.

"And Terry, I know your first instinct will be to call the police. I can't emphasize enough how bad that would be for Lawrence's health. If I hear or even sense another person is there with you, I will put a bullet in Lawrence's brain.

"One more thing—you might wonder, with me standing in the church, how I could possibly know who might be gathering outside? I admit I got lucky there. We've had a few break-ins lately, and Lawrence decided to install security cameras outside the church and the main office. Technology being what it is, these are the type of cameras that can forward a video feed to an app on your cell phone. With that app, I can see virtually everywhere on church grounds.

"Come alone, Terry, it is really better we talk in private. We'll have fun, I promise you."

"I'll be there."

He hung up, and I gave Paul a rundown of our conversation.

"You can't possibly be thinking of going."

"What other choice do I have? I don't know if he's telling the truth about the cameras, but I can't run the risk of involving the police at this stage."

He was ready to object, and I was afraid he would call the police the moment I left the room. I also needed a backup plan in case my primary—and as yet, nonexistent—one didn't work. I handed Hannah's card over to Paul.

"The number I just gave you is for the police detective who worked with me on this case. After I leave, I need you to wait one hour and then call her and explain where I am. I mean exactly one hour, no more and no less. That will give me thirty minutes to drive to the Saint Edmund's and thirty minutes to resolve this situation on my own. If I can't do it in that time, then you're right—the police will have to be involved."

Paul still looked dubious. "This is the first time we've talked in years. I don't want to lose you the same night."

"You won't, but I need you to trust me. Will you give me one hour?"

"I will. Just please come home."

I grabbed my keys and my gun and headed out the door. It was then I realized what I was doing. Time was crucial, and I was heading to a confrontation in a car that was the poster child for clunkers everywhere.

I went back inside. Paul looked at me in surprise, no doubt hoping I'd changed my mind.

"Paul, I need your car."

"Why don't you take your own?"

I was getting impatient. "Because I can't take Hannibal to something like this!"

"Who the hell is Hannibal?"

"Damn it, Paul. Just give me your fucking car keys!"

CHAPTER THIRTY-FOUR

I SHOULDN'T HAVE yelled. Paul looked stunned, but he threw me his keys. I reminded myself to apologize later as I ran out the door and found his Toyota minivan in the apartment parking lot. Paul and Lydia purchased the van shortly after the birth of their daughter, Hailee. Hailee's car seat was still securely attached to the backseat.

The van was a practical, energy-efficient option for any young couple with a child. For someone about to confront a lunatic, it went well beyond absurd.

Fortunately, it was eight o'clock, and rush hour traffic had long since ended. As I drove, I tried not to think of Hannah's reaction. She would be furious that I was doing this on my own.

The trip to Saint Edmund's took twenty-five minutes,

and it was dark by the time I arrived. The church parking lot was empty, but the lights in the building were on. I parked Paul's minivan and tried the front door. As promised, it was unlocked.

I took out my Glock as I entered. As with many Catholic churches, the Saint Edmund's vestibule was large with several side rooms for meetings and educational programs. After a quick search, I verified those rooms were unoccupied. Conscious of my limited time, I walked through another set of doors and found myself in the back of the church worship area, what my Jesuit teachers would call the nave.

I realized immediately why Samuel had insisted I enter from that side. With the church lights on, I could easily see Samuel and Father Lawrence standing together at the altar. Samuel held a gun to Father Lawrence's head, stationed where he'd delivered many sermons. Despite his mortal danger, Father Lawrence only stared at me intently. If he was trying to communicate something, I had no idea what it was.

From where I was positioned, I was at least one hundred twenty feet away from the two priests. My Glock had an effective firing range of ninety feet, one hundred for a marksman. On my best day, I was far from that. The two priests were also standing on a raised altar, with Samuel slightly behind Father Lawrence. If I fired, I'd be just as likely to hit the wrong priest. Father Samuel had staged this for a purpose, and I needed to hear him out.

"Stay right there, Mr. Luvello. Also, you can put down the gun. We both know you aren't going to shoot me from that distance."

There was no way I was lowering my gun. Samuel

obviously wanted to talk, and I needed to keep him speaking until I came up with a plan.

"I think I'll keep my gun right where it is," I said. "By the way, I know you raped that girl in Manhattan."

"You have been doing your homework. I knew if anyone found out, it would be you. So, you know I raped the girl. Tell me why you think I did it."

"With anyone else, I would say sex and power. With you, I'm guessing it was something else."

"Very good. Sex bores me, other than as a means to an end. As far as rape is concerned, any guy with a dick can rape a girl. It's not exactly an achievement."

"Then tell me why."

"I assume you've heard of the seven deadly sins. Forgetting about what the Church taught you, tell me what you think of them."

"I always thought their designation was overwrought. Pride, anger, lust—what human being hasn't felt those things? I figured they were the Church's way of laying a guilt trip on the faithful."

"Exactly! I knew you weren't a total idiot. I grew up thinking the same thing, but it wasn't until I was a teenager that I realized the one, true deadly sin."

He paused, clearly waiting for me to guess. When I remained silent, he shook his head in disgust. "Corruption, Mr. Luvello, the greatest sin of all. I may not be much of a priest, but I do believe in the soul. Once you corrupt a man's soul, you own him for life. Do you want to know why I talked Bobby into raping that girl? Because he liked her. They'd gone out a few times, and he really, really liked her. Once I realized that, I decided to shame him into raping her. It was easier than you might think. Unlike you, Bobby was an idiot. It only took a few weeks before he agreed it was his duty as a man.

"That rape was the high point of my life until this past year. I once thought I would spend the rest of my days in Manhattan, take over my father's business, and use it to take advantage of whomever I could. While satisfying in some respects, that would make me a chip off the old block. Whatever else happened, I couldn't allow that.

"Fortunately, everything changed after the bitch's mother took a shot at me. When my father came up with the idea I should join the priesthood, I immediately said no. Then I remembered the look in Bobby's eyes after the rape and how the light in them just...died. I missed that look. I figured the priesthood would give me more opportunities to find it again.

"I did find it, but it was small-scale stuff. Once I talked a man into beating his wife. He wanted to do it for years, but there was one little spark of humanity that kept him from it. Some old-time religious preaching put that spark out with no problem. Unfortunately, that sort of piddly shit got boring very quickly."

Samuel paused as if catching his breath. I took that opportunity to shift my gaze to Father Lawrence, but he remained stoic and appeared remarkably unsurprised by Samuel's long confession. Knowing Samuel's propensity to talk, I suspected Lawrence had heard the same speech just before I arrived.

Finally, Samuel continued. "There wasn't any worthwhile action until Dr. Michael Grieve came into my confessional. Someone had killed his cousin, and he felt so guilty I wanted to vomit. My opening came when he talked about his patient, a long-haired blonde who reminded him of his former girlfriend. Grieve refused to sleep with the woman, even though he thought she was interested.

"I talked him into inviting me to a session. I called it couples counseling. They were both so easy to control. I ended up making him watch while I screwed the bitch. I told him watching would make him realize his feelings were normal and should not be repressed.

"You want to corrupt a man? Make him watch while you screw the girl he likes. Once that happened, it was easy to convert Grieve's guilt into rage and his rage into murder. It was a snap, really."

"Did you kill the woman in Westlake?"

"You guessed that as well? I did kill her. I thought it would be a dry run for more, but I found that murder doesn't interest me. Like rape, killing is ultimately boring. I've always been more excited by the psychological."

"I'm curious. Who took the shot at me?"

"That was the slut. She did it entirely of her own volition. She got her hands on my copy of the parishioner list Lawrence gave you, and she followed you to one of their homes. I almost killed her myself when I found out. There was no reason to kill you then, especially when I wasn't done playing with you."

"What about the phony confessions?"

"I thought the declarations in the confessional booth added some drama to the situation. Everybody's life needs a little drama. That's why I asked you here tonight."

In its own sick, perverted way, this was fascinating. I was, however, running out of time. I'd told Paul to give me an hour before calling the police. They would be coming, and I needed to bring this to a close.

"You said you had a game for me. What did you have in mind?"

"It's simple. When we first met, I said I wanted to get you into confession. That hasn't changed. I want you to confess your sins, and I want you to feel shame. If I feel you are properly penitent, then I might let Father Lawrence live."

Father Lawrence continued to stare in my direction, seemingly unmoved by the threat to his life. Regarding Samuel, I knew he was lying. While the sadist in him might enjoy the idea of me in confession, I knew he'd called me here for more than just that. Despite his love for drama, I couldn't see Samuel as the lead in some grandiose suicide play. He had an escape planned, but I had no idea what that plan was. Samuel held a gun, but the distance separating us was as great an obstacle for him as it was for me. That being said, Father Lawrence and I were the only ones aware of his secret. If Samuel were to escape, he needed us both to die in the process.

I played for time. "What if I'm not truly penitent?"

"Then I'll give you something else to be sorry about. I would also get some closure for you sticking your nose in my business."

"Fine, let's go in the confessional, and we can talk."

His voice almost thundered from the pulpit. "Do not treat me like an idiot, Mr. Luvello. Do that again, and I'll put a bullet in this man's brain. Then I imagine you'll really have something to confess. Now say the words. You know what they are."

As he spoke, I remembered an offhand comment from

my telephone conversation with Detective Aldean. Samuel was clearly familiar with his father's furniture stores. I was guessing he had experience with his other ventures as well. With a chill, I realized just what he was planning.

For the fourth or fifth time, I considered my options. For the fourth or fifth time, I realized I had none. Samuel was right—I really had no other choice.

In my loudest voice, I said, "Bless me, Father, for I have sinned."

Then I took the shot.

CHAPTER THIRTY-FIVE

WHEN I WAS growing up, my father and I used to love watching old Clint Eastwood movies. We loved them all, my father and me, but our favorites were the *Dirty Harry* films. I was amazed how Clint, as Harry Callahan, always hit whatever he was aiming for, even with that massive 44 Magnum revolver.

Sadly, I was not Dirty Harry. As I feared, my bullet went to the right of its intended target, directly into Father Lawrence's shoulder. Father Lawrence, not expecting the impact, fell backward onto the altar. Fortunately, Samuel was equally surprised, and it took three to four seconds before he fully realized what had occurred.

I might be a mediocre shot, but I was a fast runner. By the time Samuel began to turn toward Father Lawrence, I'd almost halved the distance between us. I set myself and fired again, aiming for Samuel's chest. Shooting instructors refer to that as center mass.

Unfortunately, I didn't properly adjust for the height of the altar. While I got the center part right, the bullet went high and directly into Samuel's throat. He fell backward, a few feet away from Father Lawrence.

I ran the rest of the way to the altar and noticed Samuel's gun lying by his side. I kicked it away and stood guard as Samuel continued to bleed profusely from the wound to his throat. Given the murders he was responsible for, the irony was hard to escape. His hand clenched to his neck as he tried to stem the flow of blood, Samuel gasped my name and gestured for me to bend down. He made no move to his pockets or the gun now lying too far away for him to reach. Leaning forward against my better judgement, I heard him again gurgle out my name.

"You would just let me die, Mr. Luvello?"

"To be honest, I'm enjoying it immensely."

He smiled then, a psychotic's dying act. "Then I have given you something to confess after all."

I wasn't worried. In truth, I was too tired to feel triumph or much of anything else. I'd shot a priest and allowed him to die. If God judged me harshly for that, so be it. I worked in a career that required me to search for the worst in people. Having found that in a church, of all places, all I could think about was sleep.

In the midst of my reflection, I remembered Father Lawrence. Lying several feet to my right, Father was gamely trying to regain his footing.

As I walked over to see if I could help, the back doors of

the church blew open; the cavalry had finally arrived. Along with the police, that included at least four emergency medical technicians.

Before they reached Father Lawrence, I said, "You know, Father, I think you guys need a little work on your applicant screening."

He shook his head and sighed. "I'll get right on that."

By that time, the EMTs had taken over and started to wrap Father Lawrence's wound. I backed away, but Father motioned to me one more time.

"When I told you to trust yourself," he said, "I don't remember saying anything about shooting me."

"I'm sorry, Father. I figured that was implied."

I chalked up his reply to the shock of being injured, though I'd never previously heard those words coming from a Catholic priest. From the looks on their faces, I don't think the EMTs had either.

Hannah had entered Saint Edmund's along with the police contingent. To my surprise, Detective Roberts was there as well, although he limped noticeably. Hannah talked with the other cops surrounding Father Samuel's body without looking in my direction. She was, in a word, pissed.

Detective Roberts—Andy to his friends—came over to take my statement and said, "Nice shooting, Tex."

Everyone was a critic.

Before Andy went further, I told him to look under the altar for a bomb. The altar was a guess, but I figured Samuel would prefer something sacrilegious to a more mundane location like a church meeting room.

Andy checked, and I was right on both counts. The bomb appeared to use fertilizer as an explosive. The detonator, which they found in Samuel's pocket, was a modified version of a device used for fireworks displays.

The bomb squad was called, and they arrived within minutes. Andy then finished taking my statement. I told him what had happened, including the phone call at my apartment, Samuel's confession regarding the murders, and his desire for me to confess. Andy wrote it all down; then he glanced back at the altar.

"How did you know?"

"I didn't know for sure, but Samuel thought Father Lawrence and I were the only ones who knew his secret. He wasn't in a position to shoot me, so he had to have some other method to get rid of us. Two of his family's businesses involved fireworks and fertilizer. I figured some combination of those would make a nifty explosive.

"I think the whole confession thing was a ruse to justify getting me to Saint Edmund's. When I finished, Samuel planned on leaving the church with Father Lawrence and me still inside. He could then set off the bomb, drive away, and hope it would be days before anyone realized his body wasn't also in the rubble."

With that, Andy closed his notebook and stared briefly at Hannah before turning his gaze back in my direction.

"She's pissed at you. I'm sure you figured that out. She considered you a partner, and she thinks you violated her trust. I understand why you did what you did. I'll talk with her, but you may want to give her some room in the meantime."

I thanked him, promising I would make myself available if he had any further questions. Exhausted, I then sat down in one of the pews. As I was contemplating the night's events, it occurred to me I'd fired two shots that evening and managed to hit two different Catholic priests. While I'd killed the right one, there still had to be a record in that somewhere. I guess God did laugh after all.

I probably would have stayed in the pew for quite some time if I hadn't appropriated Paul's car. He'd be stranded at my apartment, and his wife would have a new reason to hate me. I called to assure Paul I was okay, then walked back to the parking lot.

No one stopped me from leaving the church, though I hadn't counted on the presence of the news media outside. They yelled out their questions, but I had no interest in becoming part of the frenzy this case was bound to become. To my amusement, their questions ceased when they saw me enter Paul's minivan. In their minds, nobody of consequence would be driving a minivan.

I drove home, handed Paul his keys, and thanked him for having faith in me. His belief did mean something, maybe more than I cared to admit. I summarized what had happened, including the fact that I'd shot not just one but both of his parish priests. Paul volunteered to stay the night if I wanted him to, but I figured Lydia would be mad at me enough just for taking their car to a shootout. I sent Paul home with my thanks and a promise to provide more detail the next day.

The case had been solved, and that should have felt good. Sitting alone in my apartment, I just felt empty. I told myself the feeling was natural. The biggest case of my career had ended, and anyone would experience some letdown.

I also knew that was bullshit. I knew what, or more accurately who, was behind this feeling. Andy Roberts had told me to give her some time. I would, but I wasn't sure that would make any difference. Hannah felt betrayed, and given her history, she wasn't a woman who would tolerate betrayal.

Still, I hadn't lost her yet. Tonight, more than any other night, I needed that hope. Tonight, for the first time in years, I needed to pray.

EPILOGUE

TWO WEEKS. IF anyone had told me my life could turn upside down in just two weeks, I would have said they were insane. As I'd predicted, the shootings at Saint Edmund's began a media frenzy. To my surprise, I was at its center.

It started with the photographs. Someone had snapped pictures of me as I walked out of the church that evening, likely more out of reflex than genuine interest. Then a Westlake policeman told them just who and what I was.

The resulting headlines would have made the *National Enquirer* proud. John's personal favorite, "Transgender Detective Shoots Killer Priest," was picked up by the *New York Times*. With my story now national, the *Times* and other publications called requesting a comment. I didn't return any of their messages. John objected, but I didn't want to be anyone's cause for a day.

My mother phoned, wanting to know why she had to read about my exploits in the newspapers. I promised next time I would call if I shot any more priests, but Mom was not amused. John called as well and later brought me dinner. He proved to be a true friend when we talked about everything but the case.

Despite my best efforts, I'd become the most well-known private detective in Greater Cleveland, maybe the entire Midwest. In the first week after the shootings, I received calls regarding six other cases, and I responded to the two that sounded most interesting. One was a young wife whose husband had disappeared. The facts she related made it sound like more than the usual "other woman" situation. The second call would be my first corporate case, an embezzlement potentially extending across several layers of an Akron industrial firm. As a prelaw student in college, my minor had been in finance. I figured I should finally put those skills to work.

I'd left her four messages, but the person I most wanted to hear from would not return my calls. When he'd first met Hannah, John had told me not to fuck things up. I still held out hope, but it looked like I'd managed to do just that.

I needed to keep my mind off my romantic difficulties, so I came up with a to-do list. I accomplished the first item with a phone call to Detective Aldean in Manhattan, Kansas. Ecstatic to hear of Samuel Dennert's death, he promised to buy me a beer should I ever visit the city. I told him he could thank me instead by informing the Donahue family, and he agreed without any hesitation.

I completed the next item after I received my final check

from the Jesuits. With some trepidation, I traded Hannibal in for a 2016 Volkswagen Passat. As I looked at Hannibal sitting alone at the auto dealership, I knew my mixed feelings weren't based on nostalgia. Hannibal and I had hated each other for too long to pretend about such things.

Instead, it occurred to me that Hannibal might hunt me down, like the car in Stephen King's *Christine*. That prospect would have worried me more if I weren't certain Hannibal would break down long before reaching me. After the trade, it was a relief to drive home in a car that didn't sound like an eighty-year-old asthmatic lying on his death bed.

The third item on my list was more complicated, and it required a meeting with Father Lawrence. I'd visited Father in the hospital, but I hadn't been back to Saint Edmund's since the night of the shootings. I called first to make sure he knew my intentions and then drove to the parish. The church was unlocked, and I found the confessional booth with Father Lawrence's name.

The light was on, and I stepped inside. It had been twelve years since my last confession, and the booth was as constricting as the ones I remembered from my childhood. I knelt, and the divider slid between us.

"Bless me, Father, for I have sinned."

Father Lawrence responded a little too quickly. "Why is it I feel like I should duck?"

I wondered how long he'd been saving that one. The rest of the sacrament went more smoothly, at least until Father assigned my penance. I expected the "three Our Father's and three Hail Mary's" of my youth. What I received was something completely different.

"Paul told me you and he have reconciled, and I think

that's great. For your penance, you should do the same with Lydia."

I was appalled. "You're punishing me because I shot you."

"Making up with your sister-in-law is an important step for you. The fact that it amuses me is merely a side benefit."

Father Lawrence then reminded me he was God's representative in the sacrament of confession, which cut off any further argument I might have made. Stepping out of the confessional, I found I did feel better. Maybe there was something to the sacrament after all.

Sometimes it's better to pull the Band-Aid off all at once. After calling Paul to ensure he and Lydia were home, I asked if I could come over with a present for baby Hailee. Despite my objections to Father Lawrence, it occurred to me days ago this might be a way of smoothing over the rift between Lydia, Paul, and myself.

I also knew I needed to avoid the mistake I'd made at Hailee's baptism party. Trying for humor, I'd brought Hailee a small plastic football as a toy. Knowing my personal history, Lydia and Paul were not amused.

Instead of humor, I went for nostalgia and brought copies of the two books our parents had read to Paul and me before every bedtime. Every evening, my mother would start with *Goodnight Moon*, and my father would finish up with the *Great Big Book of Dinosaurs*. While their connection always eluded me, the books were a staple of our childhood for years.

Lydia greeted me at the door, and I ended up staying for supper. Paul and I pretended not to notice her flinch when Paul handed me their baby, but that was the only glitch in an otherwise successful evening. Hailee, now almost two years old, surprised us all by saying my name. While I'd never been much for children, I found I actually liked the kid. Growing up with Paul and Lydia as parents, she would need a fun uncle. For my part, I would need someone to watch the Browns games with when John wasn't around.

I left Paul's house shortly after supper. When I arrived back at my apartment, I was shocked to find Hannah waiting for me at my door.

"Sorry for arriving unannounced," she said. "Do you mind if I come in?"

I hurriedly unlocked the door before she could change her mind. I motioned her to a chair, but she remained standing.

"I had three visitors at the station today—your friend, John; Father Lawrence; and some guy named Tomas O'Malley. I assume the last name was fake. In any case, they came to talk about you."

To my knowledge, the three of them had never met. Also, Tomas had given his real name? I was surprised, to say the least. "What did they say?"

"They said you were a pain in the ass. John was the one who said it, but you'd be amazed how quickly the other two agreed."

It was nice to have supportive friends. "Did they say anything else?"

"They said that you were worth it. Is that true? Are you worth it?"

I suddenly felt exhausted. "To be honest, there are days I really don't know."

"I think you are. The truth is, I was planning to stop by

even before your friends' visit. I've done a lot of thinking these past two weeks, and I realized I was looking at our relationship strictly in the context of my parents. I watched for any sign you weren't trustworthy, and I ignored all the signs you were. You saved my life in that house, even though it meant putting your own at risk. I'm not sure how I allowed myself to forget that."

"You saved mine right after."

"I couldn't let you one-up me, could I?"

For the first time in weeks, I was smiling. "I won't lie. It's great talking with you again."

"There's one more thing I want to ask you. You and I came together during a lot of craziness. There's nothing wrong with that, but I need to make sure we can be as good during non-crazy times."

"What are you asking?"

"I want us to back up to a bit. I want us to go out on a date, maybe even a few dates, and see how we do. I want to see what it's like to be normal."

"You think you and I can ever be normal?"

"Maybe normal is the wrong word. I want to know we can work when we're not together on a case. I'm going home right now, but I want you to call and ask me out on a date. We can even go to one of those superhero movies you like."

"I will call you. I promise."

She started to leave, then turned again to face me. "These last two weeks have been the least annoying time in my life—it's been driving me crazy. Call me, okay?"

"Count on it."

I stood in my tiny apartment and watched her leave. When we met, Hannah told me my cases were all about chasing happy endings. Weakness or not, I knew I wasn't ready to stop looking.

I also realized Hannah and I weren't living in a Hallmark movie. Our issues wouldn't be resolved with a last-minute kiss or the arrival of a puppy dog. That being said, she seemed interested in trying. That was a victory I hoped I could build on.

With my mind still reeling from the thought of a transgender Hallmark movie, I remembered the final item on my to-do list. I found the old contact information in the back of my small desk and called the number on the page. Given the hour, I expected a recording, but a human voice on the phone said, "Cleveland Gender Reassignment Program. How can I help you?"

I made my first appointment.

How does one define identity? I still don't have the full answer to that question, but I now know this procedure would be part of my response. Years ago, I signed up for the same program and backed out after just two appointments. John had called me a wimp, and he was right.

Whether it was Hannah, this case, or a combination of the two—I was different now. Father Lawrence called it trust; others might call it acceptance. For me, they were the same thing—I could no longer be something I wasn't.

I couldn't be a wimp anymore.

ACKNOWLEDGEMENTS

This book would never have been completed without the support of everyone at NineStar Press, particularly my editor, Elizabetta McKay. Elizabetta, your patience and advice were invaluable throughout the process. You made this a much better book than it was going in.

I would also like to thank Michelle Guzowski and Denise Vonderau. Your input was essential, and I appreciate it more than I can say.

A special thanks as well to all the other family members who took the time to review my manuscript, particularly Pam Glick, Michelle Joseph, Sue Hampton, Kathy Gabel, and Libby McCuan. Your counsel and encouragement meant the world to me.

About Joe Rielinger

Joe Rielinger lives in Cleveland, Ohio, with his wife, Lisa, and their two fun-loving, though often borderline crazy golden retrievers. With a lifetime love of mystery, crime, and detective novels, Joe is currently working on a sequel to his first book, *And God Laughed*. When he isn't writing, Joe likes to cook, read, and pretend he might someday learn something about training his two dogs.

Email
jarielinger@gmail.com

Facebook
www.facebook.com/jrielinger.author

Twitter
@JAR_author

Website
www.joerielinger.com

CONNECT WITH NINESTAR PRESS

WWW.NINESTARPRESS.COM

WWW.FACEBOOK.COM/NINESTARPRESS

WWW.FACEBOOK.COM/GROUPS/NINESTARNICHE

WWW.TWITTER.COM/NINESTARPRESS

WWW.INSTAGRAM.COM/NINESTARPRESS

Made in the USA
Middletown, DE
04 December 2022

16984807R00194